MW01093910

The Love Fix

ALSO BY JILL SHALVIS

SUNRISE COVE NOVELS
The Family You Make • *The Friendship Pact*
The Backup Plan • *The Sweetheart List*
The Bright Spot • *The Summer Escape*
Better Than Friends • *The Love Fix*

WILDSTONE NOVELS
Love for Beginners • *Mistletoe in Paradise* (novella)
The Forever Girl • *The Summer Deal*
Almost Just Friends • *The Lemon Sisters*
Rainy Day Friends • *The Good Luck Sister* (novella)
Lost and Found Sisters

HEARTBREAKER BAY NOVELS
Wrapped Up in You • *Playing for Keeps*
Hot Winter Nights • *About That Kiss*
Chasing Christmas Eve • *Accidentally on Purpose*
The Trouble with Mistletoe • *Sweet Little Lies*

LUCKY HARBOR NOVELS
One in a Million • *He's So Fine*
It's in His Kiss • *Once in a Lifetime*
Always on My Mind • *It Had to Be You*
Forever and a Day • *At Last*
Lucky in Love • *Head Over Heels*
The Sweetest Thing • *Simply Irresistible*

ANIMAL MAGNETISM NOVELS
All I Want • *Still the One*
Then Came You • *Rumor Has It*
Rescue My Heart • *Animal Attraction*
Animal Magnetism

The Love Fix

A Novel

JILL SHALVIS

AVON

An Imprint of HarperCollins*Publishers*

This is a work of fiction. Names, characters, places, and incidents are products of the author's imagination or are used fictitiously and are not to be construed as real. Any resemblance to actual events, locales, organizations, or persons, living or dead, is entirely coincidental.

THE LOVE FIX. Copyright © 2025 by Jill Shalvis. All rights reserved. Printed in the United States of America. No part of this book may be used or reproduced in any manner whatsoever without written permission except in the case of brief quotations embodied in critical articles and reviews. For information, address HarperCollins Publishers, 195 Broadway, New York, NY 10007.

HarperCollins books may be purchased for educational, business, or sales promotional use. For information, please email the Special Markets Department at SPsales@harpercollins.com.

Avon, Avon & logo, and Avon Books & logo are registered trademarks of HarperCollins Publishers in the United States of America and other countries.

FIRST EDITION

Interior text design by Diahann Sturge-Campbell

Waterfall illustration © Danussa/Shutterstock

Library of Congress Cataloging-in-Publication Data has been applied for.

ISBN 978-0-06-335344-2
ISBN 978-0-06-335349-7 (simultaneous hardcover edition)

25 26 27 28 29 LBC 5 4 3 2 1

The Love Fix

CHAPTER 1

I t was a terrible, horrible, no good, very bad day to die. For one thing, Lexi Clark's entire existence was still circling the drain after being fired and dumped all those months ago. Going toes up before she fixed her life would really suck.

"Ladies and gentlemen, this is your captain speaking," came a voice from the overhead speakers. "When we left Greensboro, the weather in Reno looked good, but coming in for our approach, we've got high winds and dropping temps. So buckle up, buttercups, it's going to get a little bumpy." He clicked off, and then immediately came back on, the speakers screeching, making everyone groan. "Nearly forgot the silver lining—those of you on the left get a gorgeous view of Lake Tahoe, which is deep enough to cover the Empire State Building. If the entire lake were to spill out, it'd cover the state of California under fourteen inches of water. But no worries, after two million years, the odds of that happening are pretty slim. Hold on tight, we're coming in hot."

He hadn't even finished the sentence when the plane dropped, and so did Lexi's stomach.

"I need a snack," the woman on her left whimpered. "We flew all the way across the damn country without a courtesy snack, and now I'm going to die hungry. Why didn't I just buy food?"

"Because a bag of chips cost seven bucks," Lexi gritted out, white-knuckling the armrest.

The woman let out a breathless laugh that turned into a gasp when the plane dipped again, yanking shouts and Hail Marys from the other passengers. Lexi, breaking out into a sweat, reached out at the same time as her seatmate did, their hands blindly clasping tightly to each other.

"Maybe I should try to sleep through this," the woman said. "I'm really good at sleeping."

Lexi had never understood how someone could sleep through a crisis. When did they do all of their panicking and overthinking?

Around them, the cabin turned into a cyclone, the air filled with flying debris and more screams. When she'd boarded, she'd walked past first class with a twinge of envy, thinking that she wouldn't mind a little tomato soup to soothe the soul. Especially if it was cold. Over ice. With a celery stalk.

And vodka.

But now, seeing drinks and trays whip around as their plane seemed to fall out of the sky had her stomach reversing direction, getting stuck in her throat, making her glad she hadn't eaten.

They plunged again, so hard her body went airborne, giving her the unnerving sense of being a balloon on a string—until the seat belt yanked her back.

"The universe will keep us safe. The universe will keep us safe," the woman next to her chanted softly, squeezing Lexi's hand tight enough to crack bones. "Say it with me."

Lexi didn't want to blaspheme, but she believed in the universe caring about her about as much as she believed in love.

"Say it!" the woman begged.

Fine. At this point, she had nothing to lose. "The universe will keep us safe."

A few seconds later, the plane leveled out and everyone gave a sigh of relief as the woman turned to look at Lexi with triumph. "You're good at this."

Ha. Not even close. Proving it, the plane promptly banked right hard enough to rattle her teeth and nearly roll them in a somersault and then . . . free fall.

Screams of terror pierced Lexi's ears, her own and everyone else's. They were heading down, down, down, right to rock bottom, apropos since that's where her life sat anyway.

"No!" her seatmate cried. "This isn't happening! We're *not* going to die. Not when I haven't had a single man-made orgasm in at least a month."

A month? That was nothing. Lexi couldn't even remember the last time she'd had an org—

The plane dropped again, along with Lexi's organs . . . just as they hit the tarmac.

Hard.

They bounced a few times, the cabin utterly silent now, struggling against the g-forces as they screeched to a halt at the very end of the runway.

The woman still holding Lexi's hand let out a shaky breath. "See? We did it! I'm Summer, by the way." She dug through her pocket and came up with a business card.

Summer Roberts, CPO
CHIEF PROFESSIONAL MANIFESTER

"Fifteen percent discount for friends and family," Summer said. "Contact me anytime. Do you have a card?"

She had until six months ago, when she'd still been an over-achieving, naïve art appraiser, working for a company who handled estate closure. Currently, her life was in free fall, much like the plane's approach had been.

Their pilot was talking, apologizing for the rough landing as people scrambled to disembark. Lexi grabbed her carry-on and joined the herd shuffling into the crowded terminal, heart still pounding in tune to the headache behind her eyes. For the past half hour, she'd forgotten why she was here, but it all came back to her as she made her way through the throngs of people, stepping onto the escalator that seemed to crawl down two full floors toward ground level. But for once, her impatience was gone, beaten back by a case of vicious jitters, her limbs trembling like she'd consumed too much caffeine.

She shouldn't have come. But her stepsister, Ashley, twenty-three to Lexi's twenty-nine, had begged her on their last monthly call.

And for reasons Lexi didn't want to think about too hard, she'd agreed. Over the years, she'd been back here to Lake Tahoe, and her childhood home in Sunrise Cove on the north shore, only a handful of times after leaving with her dad when she was ten.

The last time had been four years ago, for Ashley's dad's funeral. It'd been a short trip, but Ashley—and Daisy—had been genuinely happy to have her. Still, seeing Daisy always stirred up a maelstrom of complicated emotions.

Daisy was gone now, and Lexi had no idea what to expect. She pulled out her phone to access her Uber app for a ride. As the escalator slowly brought her down, she caught sight of a petite redhead—her sister—holding a huge bouquet of flowers and balloons that spelled out HAPPY BIRTHDAY, FRED! Lexi grimaced in secondhand embarrassment for poor Fred, grateful that no one would ever confuse Lexi for a flowers-and-balloons kind of girl. She was more of a please-don't-bring-attention-to-me girl.

"Lexi!!" Ashley bounced up and down in excitement. "Welcome home!"

Oh boy. The escalator ended and she stumbled off, thanking the guy who reached out and steadied her without taking her eyes off her sister, who was still bouncing around in a white tank top and flower-power skirt. "Ash? What are you doing here?"

"Picking you up, silly!"

Lexi eyed the balloons. It wasn't her birthday, nor was her name Fred. "Did you steal those?"

"Didn't have to. The grocery store gave them to me for free. The clerk told me the wife ordered them for her husband but caught him cheating. Just another reason I don't date anyone with a penis." Ashley grinned and threw herself at Lexi, hugging her hard, smelling like cotton candy and forgotten dreams as she rocked them back and forth, making little happy noises. "Hi! It's really you! You're here, you're really here!"

Lexi, who thought she'd buried her emotions a long time ago, found her arms coming up to return the hug. Feeling eyes on her, she lifted her head.

The guy standing at Ashley's side, the one who'd steadied Lexi off the escalator, was watching, quietly assessing, and . . . amused? Tall and leanly muscled, he wore jeans and an untucked button-down with the sleeves shoved up to his elbows. His wavy dark brown hair was on the wrong side of a cut, and there was more than a few days' worth of scruff on his face, but it was the flash of mischief in those shocking blue gray eyes that held her.

Everything inside her stilled at the sight of her childhood nemesis and one-time crush—okay, *two*-time crush, but who was counting? Dammit, she was. She was also lying to herself, because it was an ongoing crush. As in still current.

Heath Bowman, whose eyes got her every single time, those searing, knowing eyes, and that smart-ass smirk—

"She's turning purple, Ashley," he said mildly. "Might want to let up on the grip."

The easy affection in his tone gave away how much he cared about Ashley. Anyone who'd ever met Ashley cared about her, deeply. It was impossible not to.

At whatever Heath saw on Lexi's face, his mouth quirked on one side, an expression disarming enough that two women walking by tripped over each other. "Been a while, Lex."

Not long enough . . . "And you're here why?"

"Oh," Ashley said. "He's here as my emotional support."

Lexi's heart stuttered as she turned to her sister. "Why? What's wrong?"

Ashley shored up her expression and quickly shook her head. "It's nothing, don't worry."

Too late. Plus she was a professional worrier. But Lexi would get it out of her later, in private. But if someone had set off Ashley's debilitating depression again after she'd been free of it for years now, Lexi prepared to go to war against them. "You didn't have to come get me," she said in her softest voice, one she didn't get much use out of these days. "I planned to Uber. Neither of you needed to take away from your jobs."

"I didn't," Ashley said. "School just got out for summer. I would've loved to teach summer school for the extra paychecks, but kindergarten doesn't offer it."

Lexi turned to Heath. He lifted a broad shoulder. "Being a nine-to-fiver isn't my thing."

Once upon a time, *everything* had come easy to him, making friends, melting teachers' hearts, schoolwork . . . and she'd crushed on him hard. He'd continued to skate on that charm and charisma from childhood right into adulthood, where last she'd heard, he was an attorney. "What happened to trial law?"

Another shrug. "Wasn't for me."

Ashley slid her arm into Lexi's. "As for why we're here, I wanted you to have a big welcome committee when you arrived, surrounded by people who love you."

Lexi bit back the urge to point out there were only two of them here, and she'd have bet her last dollar that the taller of them had been dragged against his will. No way did he come willingly, not after their last . . . encounter.

"I know you're far too busy for a visit, but . . ." Ashley glanced at Heath. "Well, there're some things we need to fill you in on."

The "we" was deeply disturbing. Lexi had dropped her duffel bag while they talked, but reached down for it now, ending up in a tug-of-war with Heath.

Ashley laughed. "Mom always said you two could argue over what color the sky was. I didn't believe her."

There'd been a time when Lexi had been rotten enough to resent a six-years-younger Ashley, Daisy's stepdaughter from her second husband. But that had been more a reflection of Lexi's complicated feelings about Daisy and nothing against Ashley, whose genuine sweetness and affection always tore Lexi's walls down with shocking ease. "That was all a long time ago. We were stupid kids then."

Her sister smiled. "If bygones are truly bygones, then where's the nice-to-see-you-again hug?" She nudged Lexi right into the man. Repugnant, she told herself, but that was yet another lie. As she brushed up against his warm, solid frame, something warm unfurled in her gut as if there was a live wire between them. She blamed Heath for being too sexy for her peace of mind. The only thing that made her feel better was how he stared down at her, his amusement gone, something pensive in his gaze now.

Ha. He felt it too. Good, because if she had to suffer, then so did he.

"It's nice to see you," he murmured.

She blinked at the words, at his surprisingly genuine tone, which threw her off. She could count on one hand the number of times she'd seen him since their childhood rivalry, and for each of those times, she'd managed to make a fool of herself, something she did not intend to repeat, ever. She didn't have the bandwidth for him. Whether that came from her currently empty confidence tank or exhaustion, it didn't matter.

But then he leaned in close, and she found herself more breathless than she'd been during the rough plane landing. He smelled good, dammit, and she could feel the easy strength of him. She blinked slow as an owl, head spinning, because those eyes, they were warm and kind, and her own smile came utterly unbidden.

Which was when he whispered, his warm breath barely grazing her earlobe, "*Shotgun . . .*"

CHAPTER 2

I t was a forty-five minute drive from the airport, and Lexi spent each of those minutes staring out the window while refusing to look at Heath. She'd forgotten how stunning the Tahoe National Forest was, the deep jade pines lining the lower ridges, leading to jagged, granite-faced peaks that in turn vanished into fluffy white clouds lazily floating across the azure sky.

They were in Daisy's old, beat-up '72 Chevy truck, a relic from Lexi's childhood. It had a cracked windshield, an eight-track player, a passenger window that wouldn't open, and an ignition that only turned if you asked it real nice. She sat squished on the bench seat between Ashley and Heath. Every single left turn had plastered Lexi up against Heath's body and made her grind her back teeth. They'd be powder by the time she got to Daisy's.

When they hit Lake Tahoe's north shore and drove into the small mountain town of Sunrise Cove, Lexi's belly quivered with nerves. On the main street, the lake shimmered with whitecaps on her right, the quaint shops and cafés on her left resembling a Swiss Alps village. "Hasn't changed much."

"Hey," Ashley said. "We've got *two* grocery stores now. *And* a roundabout."

She made another turn, this one tight, taking a lot of muscle to do it. Sure enough, the movement knocked Lexi into Heath, her elbow digging into his gut.

It was *almost* an accident.

He'd clearly been just trying to rile her up with the earlier "shotgun" comment, since they were all in the front seat, but she had a news flash for him—she was *already* riled up.

Just being here did that.

Ashley stopped the truck in front of their childhood house at the same time that her cell started playing U2's "With or Without You."

"Love this song," Ash said, pulling out the phone to sing along for a few bars before slipping it back into her pocket without answering it.

"Anyone important?" Lexi asked wryly.

"Absolutely not."

Lexi decided she could learn a lot from her baby sister.

Ashley was eyeing the driveway, which already had two cars in it.

"The Ramos family across the street has teenagers, and too many cars," Ashley said as she attempted to parallel park. "They pay me for use of the driveway." She cranked the steering wheel and ended up with two wheels up onto the sidewalk. "Dammit."

"Why don't you use the garage?" Lexi asked.

"It's packed to the gills with a bunch of Mom's stuff, and I didn't want to go through it all alone." Ashley turned the steering wheel the other way, and the car groaned as it fell off the curb with a lurch. "Don't say it," she warned Heath, who lifted his hands in a surrender motion.

Ashley studied all the mirrors and gave it another go. Aaaaand again, they went up onto the curb with teeth jarring precision.

"Crap." Ashley knocked the back of her head into the headrest a few times before turning to Heath. "You're up."

"No way. You made me promise not to save you from parking hell again. I had to pinky swear on Mayhem's life."

"Who's Mayhem?" Lexi asked.

Ashley slid out of the truck and jabbed a finger at Heath. "I take back the pinky swear."

"You can't take back a pinky swear."

Ashley glared at him. The cute little puppy with her sharp little puppy teeth out.

Apparently unconcerned about getting bitten, Heath gestured to Lexi without even looking at her. "It should be her turn."

"Oh, no," Lexi said. "I don't parallel park either."

He lifted a brow. "What if it's the only parking space available and you're late to, say, a dentist appointment?"

"Then I miss the dentist appointment."

Shaking his head, he slid out of the truck. "Good luck," he said, and it wasn't clear which sister he was speaking to before he strode off, leaving Ashley standing in the street and Lexi alone in the truck.

Ashley stood with her hands on her perfect little hips as she yelled after Heath, "Where do you think you're going? The three of us have a meeting!"

"Your teacher voice won't work on me. And there's no meeting until you two talk first." And he kept walking.

"Not funny!"

Heath merely flashed Ashley a grin that said he found it very funny.

"Get back here!"

"Need my laptop, princess." And then he got into a much, *much* newer truck that was *perfectly* parallel parked on the other side of the driveway and drove around the block home.

Ashley looked at Lexi with desperation.

"No," she said.

Her sister bit her lower lip, and were those unshed tears in her eyes? Dammit. Grumbling, she slid across the bench seat and gripped the steering wheel.

Ashley's smile came so quick that Lexi narrowed her eyes. "You played me."

"I can't get another ticket. My insurance will go up again. And I'm already doing the whole robbing Peter-to-pay-Paul thing every month."

Lexi's heart pinched. And . . . she put the truck into gear. *Sucker.*

Ten long minutes later, she was sweating, but the truck was properly parked. And it'd only taken a few hundred attempts. She followed Ashley into Daisy's house.

Nothing much had changed over the years, which meant like always, it was basically walking into a portal back to her ten-year-old self. The furniture was worn but inviting, but there was also a whole bunch of . . . well, stuff. Daisy had *loved* stuff. As a kid, it'd made Lexi feel claustrophobic, but as a grown-up, as a professional appraiser, she looked around with different eyes than younger Lexi had. Still, if there were anything here of value, it'd long ago been buried under layers upon layers of crap.

"It's a hot mess," Ashley said self-consciously. "But I never felt comfortable going through and getting rid of stuff without knowing what you might want."

Guilt hit her. "You didn't have to do that. Wait for me, I mean. She's been gone a year."

"I know, but I didn't mind waiting."

"And if I'd never come?"

Ashley turned from setting down her purse on a foyer table, surprised. "Well, of course you would have come eventually, even if I hadn't asked. Right?"

Not touching that land mine, Lexi turned from Ashley and assessed the room. In her job, she'd gone into homes, usually shortly after someone had died, right into the heart of a family who was grieving, to put price tags on the deceased's belongings. In order to be effective, she'd learned to disengage and dissociate. But as it turned out, it wasn't a two-way switch that she could easily turn back on. She pointed to the makeshift lace curtains blocking off a full corner of the room. "What's that?"

"My way of covering stacks of boxes of Mom's stuff so I don't have to look at them every day." Ashley didn't meet Lexi's gaze. "The boxes gave me anxiety."

"Why not go back to your apartment? Why stay here if it's too hard?"

"This is free, and my apartment wasn't. Nice job on parking, by the way. You only hit the curb on the first two tries. Heath would've been impressed."

Lexi laughed roughly. "I doubt that. And nice subject change."

"And here's another . . . What's up with the tension between you and Heath?"

Lexi looked away. Heath had been the boy who'd beaten her at everything: their kindergarten ski race, their first-grade spelling bee tournament, the third-grade class presidency—he'd cheated by handing out candy for votes.

And then years later, she'd come back in her early twenties

for one of Ashley's birthdays, he'd slow danced with her, and somehow her childish irritation at him had turned into a crush.

A one-way crush. Which was embarrassing enough, but not as embarrassing as their next encounter in her midtwenties, when she'd made a move on him.

And gotten her heart stomped on.

Not that she'd ever admitted such a thing. "There's no tension between me and Heath. What are you even talking about?"

"I'm talking about how you both pretend everything's fine when it isn't. It started five years ago, when you came for my high school graduation."

"We don't need to revisit—"

"Oh, but we do. I found you two making out."

True story.

"I was so excited," Ash said. "You guys were together that whole week you were both home, and then you broke up with him. When I asked why, you told me he was a horrible kisser. Which I know is a lie, given the kiss I witnessed between you. Obviously, you didn't want to talk about it. What I don't know is why."

Not Lexi's finest moment, that was for sure. After the graduation ceremony, she'd gotten talked into a party at the lake. Once night had fallen, Ashley and her friends had turned up the music and started dancing beneath a sliver of a moon and trillions of sparkling stars.

In a very weak moment, Lexi had found herself dancing too. With Heath.

It'd been very late when the music slowed, changing into a seductive, sexy beat. She'd been stupid enough to get swept up by that, by the easy strength she'd found in his arms, by those bedroom eyes, and . . . gah, this was still so embarrassing . . . she'd kissed him.

He'd stilled in shock, and before she could run off in humiliation that she'd misread him, they'd been caught by Ashley. Ashley, who'd wanted her two favorite people to be together more than anything. Taking in the horror on Heath's face, Lexi had come up with the story about him being a bad kisser. She'd done it to save face, but it'd backfired, because Ashley had been mad at Lexi for "hurting" Heath.

Heath, who'd remained silent on the entire matter, the ass.

Lexi still resented the hell out of him for that, because he'd come out smelling like a rose and somehow she'd been the bad guy. "We didn't discuss because there's nothing *to* discuss."

"Okay, then, what about when you came the next year for my dad's funeral? Four years ago now. You two iced each other out."

Not exactly true. Heath had been dating someone, but he'd been friendly and open with Lexi.

She'd been the only icy one, and frankly, that had been embarrassment from the year before, along with a second emotion regarding him being in a relationship that she tried very hard not to think about. "Old history. Now, can you please tell me whatever it is that you're not telling me?"

Her sister bit her lower lip. "Wine? How about some wine?"

"Maybe later." Definitely later. "And what did you mean before when you said we have a meeting?" She'd prepared herself to deal with Ashley. Just Ashley. To deal with Heath as well, she would have liked advanced notice.

In writing.

Her sister had moved to the fireplace to stare at . . . Oh dear God. "Is that . . . Daisy?"

Ashley nodded at the urn on the mantel. "She wanted to be cremated, but never said what we should do with her. I think she's happy there, keeping an eye on things."

Lexi stared at the urn. Whenever her dad had sent her here to Sunrise Cove to visit Daisy, which hadn't been that often, she'd resented it. Resented that she had to spend time with her mom, who'd broken just about every promise she'd ever made. But it was during her own visits here that she'd also spent time with Daisy's new husband and daughter. Ash's dad had been a good man, and Ashley . . . Well, Lexi defied anyone not to immediately love that girl, but Lexi had still always felt like an outsider here. She still did. Her dad had passed eight years ago now. She knew it was natural to outlive your parents, but to be truly untethered by blood relatives felt odd, to belong nowhere and to no one. It'd taken her a while to get used to it. And what had she done? Given her heart to yet another person, one who'd *also* been full of broken promises.

Maybe she'd been slow on the uptake, but she'd eventually gotten the message—keep her heart locked up tight.

"You look tired." Ashley smiled gently when Lexi's gaze flew to hers. "Why don't you drop your stuff in your room. I'll pour us some wine to celebrate."

"What are we celebrating?"

"Your homecoming, of course."

"You know I'm only here for a week, right?"

Ashley made a hum of agreement, but it also sounded like a wordless *we'll see*.

"A week, Ashley. It's all I've got." Another fib, but not wanting to get into it, she moved down the hallway, which was lined with pictures. Pictures of . . . *Lexi*, and shock froze her in place. There, her middle school graduation. Another of her in the hospital after a freshman bout with mono that had turned into pneumonia. Then of her grinning wide at getting her driver's license. Her high school graduation. Her college graduation . . .

All in or near Greensboro. "Where did these pictures come from?" she called to Ashley.

"Found them in Mom's things."

Daisy hadn't been to any of these events. Lexi, tired of all the broken promises to visit in Greensboro when she'd been so young, had stopped inviting her mom. Had in fact told her outright not to come.

"Your dad sent them. I have the letters that came with if you want to see them."

Lexi had no idea what she wanted. The back door opened, and an unbearably familiar husky male voice said, "I didn't hear anything blow up, so I assume she took the news well."

Heath. And . . . *news?*

"I haven't told her yet," Ashley said.

Next came the sound of paws scrambling on the kitchen floor, accompanied by heavy panting that Lexi was pretty sure didn't belong to Heath.

"Mayhem, sit," Heath said with such calm authority that Lexi nearly sat. "Good boy." Then he presumably spoke to her sister, his tone reproachful. "Ash."

"I know! But Lexi's not okay, Heath. She's not."

"How can you tell?"

"Very funny," Ashley said. "But I'm right. Something's wrong, and I don't want to add to her burden."

"Ash, this is a burden that *both* of you were meant to bear, not just you."

This did not sound good. Needing a moment, Lexi quietly opened the door to her childhood bedroom and slipped inside.

Another time warp, from the NSYNC poster to her second place trophy from the first-grade spelling bee that still sat on the scarred particleboard desk.

A shrine to her childhood.

She dropped her bag on the bed, yearning to climb in after it and close her eyes and not wake up until next year, or better yet, after her life had improved, however long that took.

A week. She'd promised to stay for a week. She'd use this time to quietly regroup without admitting what a shambles her world had become. As the older sister, she was the one who should have her ducks in a row. All she had to do was find them.

CHAPTER 3

Heath hadn't been born with patience. Nope, it'd come to him slowly, painfully, over time. So waiting for Lexi to come back into the living room? Simple enough. Keeping Ashley calm? Not nearly as easy. "You're wearing out the floor. It's going to be okay, you know."

She stopped pacing the length of the living room and whirled to face him, her hands clenched together in front of her. "You don't know that."

"Have I ever lied to you?"

She raised a brow. "Several times."

"Name one."

"When you told me I could come out of the closet and not lose any friends."

His expression darkened. "The people who didn't stand by you were never your friends."

Ashley dipped her head in acknowledgment of that. "Okay, how about when I wanted to backpack through Europe for a year instead of going straight to college and you said I absolutely should. That was one big fat fib."

He shrugged. "More like reverse psychology. And you're welcome. You got your educator credentials in three years, and you love teaching."

"I do," she admitted. "But this, with Lexi. Not telling her the truth of why I asked her to come until now? I don't see how it's going to be okay."

"That was a choice *you* made," he reminded her gently, *always* gently with Ashley, whom he considered a baby sister, one who hadn't quite found her way back to herself after getting hurt in her last relationship.

Ashley sighed. "I should've told her everything from the start. So please tell me how it's going to be okay."

He smiled. "Because you always make everything okay."

"You're going to stay and help me explain?"

"Whatever you need." And he meant that. Daisy had given Heath stability when he'd had none, strength when he couldn't find his own, and the safety net of the family you make. So hell yes, by extension, he'd always help Ashley however he could.

Because as he knew all too well, everyone made mistakes. He was counting on that very fact to be the bridge between the sisters.

They heard footsteps coming down the hall. Mayhem, who'd been sleeping on Heath's feet, sat up, tail thumping in excitement at meeting someone new. Since this often involved a nosy nose to the crotch, Heath grabbed him by the harness.

When Ashley sucked in a nervous breath, he murmured, "Just be you," as Mayhem excitedly danced in place.

Lexi stopped in the doorway. The sisters, not being blood related, looked nothing alike. Ashley barely came up to his shoulder, all soft, warm curves, usually dressed to match her free spirit and the wild red waves that hung down her back.

Lexi had at least six inches on her, her straight honey-brown hair hitting her shoulders, perfectly matching honey-brown eyes that gentled when they landed on her sister but turned chilly for him.

Not a surprise. He'd earned that chilliness.

"Who's the cutie pie?" Lexi asked of the massive yellow Lab Heath held back from licking her to death.

He slid her a smile. "I *knew* you thought I was cute."

Lexi gave an impressive eye roll, and he laughed. "This is Mayhem. Officially, he belongs to Grandpa Gus, but he's mostly my problem."

"Is he friendly?"

"Psychotically so."

She dropped to her knees, holding out her hands. Stunned by the melting Ice Queen, Heath let go of Mayhem. "Be good."

"I'll try, but no promises," Lexi said, making him laugh. How had he forgotten that beneath her tough exterior lived a warm, sexy, funny-as-hell soul?

Mayhem wiggle-butted his way across the room, throwing himself down onto the floor at Lexi's knees, going toes up for a belly rub.

"Aw, look at you," Lexi said on an easy laugh that Heath hadn't heard since they'd been kids. "Who's a good boy?"

There hadn't been a single day in Mayhem's life when he'd been a good boy, but Lexi sat on the floor so the eighty-five-pound dog could climb into her lap and told him, "*Such* a good boy."

Mayhem gave her a lick from chin to forehead, then farted audibly. It was an impressive one too, lasting a good five seconds, startling the dog into craning his neck and staring at his own hind end.

Lexi snorted and waved a hand in the air, fanning it away.

The young girl Heath had once known was a bratty, know-it-all, angry, undersize half-pint.

Now she was anything but.

No, scratch that. She was possibly still angry.

But the rest? Gone. In that little kid's place, a beautiful, albeit quietly contained, woman had come down that airport escalator like she'd owned it.

It wasn't often he couldn't get a bead on someone. He'd made a career out of reading people. It was what had made him so effective as an attorney. At least until living in the fast lane had turned him into someone he hated so much that he'd left it all in his rearview.

But he couldn't get a bead on this Lexi at all.

Lexi rose to her feet, which took some effort, given that Mayhem had put all his weight on her. The dog now stood at her side, staring up at her adoringly, tongue lolling.

"We need to talk," Ashley said.

Lexi nodded, eyeing Ashley on a chair, then Heath on the couch, not making a move toward either of them. "What is it?"

"It's about Mom."

Lexi's eyes shifted to the urn. "Okay. What about her?"

"We didn't have a service or celebration of life." Ashley swallowed hard. "She always said she didn't want that because no one would come, and she asked us to honor that wish."

Lexi nodded. "The attorney told us last year after she passed."

"She'd burned a lot of bridges with the gambling," Ashley went on. "Borrowing from friends, not paying anyone back, but at the same time, kept gambling . . ."

"Do you think I don't know all this? It's why we . . . didn't see each other much."

Ashley shifted anxiously on her feet. "She felt really bad about it, about all of it."

Lexi shrugged. "Speculation."

"She did." Heath sensed the heavy weight of Lexi's annoyance at his interruption in what she clearly felt was none of his business. "She was sick about it, actually."

Lexi opened her mouth, probably to blast him, but Ashley stood. "She won the lotto. Shortly before she died."

Lexi stilled. "She did? How much?"

"I don't know, just that she won big."

"No." Lexi shook her head. "That can't be. You're the executor, you know better than anyone that the only assets she had were this house and the truck."

Ashley swallowed hard and sent a quick glance to Heath. "Actually, I passed on the responsibilities of being executor. Mom had made a provision in the will that I could do so if I wanted. I was so overwhelmed, and not sure I could do the job justice, so I passed it to Heath."

Lexi's brows raised, but she said nothing.

"Apparently, there was something the attorney held back at Mom's request," Ashley said. "A separate provision, which was left out initially, not to be known until one year after her passing. I don't know why, and I just found out last week. That's why I called you to come out here. She split her lotto winnings into six parts, each going to someone she wanted to pay back for one reason or another. We were left six sealed envelopes to deliver, one at a time, once a week, until it's done."

"We?"

"You and me."

Lexi shook her head. "I can't just stay here for six weeks. I've got a life to get back to."

Something about that last sentence rang untrue, but Heath didn't know this version of Lexi enough to even guess at what she might really be thinking.

Ashley stared down at her tightly clasped hands. "I know you only took a week's leave, but I'm hoping you might be willing to extend it."

"You should've told me this before I got here. But . . . you didn't, because . . ." She studied her sister. "Because you wanted to make sure I couldn't say no."

"Correct," Ashley whispered.

Lexi gave a shocked shake of her head, as if she couldn't believe this. Mayhem, feeling the tension, whined, and Lexi reached down, setting a reassuring hand on top of his head. "I can't just ask work for more time. Nor can I afford to fly back and forth every week for the next six weeks to do something that Daisy didn't even have the decency to give us a heads-up over."

"Actually," Ashley said, "I think Mom meant for you to stay here the whole time. As for why we weren't told when she died, I'm guessing she wanted to wait the year so that our grief would be dulled enough that we'd agree to do this."

"You mean me, so that *I'd* agree to do this," Lexi said. "It's an unfair request."

"For what it's worth, I agree." Heath stood and met Lexi's angry gaze. "It *is* unfair. But make it she did. So now, I suppose, you've got a choice. To do as she's asked, or to turn tail and run."

Lexi's eyes narrowed dangerously. "I don't run."

"So then you're in."

"I didn't say that."

He nodded. "Well, then, if you're on the fence, here's something to sweeten the pot. Whatever's left from her winnings

after you two deliver the envelopes is to be divided equally between both of you."

"How much?"

With that poker face, she'd be a most worthy opponent in
court, not that he intended to ever set another foot in a courtroom. "That's not to be disclosed until it's time."

Lexi studied him for a beat. "Are the envelope recipients all
local?"

"No, there are a few that will require a road trip."

She appeared to think about that. "Why can't we mail them?"

"That's not how Daisy wanted it done. She didn't want any
of the recipients getting advance warning. If they're not home
when delivery is attempted, we'll figure something else out."

"And you care why? What's in this for you?"

"I made a promise," he said.

She didn't look impressed. "So? My mom was the master of
breaking promises."

"Not to me, she wasn't."

Her eyes chilled. Hooded. "Well, good for you."

"Lexi," Ashley said softly. "It's Mom you're mad at, not him."

Heath gave a low laugh. "Oh, she's mad at me too, trust me."

"For what?" Ashley wanted to know.

"For one thing, I was an asshole kid."

Lexi shrugged. "So was I."

He held her gaze. "I liked you as a kid."

"*No one* liked me as a kid. And it was a long time ago. The
person you knew then, that was season one me. I got canceled,
needed a rewrite."

A low laugh escaped him. "Same."

She was still considering him when Ashley said, "*All* kids
have their moments. As a teacher, I'm an authority on that.

Whatever either of you pulled all those years ago, it's in the distant past."

"It wasn't *all* in the distant past," Lexi murmured.

"Anything before today is in the distant past," Ashley said. "It's a new day."

And this. *This* was why he'd defend Ashley until he didn't have a breath left in his body, even against her sister if he had to. Ashley might be young, but she was also an old soul.

But Lexi . . . He had an entirely different connection with her, one that had always been undefined. That is, until that kiss five years ago, when she'd rocked his world and threatened to turn it upside down. He'd done his best to cut off his feelings for her. And then today happened. That hug in the airport. In the blink of an eye, their chemistry was back, and he knew she'd felt it too.

Lexi crossed her arms. "So these six envelopes, they're the real reason you asked me to come out here? You said it was because you missed me."

Heath heard pain in that statement. Surely Ashley did too, but she met her sister's gaze evenly. "You have no idea how much I missed you. Stick around this time, and maybe you'll get the idea."

Lexi took that in, but when she spoke, she ignored what Ashley had said, either unwilling or unable to believe. "So she really just expected us to deliver these letters for her? Letters she kept hidden from us until now."

On this, Heath felt every bit as frustrated as Lexi, and wasn't that ironic. They'd rarely agreed on a thing.

"I don't understand why she'd do this," Lexi said. She looked at Heath. "Or why you'd be a part of it."

How to explain? His grandpa's house was one street behind

Daisy's. Their backyards butted up against each other. His mom died when Heath was ten. Since his dad had abused alcohol to cope, turning himself into a mean, menacing drunk, Heath and his younger brother, Cole, had spent much of their time at their grandpa's. Daisy used to bring them casseroles for dinners, and often baked them cookies to take with their school lunches. In later years, when Heath had worked hellishly long hours and Cole had been facing a health crisis of his own, Daisy had helped out as needed.

Heath honestly had no idea how he and Cole would've gotten through without her. "She had congestive heart failure when she won the lotto jackpot, but hadn't told anyone. She knew she could possibly have a few more years, but maybe not. She had a small life insurance policy. She had a trust created and made that trust the beneficiary of the payout, as well as her winnings." He paused. "I managed the trust for her. It was the last thing she asked of me, and I couldn't tell her no."

Lexi merely snorted. "Ironic, since she had no problem telling people no. She told me no too many times to count."

Ashley leaned forward. Earnest. Sweet. Wanting to make this better, and not yet realizing she couldn't possibly do that. "She'd made changes, Lexi. She wasn't the same person you knew."

"In my experience, people don't change their spots." She looked at Heath. "Mr. *Shotgun*."

He couldn't help it, he laughed. She was just as feisty and stubborn as ever. He'd loved competing with her over . . . well, everything.

And apparently he still liked it.

"Is that all, then?" Lexi asked. "This meeting's adjourned?"

"Not yet." Heath gestured to the couch. Her jaw tightened, but she sat, crossing her long legs. She didn't burrow in, like

Ashley did. Nope, her spine remained rigid. Braced to hate everything about this.

And she would indeed hate everything about this. He actually didn't know much about her childhood in this house other than the few tidbits Ashley and Daisy had doled out over the years. He knew her dad had been a prick and that Lexi had been moved across the country to be raised by him.

Daisy had admitted more than once in the years since how much she regretted that her addiction had led to her ex getting to keep Lexi.

He had zero idea how Lexi felt about any of that, but given how closed off she'd been since arriving, he knew it cost her to be here. "As Ashley said, there are six envelopes, six people Daisy wanted to make amends with but ran out of time." He pushed an envelope across the coffee table. "This is the first one."

Lexi didn't so much as look at it. "I think she was looking to push Ashley and me into spending time together, but she doesn't get to dictate that from the grave." Again, she glanced at the urn. "Correction: from the mantel. I can't just stay, and it's wrong to ask it of me."

"I hear you," Ashley said. "And I don't know why she wanted it that way, but she did. Maybe . . . maybe you could talk to your boss. Maybe they'd let you extend your leave, or work from here."

Again, something came and went in Lexi's gaze, too fast for Heath to identify. She turned her head, raising her chin as if daring him to push her into this. But that wasn't his job. She'd either do it, for her mom, for Ashley, or . . . she wouldn't.

"I'm sorry," she finally said. "I can't. Let's just deliver the envelopes this week, then split what's left between us and go back to our own lives."

Ashley opened her mouth, then shut it before standing and walking out of the room.

Mayhem jumped onto the couch taking her spot, setting his big fat head on Heath's shoulder.

Lexi eyed the empty doorway where Ashley had vanished. "I'm guessing," she said quietly, "that this is where you tell me I'm being an ungrateful, horrible sister."

He shook his head. "You have to protect your life, your livelihood. I get that. I also get that it truly is an unfair ask. But I'll say this. Your sister thought, or hoped anyway, that you were here to be her sister. Not to get whatever money is coming your way and go."

Her eyes narrowed, the ones that could slice open a vein or, as he'd caught more than once, reveal a fathomless, hidden pain. Right now though, she was still giving him nothing.

"She's been counting the days until your visit," he said. "It's all she's talked about, having you here. So all I'm asking is that you do your best not to break her heart."

"Why do you care?"

"She's family to me."

She rose to her feet. "Then maybe you should deliver the envelopes with her."

"Daisy didn't ask for me. She asked for you." He paused, watching her absorb that. "When you first left," he said, "Ashley used to get so lonely for a sibling, she'd follow me and my brother around. She became the third musketeer."

"I didn't leave."

"What?"

"You said 'when I left,' but that's not what happened." She looked away. "It wasn't my choice."

His teen years had been harrowing to say the least, and so had finding a way to get through college, pass the bar, and make a name for himself. He'd learned to keep a wall around his heart, learned to operate from a place of logic at all times, not emotion. Except right now, while taking in Lexi's words and the aching hurt behind them. "I'm sorry."

She shrugged.

More than a little unnerved by how much he wanted to reach over and take her hand, he leaned back instead.

"Ashley should have told me the truth about why I was coming here," she said.

Another thing they agreed on.

"You don't want me to hurt Ashley," she said. "I don't want that either. I'll do what needs to be done, and then I'm out."

"You're going to stay," he said with surprise.

"I don't see much of a choice. It's not right to make Ashley do this by herself." She moved to the living room window, looking out, arms crossed, posture stiff.

There was no lake view from this house, just the wild, majestic mountains, which told their own story. They also had a way of calming the soul, quieting distress. At least, that's what they'd always done for Heath. "What can I do to help?"

She said nothing.

"Don't feel like sharing with the room?"

This won him another shrug. "Don't take it personally. I'm not into trust."

He smiled. "Finally, some honesty."

She didn't turn to him, but she didn't have to for him to feel her roll her eyes, and it gave him a reluctant smile. He had no idea what it was about her, what it'd *always* been about her, that spurred him to ruffle her feathers, push her, goad her, challenge her to reveal her real self to him.

She turned then and caught him staring. And instead of being amused, her eyes chilled. "We're not doing this, not this time."

"*This?*" he repeated.

"Yes, this." She gestured between them. "No kissing. No fake relationship. No relationship at all. You're just Daisy's messenger, right? So no need to know what's going on in my head. Or in my life. And I don't need to know what's going on in yours, whether you're seeing someone or not. It doesn't matter."

"I'm not," he said, "in a relationship. And if you decide you want to know what's going on in my life at any time, just ask."

She stared at him for a long beat, but didn't speak.

In the silence, Mayhem farted again. Resigned, Heath rose. "I'm sorry, I've got to take him out before we have to fumigate this place."

She waited until he was nearly at the door. "Ashley's lucky to have you at her back." And with that, she vanished down the hall, leaving him to wonder when was the last time someone had *her* back.

CHAPTER 4

A rooster crowed loud enough to peel skin back, and Lexi jerked awake and very nearly out of her own body. Gasping, she put a hand to her chest to keep her heart inside her rib cage and pried open her eyes. There was just enough of dawn's light to jump again at the teenage members of NSYNC smiling down at her from that ancient poster on the wall.

"Cock-a-doodle-dooooo!"

With a groan, she pulled the pillow over her head. "What the actual f—"

"His name's Cluck Norris."

Lexi yanked the pillow off her head and peered bleary eyed at Ashley, standing in the doorway, looking far too chipper and put together for . . . She took in the circa 1990s digital clock's red numbers on the dresser. "Oh my God. It's six. *In the morning.*"

"Yep." Ashley sipped from a mug of what looked and smelled like the coffee that Lexi could use more than her next breath.

"Why?" was the only word she could manage.

"Because I'm excited." Ashley, the caffeinated bee-yotch, grinned. "You're here. You're really here."

They'd stayed up late last night, just the two of them, sitting in the kitchen with not enough ice cream (dairy-free, but beggars didn't get to be choosey) and way too much wine, if her headache meant anything. As they had all their lives, they stayed away from problematic topics, instead mooning over their favorite TV shows, books, and which celebrities were their future spouses.

Lexi claimed Idris Elba.

Ashley claimed Emily Blunt.

No matter that they were both already married . . . When Ashley had finally gone to bed, Lexi still hadn't been tired. She'd flipped on the small TV over the dresser. Unable to find the remote, she'd been stuck watching a documentary on Ted Bundy, and gave herself nightmares.

Or maybe that was from agreeing to stay here for the next six weeks. Insanity, really. She'd been subleasing a room in a large house the past month, with five others. All hardworking people who'd been nothing but nice, if a bit distant.

Okay, maybe the distant one had been her.

In any case, the rent would be going up next month, and she'd given her notice. Which meant on top of everything else wrong in her life, she was soon to be homeless.

Cluck Norris did his screeching thing again, and she nearly fell off the bed.

Ashley laughed so hard she had to set her coffee down on the nightstand. She was still cackling when Lexi sat up and scooped the coffee, claiming it as her own.

"Rude," Ashley said.

"So is that damn rooster. When did you get him?"

"Oh, Cluck Norris isn't mine. He gets in through the break in our fence to eat my homegrown romaine lettuce."

Lexi blinked. "You grow lettuce?"

"I grow a lot of things. Those trees along the back? They're crab apple trees. You should taste all the stuff I cook with the fruit they provide."

Once upon a time, all Ashley would eat was junk food. She'd believed sugar was its own food group. Now there was no junk food in the entire kitchen—yes, Lexi had looked—with the exception of the coconut ice cream, which hardly counted. "Who are you, and what have you done to my sister?"

Ashley gave a small but genuine smile at the "sister" comment, but only shrugged. That wasn't unusual. But the break in eye contact was. "People change," Ashley finally said.

"Not in my experience, at least they don't change in the ways that matter." Lexi paused. "You're pale. You feel okay?"

"Of course. I'm fine. Why?"

"Because you're in a big, baggy sweatshirt instead of one of your flower-power skirts."

"It's laundry day." Ashley shrugged again. "Plus, I love sweatshirts. Am I wearing a bra? Who knows. Am I wearing what I wore to bed beneath it? Maybe . . . It's anyone's guess." She paused. "Did you mean it?"

Lexi didn't need clarification. "Yes. I'll stay and do what we have to."

"And your job? You'll be able to extend your leave?"

Lexi worked at keeping her expression blank, since she'd lied about the taking leave part. She'd been flat-out fired. But that was a story for another day. Or never. "I'll make it work." And before any more questions came at her, she added, "I don't break my word."

"True," Ashley said. "You never once flaked on a promise to visit. Because you rarely promised. Or visited."

Lexi felt the one-two punch of those words. "I came when I could. And I didn't want to be Mom, promising to come to my middle school graduation and then not showing up. Promising to be at my dance recital and then not showing up. Promising—"

"I get it." Ashley hugged herself tightly. "And I know how hard it was for you to grow up without her, but—"

"If you're about to tell me she did the best she could, save your breath."

Ashley flushed.

And this. *This* was why she and Ashley shared wine and ice cream, not deep emotions. Suddenly exhausted all over again, Lexi flopped back onto her pillow. "I take it going back to sleep isn't going to happen."

In answer, Ashley tossed an envelope onto the bed.

Their first delivery.

"I thought you might want to get the clock ticking," Ashley said.

Lexi read the name on the envelope. "Margo Schutz."

"She lives in Placerville. It's a two-hour drive, give or take. I'd like to leave in the next half hour, I've got a class later this afternoon."

"A class?"

Ashley turned back from the door long enough to say, "You told me last year, after I expressed being bored with my life when I wasn't teaching, that I should expand my horizons. So I did."

"What kind of class?" Lexi asked, but the door had already been shut.

She showered quickly. Not because she wanted to, but because after four minutes, the hot water ran out. It might be summer in Tahoe, but the mornings felt like the North Pole, and today was no exception.

The house felt silent and empty, so she headed outside.

Still no Ashley, but when she peered in the side window of the truck, she saw the keys in the ignition. She reached for the handle to open the door, but froze at the spider nestled in the handle.

Correction: *massive* spider.

With a squeak, she jumped back, hand to her pounding heart. "Why are you so big?" Since no one answered, or miraculously appeared to save her, she looked around for something to knock the spider loose. Grabbing a stick lying on the wild grass beneath the sole towering pine in the front yard, she eyed her multilegged, hairy opponent again. New problem. The stick wasn't nearly long enough. Probably no stick would be long enough. So instead of knocking the spider off, she chucked the stick at it.

She missed, but the spider flew into the air and . . . vanished.

With a startled scream, Lexi flapped her hands over her entire body, certain it was crawling on her—

"Ah, the spider dance."

Why. Why in the world did it have to be him to find her? "If you laugh, I'll find the spider and put it in your bed."

"No, you won't. You'd have to touch it."

Opening her eyes with a sigh, she turned to face Heath.

He stood there in another pair of sexy jeans, battered running shoes, and a black T-shirt acting like it was its job to perfectly emphasize his broad shoulders and flat belly—which, for reasons she didn't want to think about, annoyed the crap out of her.

He smiled. "My bed, huh?"

"I didn't say bed. I said head. I'm going to put it on your head."

When he laughed, she crossed her arms. "What do you want?"

He held up a finger, signaling he wanted her to hold on to

that question. Then he knocked the spiderweb she hadn't even noticed from the truck's door handle. "Listen up, spiders," he said to the morning air. "I know you do good things, but you've got to stay out of sight or risk death by teeny, tiny stick."

Lexi sighed. "Again, *what do you want?*"

He faced her, smart enough to make an effort at swiping the smile off his face. "Just making sure you ladies don't need anything before you head out."

"In fact, I do need something," she said.

"Name it."

Name it? Was he nuts? "It's your turn to do something embarrassing."

He slid his hands into his jeans pockets. "I don't do embarrassing."

Of course not. "Okay, well, this has been a whole bunch of fun. Buh-bye, now." She turned back to the truck to get in, then hesitated because she still had the heebie-jeebies. She literally couldn't force herself to touch the door handle.

"Worried the spider left behind a mate?"

"No." She bit her lower lip. "I'm worried about the spider cooties."

"Naturally." Coming close, he opened the door for her and, with his free hand, gestured grandly, offering a mocking bow while he was at it. She accidentally bumped her arm into his and . . . Why in the world did he smell so good? His hair was damp and curling against the nape of his neck. He'd just gotten out of a shower. And why that made her mind spin, she had zero idea. She tossed her purse behind the driver's seat before looking at him, finding him with his head tilted back, face to the cresting sun, eyes closed, a hint of contentment on his face as the light breeze rustled his hair.

Damn.

Luckily, before she could further humiliate herself by getting caught drooling, Ashley came out of the house, stopping short at the sight of them. "Are we fighting some more, or . . ."

Lexi glanced at Heath, and realizing just how close they stood, she jumped back.

He just smiled at Ashley. "No fighting."

Ashley beamed at him as she climbed into the passenger seat.

Okay, so clearly, they both adored Ashley, and just as clearly, that meant Lexi had to play nice with Heath—at least in front of her sister. She yanked on her seat belt and cranked the key.

Nothing happened.

"She likes to play hard to get," Ashley said.

Lexi turned the key again. This time, the truck roared to life with a little sputtering and a whole bunch of smoke. "Uh . . ."

"Betty's just cold," Ashley said.

"Betty?"

"That's her name. Try again."

Lexi had her doubts, but she put the thing into gear and hit the gas, only halfway sorry when Heath had to jump out of the way or risk getting his foot run over.

"You did that on purpose."

Lexi slid Ashley a look of innocence.

Ashley snorted. "Whatever, I'm not going to let you ruin this. It's going to be fun." Turning in her seat, she waved goodbye to Heath.

Fun? Was she kidding? At the end of the street, Lexi turned the wheel and . . . nothing happened.

"You parked this beast yesterday, you know there's no power steering. You gotta really crank it," Ashley said.

Dear God. It took both arms and just about every other part

of her body to muscle the truck into the turn. By the time they hit town, Ashley had waved to no less than five people. At each stop, she gestured for other cars to go first, even when they had the right of way. "If you keep it up, you're *definitely* going to miss your class," Lexi muttered.

"I've got faith in us."

Good thing one of them did.

CHAPTER 5

Two and a half hours later on the dot, Lexi pulled over a few houses down from the address listed on the envelope. She and Ashley stared at the small cabin in silence.

"Since you got to drive, I get to hand over the envelope," Ashley said.

"I drove the truck because—"

"Betty."

Lexi drew a deep breath for patience that didn't come. "I drove *Betty* because your driving makes me carsick."

Ashley gasped, affronted. If she'd been an old lady, she'd have been clutching her pearls. "My driving's perfect."

"Tell that to all of Betty's dents."

"Hey, she's bigger than a battleship." Ash patted the dashboard. "Not that size matters. Even old as you are, you're beautiful."

"First of all, I love old things." Most of the time she loved them more than people. "Also, beautiful's a stretch. And I stand by my decision to be our designated driver."

"You're as bad as Heath."

Lexi's mouth dropped open. It was her turn to clutch the metaphorical pearls. "You take that back. I'm *nothing* like Heath."

Ashley laughed. "Are you kidding? You're both stubborn, like to be the best at everything, and—"

"You two are close."

"Very." Ashley's amusement faded. "He's been like a brother to me."

Lexi already knew this. Every phone call was all "Heath this" and "Heath that," and . . . and damn. She was jealous. Not of their relationship, but of their ability to have relationships in the first place.

Ash was watching her think too hard, and put a teasing tone in her voice when she said, "You're also both I-told-you-so people—"

"I am so *not* an I-told-you-so person!"

Clearly pleased at the response she'd elicited, Ashley laughed. "Okay. How about this. Every time you find yourself about to roll your eyes or tell someone they're wrong, you make a little check mark in your head. At the end of the day, tally it all up— and *then* we'll finish this conversation."

Lexi had to catch herself from rolling her eyes. "Fine." She paused. Worried. "Wait. Do you and Heath ever talk about me?"

"No, and that's on purpose because I know you're a private person. I think I've mentioned your job a few times, but that's about it."

The job that wasn't even a thing anymore. In the six months since she'd lost it, all she'd been able to do was pick up small, short-term jobs here and there, and just thinking about it and the state of her bank account nearly brought on a panic attack.

"I know you and Heath have your issues, even if neither of

you will talk about whatever happened. But I think being here will be good for you."

"How so?"

"You isolate yourself in your work. And I get it, you study objects, piece together their histories. Which is lovely, but objects can't talk to you or keep you company. Imagine how much more interesting people might be than things, Lexi. Imagine if you actually dug deeper into personal connections."

"You want me to connect with Heath? Not going to happen."

"Why?"

"Because . . ."

Ashley raised her brows, waiting.

Lexi blew out a breath. How to say that she'd always wanted to connect with him, that he'd been the one to back off. "Look, clearly you want me to know something. Just say it."

"That would be cheating. All I'm saying is just get to know him—"

"I know him."

"As who he is now," Ashley said. "And you sound awfully defensive. It's a lot of energy to put behind someone you claim you don't want to connect to."

"The entirety of my energy toward him is indifference."

"Uh-huh. Is that what all the kids are calling it these days?"

Lexi had to laugh. "Hey, of the two of us, *you're* the kid. You tell me. Come on." She undid her seat belt. "Let's get this over with."

They knocked on the front door, and it was answered by a fifty-something woman in jeans, a plaid jacket over a sweatshirt, hoodie up, holding an ax.

Lexi and Ashley both took a huge step back.

The woman studied them. "Are you the people who come around and want to talk about the Lord and Savior?"

"No, ma'am," Ashley said. "Are you an ax murderer?"

"Nope."

"Are you Margo Schutz?"

The woman's eyes narrowed suspiciously. "Who's asking?"

"I'm Ashley Fontaine." She smiled sweetly. "Daisy Fontaine's daughter. And this is Lexi, my sister. We were hoping we could talk to you."

"Daisy's girls? Well, if that don't beat all." Margo stepped back for them to enter, and to Lexi's horror, Ashley did just that.

"Get back out here," Lexi whispered. The woman was holding a damn ax, and looked as if she knew how to wield it too. *What are you doing?*"

"What Mom asked of us." Ashley smiled at Margo. "We've got something for you. Is there somewhere we could sit for a moment?"

"You're the teacher who's also an artist."

Lexi turned to look at Ashley. "You're an artist?"

Ashley lifted a shoulder. "I dabble."

How did she not know this? *Because you don't connect, because you let your relationship with her be superficial only, because you're an emotional coward . . .*

"Your mom gave me one of your paintings for my birthday right before she died." Margo's smile faded. "She was always doing that, giving her friends little gifts. It's hanging in my den."

"Oh, I'd love to see it," Ashley said warmly.

"Sure! Follow me."

"Seriously," Lexi muttered beneath her breath, catching her sister's hand. "Have you not seen a single horror movie?"

Margo turned back with a knowing look. "Your mom told me all about you too Lexi."

Lexi froze, feeling like she was ten all over again. Ten, and a troubled, tumultuous, messy handful.

Margo smiled at whatever look was on Lexi's face, but her voice was kind. "She was so proud of you when you got that fancy degree."

Ironic, since the reason Lexi almost didn't go to college at all had been Daisy's fault.

"And then, when you landed your dream job . . . She was over the moon."

A job that she'd lost due to her own stupidity in trusting the wrong person . . . Maybe the apple really never fell far from the tree. She'd worked so hard to lose the pandemonium in her life, but she'd failed, like she had at so many other things. Her mom's life had always been crazy chaos, and it was that, that single trait Lexi had somehow taken on as her own, that she hated more than anything.

Margo's warm gaze encompassed both Lexi and Ashley as she put a hand to her chest—only one since she still held the ax in the other. "She was so proud of you both that she could've just burst."

Lexi thought about the pictures hanging on the walls at Daisy's house. Her mom had kept up with her more than she'd ever imagined, with her dad in cahoots, clearly. He'd worked a lot, and Lexi had been young, not to mention an introverted kid who hadn't opened up easily. Or at all. She figured he'd been frustrated by her, but maybe she'd been wrong. Either way, she had no idea how to reconcile the parents she'd known with the things she'd learned in the past two days.

Margo led them to a small den and pointed proudly to a

painting, an aerial view of a wave spilling onto sand, the stunning blue of the water, the white chop of the sea-foam, the graininess of the sand making Lexi feel like she stood there, right there, smelling the ocean air. Her mouth fell open. "How did you make it so . . . three D?"

"A spatula and sponge," Ashley said.

"I can't take my eyes off it."

Margo smiled. "Me either."

Lexi could feel the emotion that had gone into the painting, and the longer she stood there, the more her stone heart melted. "It's . . . amazing. *You're* amazing."

Ashley beamed. "Thank you." She turned to Margo. "And thank *you* for letting me visit my work. I miss them when they're gone." And then she gently took the envelope from Lexi's fingers and handed it over to the ax murderer.

Margo looked down at her name. "This is your mom's handwriting."

Ashley smiled and nodded.

"Please, sit," Margo said, and sank to the couch, staring a moment longer at the envelope before opening it, surprising Lexi when she read it out loud.

Dear Margo,

Hello, darling! I know you don't want a thank-you, but you'll have to bear with me. I need you to know that your friendship meant everything to me. As did your kindness and generosity. I know you didn't expect to get paid back for those things, but . . . tough.

You know that we met during a time in my life where I lived by the motto "go big or go home." You also know I went big, and lost. I wanted to go home but didn't even have bus money. And then this big rig pulled up alongside of me where I stood in the icy rain, in front of an off-the-beaten-path casino, and you hopped out and offered me a ride. We talked about our kids and how you wanted them to be the first in your family to go to college, only you had no idea how to pay for it. So I'm hoping this covers everything they might need when the time comes. Thank you, my friend.

Love,
Daisy

So not an ax murderer, then. Margo was a truck driver. One who was currently clearly trying and failing to swallow back tears. Finally, she peered into the envelope and pulled out a check. With a gasp, she dropped it like it was a hot potato.

Lexi bent down and picked it up, then had to school herself not to react. There were a lot of zeroes. She flipped it around so Ashley could see.

Her sister gasped.

"Yeah," Margo said, stunned.

Lexi leaned into Ashley. "How much did you say Daisy won?"

"I don't know. She never told me. But damn. Good for her. And good for Margo."

Lexi didn't want to rain on anyone's parade, but there was something in her gut that she didn't like. Jealousy? No, that didn't quite fit. She honestly didn't begrudge Margo a damn thing. So what, then? Unbidden came the memory she'd buried deep, of that time when she'd gone to pay her first quarter college tuition, only to discover that the trust her maternal grandma had set up for her had been emptied—by the only other person who had access to that account.

Daisy.

She'd gambled it away years before and had never said a word. Maybe because by then Lexi, tired of Daisy's broken promises, had asked her mom to stop promising to visit, since she wouldn't actually show. Stop making plans to call, since she wouldn't actually call. Stop everything.

And Daisy had. The one and only time she'd ever done what Lexi had asked.

They'd seen each other when Lexi had come west to visit Ashley, and everything had been fine as long as she didn't let Daisy try to apologize and make more worthless promises.

"I'm not taking this." Margo shoved the check at Lexi.

"What?" Lexi shook her head. "No, it's for you. You have to take it."

Margo laughed so hard, she had to swipe tears from her face. "Honey, I'm twice your age. I don't have to do shit that I don't want to. And I don't want to take your mom's money. I'm incredibly touched that she even thought about me in the end, but me and mine are good. I want you two to keep it."

"We couldn't—"

Margo shrugged and stuffed the now folded check into Lexi's front jeans pocket. "So then give it to someone in need. Pay it forward."

Lexi was stunned. It had never occurred to her that someone might turn down Daisy's offering. Not to mention, Heath had made it clear—they had to deliver each of the envelopes before they could get out from under this task Daisy had left them. "But you have to—"

"Honey, I really don't." Her smile softened her words. "Lovely seeing you both in person. I hope you don't mind letting yourselves out, I'm far too comfortable to move."

Lexi opened her mouth to argue, but Ashley murmured a goodbye from them both and tugged her out of the den. They were halfway through the living room when Lexi caught sight of a lamp and sucked in a breath. "Ash," she whispered. "That's a porcelain tabletop Lladro lamp. One of the rarest ones out there."

"So?"

"So . . . I'd have to look into it, but in that condition, it's worth easily fifty thousand dollars."

Ashley stared at her. "No wonder Margo didn't want to take Mom's money."

Lexi shook her head. "She didn't take the money because she's a good person who refused to take advantage of an old friend." She turned and went back to the doorway of the den. "Margo? You know that beautiful table lamp in your living room? The one by the couch?"

"I sure do. Picked it up for a song at a local thrift shop. Why, you like it? Take it. It's yours."

"No, I couldn't," Lexi said. "Because I'd be robbing you. If it's what I think it is, it's worth a lot of money."

Margo smiled. "No shittin'?"

"No shittin'."

"How do you find out if it's what you think it is?"

"I could make a call," Lexi said.

"Go for it."

Lexi pulled out her phone and thumbed through her contacts looking for Elaine, who worked for the company she had been unceremoniously fired from. In fact, Elaine worked directly for

Lexi's ex. They hadn't spoken since she'd been shown the door, but they'd been lunch buddies for several years, and had been close. It'd be okay, she told herself. Elaine would be happy to reconnect . . . she hoped. But as the phone rang, she stopped breathing and her nerves started jangling. Just as the second ring started, she got kicked over to voicemail.

Her stomach rolled, but with both Margo and Ashley looking at her expectantly, she smiled. "She's in a meeting. I'll do some research and get back to you, if you'd like."

Margo waved a hand. "Honestly, don't trouble yourself on my account."

Ashley didn't say anything, but Lexi could tell by the look on her face she knew something was wrong. "Whatever you do," Lexi said, "take it to a reputable place to get its exact worth before you cash it in. I don't know any local experts—"

"You," Ashley said. "You're an expert."

Ashley's easy belief, when Lexi no longer believed in herself, warmed one of the cold, dark corners of her heart, but she shook her head. "You could try one of the larger auction houses that are known for being both good and fair."

Margo stood and walked to Lexi, cupping her face. "You could've ripped me off, but you didn't. You're good, straight through." She smiled. "Just like your mama was."

They were outside when Lexi found her voice. "Daisy will probably haunt us for not forcing Margo to keep the check."

"Why are you acting like the money is evil?"

"On the contrary, money isn't evil." People were. "But how do you think Daisy won the lotto? Do you think she was walking by a gas station and a winning lotto ticket just happened to fall into her hands? No. She was still gambling."

Ashley flushed a bit. "To be honest, I never gave it a second thought. Mom had her five-year chip. She carried it in her pocket every day and showed anyone who would listen. She wasn't gambling again."

"Ash . . . grow up." The minute the words left her, Lexi grimaced, hating that she felt like she'd just kicked a puppy. "Daisy was an addict, through and through. If she hadn't died, the money would've been gone faster than you could blink, because she—"

"No. Stop. Just stop." Ashley looked close to tears. "I told you she was clean. Stop holding her past against her."

They got into the truck, the silence hostile between them for the first time . . . ever.

Ashley crossed her arms. "You know what? I'm not doing this with you again."

"This?"

"Delivering the rest of the envelopes."

Lexi felt the arrow hit its mark right in the center of her chest. "If we don't, we don't get whatever money is left."

"Good. I don't want it anyway."

Lexi didn't say anything to that. Not when, at the end of the day, she *needed* whatever scraps were left, no matter how little that might be—a fact she absolutely hated herself for. "Ash—"

"Save it. No one will know if we don't do these together, so feel free to do what you gotta do."

They rode home in silence, and when Ashley walked into the house without looking back, Lexi ended up on a walk by herself. She hadn't meant to start a fight. Just as she hadn't meant to be rude to Heath. She had no idea why she wore armor that didn't let anything penetrate. She really didn't, especially since, if she had to be here in Sunrise Cove, she didn't want to start off on the wrong foot. Realizing she'd walked partially around the block, she paused in front of a house with a porch that currently held one Heath Bowman.

He was doing something on his phone, though he looked up when she approached, his eyes both surprised and amused.

The amusement somehow made her irritation bubble up again, even more so when he didn't speak, just raised a single brow.

Fine. She'd go first. "I have a few things I want to say."

A small smile curved his mouth. "Don't let me stop you."

"We're grown-up now. We don't have to continue being enemies."

"Enemies," he repeated.

"Okay, frenemies."

Again, he just looked at her. To fill the silence, she said, "Look. I know I haven't always been super nice . . ." She broke off. Assigning blame wasn't going to help her case.

This earned her another smile. "Oh, don't stop there."

"Fine. I told Ashley that you were a terrible kisser. Whatever. You started it by looking so horrified that I kissed you in the first place."

"'Horrified' is the wrong word."

"What's the right word, then?"

He opened his mouth, and then shut it again. Shook his head. "What does it matter now? We've always brought out the worst in each other. Let it go."

"Are you talking about the next year, when I came out here to visit Ashley and it happened to be your birthday? I swear, I didn't mean to mash your plate of cake into your face. I was just walking by and I tripped. Besides, you were dating that brunette with the fake boobs. You never even noticed me."

He smiled. "Brandy. She was nice."

"Uh-huh." Lexi crossed her arms, feeling ridiculous.

"And when we were kids?"

Right. She'd been even worse back then. "Do you mean the time I told Julia Benson that you didn't like her when you did?"

He clasped a hand to his chest. "Broke my heart."

She rolled her eyes. "You lived."

"What about when you tattled on me when I cheated on that fifth-grade science project? I had to redo the whole thing."

"You'd gotten one of the older neighborhood girls to do it for you!"

He grinned. "I'm seeing a pattern here. You're a jealous little thing."

For a beat, she froze, because . . . it was horrifyingly, humiliatingly true. Tossing up her hands, she whirled to go, because nothing about this little trip down memory lane had been any fun.

"Friends," he said.

She turned back. "What?"

"We weren't enemies. We weren't frenemies. We were friends." And with that, proving he was infinitely more mature than she, he walked into the house and shut the door.

CHAPTER 6

Two days later, Heath finished fixing Mrs. Yates's leaky roof. Grandpa had a crush on the woman, and said he'd climb the ladder and do it himself if Heath couldn't fix it.

So Heath had fixed Mrs. Yates's roof. He now had three splinters, a bruised shoulder, and a sore back, but the job was done.

And the truth was, after all those years in a courtroom, where sometimes the bad guys won and the good guys lost, where often there was no closure . . . he loved physical labor. Loved working with his hands. Loved being outside and accomplishing something tangible.

He shifted in the hammock in his grandpa's backyard, drinking a beer, watching a few puffy clouds cross the sky. Mrs. Yates's roof was just the latest in a long line of renovation jobs he'd taken on since coming back to Sunrise Cove. In fact, he was just as busy now as he had been as a lawyer. He couldn't even remember the last time he'd had thirty minutes to himself to think, or had enjoyed even a moment of peace. Or stayed at his own place up in Hidden Hills. When his grandpa had gotten sick, it'd immediately been all hands on deck. That had been almost two years ago now. His grandpa was better—unless his bad attitude counted—but he still couldn't live on his own. Nor could he handle all the stairs at Heath's—

A movement on his left caught his eye, and he had just enough time to yell, "Mayhem, no—"

Too late.

The dog took a flying leap, landing with his full weight on Heath's stomach, but smart enough to flatten himself out so they didn't tip.

Still, all the air whooshed from Heath's lungs. "*Ouch*. You need to go on a diet."

Mayhem licked his chin, blowing his hot doggy breath in Heath's face before laying his big, heavy head on Heath's chest, those chocolate-brown eyes filled with so much love it almost hurt to look at him. "That's cheating, looking at me like that."

"He looks at you like that because you're the best thing that ever happened to him." Cole stepped out of the kitchen and onto the back porch. "He remembers who pulled him out of that shelter the day he was to be euthanized and gave him to Grandpa as an emotional support dog."

"That was forever ago in doggy years."

Mayhem licked Heath's ear, and Cole smiled. "He's never forgotten." He gave Heath a loaded look. "None of us have forgotten."

Heath sighed. Not going there. "Don't you have something to do?"

"Of course." Cole grinned. "My wife."

"You work twenty-four seven, and you have a toddler who thinks he's a wild wolf cub. You don't have time to do your wife."

"I make the time. How do you think I've got one kid with

another on the way?" Cole grinned when Heath made a face. "What, you've got something against healthy relationships? Oh, wait . . ."

"Smart-ass." Heath looked around his grandpa's large yard, which was in full summer garden mode with all of his and Ashley's hard work coming to fruition. On both sides of the fence, using both of their yards, they had strawberries, broccoli, snap peas, lettuce, cherry tomatoes, and more. It'd been backbreaking work, but somehow also one of the most rewarding things he'd ever done, growing something as real as food with his hands instead of a court memo or brief.

Cole took in the garden and shook his head, marveling. "I don't know how you did it, but you managed to take a piece-of-shit, overgrown yard and turn it into something remarkable. The peace and quiet alone is amazing."

"Peace and quiet? Are you kidding me? You've met Grandpa, right?"

"Hey, Misty and I offered to take him in."

"Right," Heath said on a laugh. "Matty was a newborn, and your wife was going through postpartum. A stubborn old man who refuses to wear pants and watches football at maximum volume would have been a huge help. He also gripes about everything I cook and throws things at me when he gets mad—which is a lot, by the way."

"At least he couldn't hit a barn standing right in front of one."

Heath snorted. "There's that."

"My point," Cole said, softer now, all signs of kidding gone, "is that I owe you."

"No, you don't."

"Misty says I do, and since that's not the hill I want to die on, I'm siding with my wife."

"Fine. I need a favor. I've got a basketball game tonight."

"Is that old men's rec league?"

"Ha ha. I need you to watch Mayhem and Grandpa."

"Sure." Cole pulled a doggy biscuit from his pocket. Mayhem stood up—on Heath's chest.

"No—" Too late. Mayhem took a flying leap off the hammock. Heath gripped the side ropes to no avail. For several heartbeats he held on through the wild swinging, and then . . .

He lay face-first in the dirt with Mayhem helpfully licking his ear. He slid the dog a look. "Your name should've been Menace."

This earned him another slobbery kiss.

Heath pushed himself to all fours and assessed. He was fine, but his beer was not. He nudged Mayhem away, sliding a fulminating look to his brother, who, the ass, was bent over, hands on his knees, laughing like a buffoon. Rising to his feet, Heath dusted himself off and then pulled something from his pocket. His brother wasn't the only smart-ass in the family. Heath whistled to get Mayhem's attention, waving the doggy biscuit before chucking it at Cole, just high enough that his brother had to jump for it. And as he came down, treat in hand, Mayhem pounced, his front paws giving Cole a junk punch.

Cole dropped to his knees, hands over his crotch.

Satisfying.

"Seriously, Heath?" Misty waddled out the back door of the house. She'd been a high school track star, but at the moment, she was about two years pregnant. When she made it to them, hands on hips, she nudged her high school sweetheart husband. With her foot. "First of all . . ."

Heath winced. "You should run," he suggested to Cole.

"Run?"

"She said 'first of all,' which means she's prepared research, data, charts, and is about to destroy you."

Misty rolled her eyes. "Don't make me laugh. I'm too mad."

"Again, or still?" Cole asked.

Misty sighed. "Never mind." She eyed the body part he was currently holding on to. "What if I want a third kid someday?"

Cole groaned and flopped to his back like a beached fish. "You said you were done after this one." He reached up and gently rubbed her belly. "That I ruined your figure and gave you hemorrhoids."

"And you wonder why I don't want kids," Heath said, and dramatically held out his hand, palm up, like, *See exhibit A*.

Misty pointed at him. "And you. You can forget me making you my world-famous, best-on-the-planet chocolate chip cookies ever again."

"He started it."

"Did not," Cole said.

"You're both children." She turned back to the house. "Matty's asleep on the couch. If either of you wakes him, I'll castrate you with a dull knife." Then she tottered back inside.

Cole sat up with a grimace. "I'm pretty sure she was kidding. At least about the castrating."

"And the cookies?"

"Oh, she definitely meant that." Cole rubbed his eyes. "I'm exhausted."

"You knew what you were getting into when you had children."

"Did I? Did I know I'd be arguing with a two-year-old that we don't lick people's feet? That we don't touch poop? That we sleep when it's dark?" He looked Heath over. "I'm the exhausted one, but you look like shit."

"Thanks, man."

"No, I mean it," Cole said, eyes solemn. "You're working too hard. Again."

"There are worse things."

Cole shook his head. "When you were doing your attorney thing, you let the job steamroll over your entire life, wrecking your health in the process."

"I did not."

"You did." His brother's eyes were serious now. "You were having daily chest pains. You even blacked out a few times. The doctor assured all of us you weren't having heart attacks, but he also said that the stress was nearly as bad for you. He not-so-lightly suggested you de-stress your life."

"And I did."

Cole nodded. "Some. You broke up with Talia because she wanted more from you than you could give. You quit the job that was killing you slowly. You moved back and said you were done with all that."

"And I am. I'm still here, aren't I?"

"Yeah, but you didn't exactly slow down." Cole shook his head. "Now you're helping me fix up my house before the baby comes, and don't think I don't know that you're also helping half of this neighborhood with their renovations—"

"Mostly just making suggestions."

"Yeah? Is that what you call it when you build an entire in-home elevator for Mrs. Tyler? Or when you put in a wheelchair ramp for Wes Scott's son?"

"So I like working with my hands," Heath said.

"And I know damn well you've helped some of the local businesses with various legal things."

"Consulting here and there for people who can't afford legal help when they need it. I won't apologize for that. For giving back to this town and the people in it when they helped us at our lowest point."

Cole met his gaze, eyes shadowed with the memories, most of them bad. Feeling like a dick for dredging them up in the first place, Heath tipped his head back to look at the sky again. Watching the clouds float was better than the anxiety meds he'd weaned himself off now that his job was no longer slowly killing him. Was there anyone on the planet who could get to him like his brother? No. But there was also no one he trusted more. "I'm okay," he said softly. "And I like to help. I like to feel . . . valuable—"

"Heath." Cole's voice was quiet, pained. "How can you doubt it? Wait. Don't answer that." He moved closer to where Heath had sat down on the ground to hug Mayhem. "This is Dad's ghost again, right?"

Heath closed his eyes, leaned his head back to let the sun warm him. Mayhem gave a soft whine and nudged up as close as he could get. "Like he doesn't haunt you too."

"Of course he does. He was an angry asshole drunk." Cole paused until Heath turned his head and met his solemn gaze. "One that you protected me from. You're the one who bore the brunt of his violence."

"Not talking about it."

"Works for me. Just know this. I get that he made you doubt your worth on a daily basis, but you've got enough money put away for several lifetimes. You helped me and Misty get into a mortgage we could afford. You take care of Grandpa to save my marriage. You're there for anyone who needs you. You've more than proven yourself, so it's time to give up the Superman complex—"

Heath pinched the bridge of his nose. "Cole?"

"Yeah?"

"Shut the fuck up."

Cole laughed softly, and the both of them heard Daisy's old truck on the street behind them. Craning their heads, they could see through the chain-link fence and down the side yard of Daisy's house as Ashley hopped out of the passenger side and yelled at Lexi, "I told you, I don't need your help!"

"Ash, you had two credit cards rejected at the gas station. So I swiped my card. No big deal."

"I'm not a charity case!"

"But I'm using the truck too," Lexi said. "And I always pay my way."

"You've paid for everything since you got here. It was *my* turn." Ashley jabbed a finger at her. "And we both know you're only doing all this so I'll take back what I said about being done delivering the envelopes with you. All you care about is getting whatever money's coming to us and leaving. Well, take Margo's and just go already." And with that, she stormed up the front walk.

"My point is that you need that money too!" Lexi yelled.

Ashley's answer was the sound of the front door slamming shut.

The brothers looked at each other.

"So much for peace and quiet," Heath muttered.

Cole snorted. "She really grew up to be hot as hell."

Heath turned his head and gave Cole a deadpan look. "You're married, asshole."

Cole laughed, and Heath knew he'd been had.

Cole was still grinning. "You still like her."

"Just watching the fireworks."

"Enjoy it, since it sounds like she might bail at any time."

Heath shook his head. "Not before she sees this through. She's too smart to do that. And stubborn." And so damn alluring. Something about her flashing eyes and irritation at all things ridiculous drew him right in. Feeling his smugly smiling brother still staring at him, he rolled his eyes. "What?"

"It's interesting, is all. I'm glad she's here, since your social life is nonexistent."

"Maybe my social life is something I've kept to myself."

"I might believe that if you'd gone on even one date in the past few months."

"Look where dating's gotten me. Nowhere close to a family like the one you've got."

Cole's brows vanished into his hair. "You want a family?"

Shit. "No." Yes . . . "*Maybe.*"

Cole stared at him for a beat. "Should I be worried about you?"

"I'm the big brother, remember? It's my job to worry about you, not the other way around." Rising, Heath headed for the back fence. "You should go inside and make sure Misty isn't sharpening a knife. Maybe make her that peach tea she likes and get her to put her feet up."

"Heath."

He kept going, shutting the gate on his brother's oath. Cole meant well, but there were still things Heath didn't want to talk about.

Ever.

He headed through Daisy's side yard toward the truck. Ashley had been avoiding him for a couple of days. He still had no idea what had happened with the first envelope delivery, but now he also wanted to know why the sisters were fighting.

He didn't realize Cole had followed him until Lexi, still in the truck, saw them coming and lightly banged the back of her head against the headrest.

His brother waved at her. "Hey, Lexi. Long time no see."

She didn't smile. "The last time I saw you, you'd just peed your pants."

Cole grimaced. "Third grade wasn't exactly my year. And I saw you the last time you were here, remember?"

She gave a small smile. "You're right. My mistake."

Mistake, his ass. Heath chuckled, ignoring Cole's dirty look. Then his brother turned back to Lexi. "So what's going on with you and Ashley?"

"It's not our year," she said dryly.

"What happened?" Heath asked. He could feel Cole's eyes on him, head tilted with far too much interest at his serious tone.

"And *you*," Lexi said, clearly annoyed as she ignored his question.

"Me? What did I do?"

"Oh, I know this one," Cole said, raising a hand. "Nothing. He did nothing except lie around in the hammock like some lazy off-season ski bum."

"Hmm," she said.

Cole's smile faded as he clearly realized that while he'd been just joking around, he'd somehow stepped in it. He glanced uneasily at Heath, who just smiled, deciding not to even attempt to change Lexi's opinion of him, instead leaning into a false narrative he'd actually cultivated. Because as long as she was on the fence about him as a human being, he could tell himself he wasn't into her. A lie, of course. He'd always been into her, far more than was good for either of them.

"Uh . . ." Cole took a step back. "I've got to get going. It was nice to see you, Lexi." He grabbed Heath's arm. "Need to talk to you real quick."

Heath let himself get pulled back to the fence. "What?"

"So that went well."

Heath shook his head. "Seriously? That's what you wanted to talk to me about?"

"That, and to mention that for someone as smart as you are, you've retained nothing you've ever learned about women."

Heath crossed his arms. "Do tell."

"You obviously like her, and yet all you do is bait her. Why?"

Heath pleaded the Fifth. Mostly because he had no idea.

"Look, you should let her see you. The real you."

As if revealing the deepest, most intimate parts of himself were something to throw around with Lexi, who no doubt would fling them right back at him. "You don't know what you're talking about."

"You sure about that?" his brother asked. "Because you never agreed with Daisy's idea to leave the sisters these tasks. You even told her so, more than once. You worried about Ashley having to face Daisy's murky past, and yet now you're encouraging her to do it so that, what? You can keep Lexi here for six weeks instead of standing in her wake as she once again vanishes back to the East Coast?"

"Enough. *Shit.*"

Cole crossed his arms. "You going to deny it?"

They stared hard at each other for several painfully long seconds, enough time for his brother to flash him a knowing grin. "Didn't think so."

Heath's insides tightened, a part of him wanting to swipe that smug superior look right off Cole's face—with his fist.

Cole just laughed. "You want to have a go, old man? Like we used to?"

Heath turned his head and met Lexi's gaze. Since she was still in the truck, still wearing sunglasses, he couldn't see much of her thoughts, but he didn't need to because he could sense her unhappiness.

Not good.

He'd been sitting on this plan of Daisy's, along with the envelopes, for nearly a year as requested. And after all the woman had done for him, he couldn't fail her on this. Not when he knew Daisy's motivation behind the envelopes wasn't about her, but about Lexi and Ashley spending time together, learning to be there for each other, becoming sisters of the heart.

Obviously, that wasn't going well. They needed a bridge, and he had a feeling that bridge was named Heath. Great. And since Lexi didn't appear to be in any hurry to get out of the truck and face her sister, he strode away from Cole and back across Daisy's yard, where he helped himself to the seat Ashley had vacated.

"No," Lexi said, pointing for him to get out. "I'm going to the grocery store. Alone."

"What happened between you and Ashley? Does it have something to do with delivering Margo's envelope? Neither of you have told me how it went."

Her mouth tightened.

Oh good, they were going to do this the hard way. Reaching over, he pulled off her sunglasses.

Those honey eyes narrowed, glittering dangerously as she snatched the glasses back. "Get out," she said. "I'm in a hurry."

"For groceries?"

She grimaced and he laughed. "Yeah, first rules of lying out of your very fine ass—you have to keep track of said lies."

She muttered something under her breath about damn nosy neighbors with sexy indolent smiles who thought they were God's gift.

"Sexy, huh?"

"I also said indolent," she snapped.

He shrugged. She sure as hell wouldn't be the first person to underestimate him.

"Are you getting out or what?"

"Or what." He could practically see the steam coming out of her ears. "I could use a few things from the store."

"No. Sometimes I get road rage walking behind people in the aisle. I don't need an audience."

He smiled. "Sounds like fun."

Lexi ground her teeth. "Fine, I'm not going to the grocery store. I'm running an errand, and I don't want to discuss it."

"I'm a great wingman."

"Are you a *silent* wingman?"

"I can be."

She pointed at him. "Not a single word."

With a salute, he buckled up, adjusted the seat, and rolled the window down.

"Please, by all means, make yourself at home while you encroach on my life." Muttering something about nosy-ass neighbors, meddling sisters, and mothers with agendas, she put the truck in drive and hit the gas.

There was something about watching her concentrate. Maybe it was the way she furrowed her brow in displeasure when she got cut off or how she looked in a tee, jean shorts, and wedge sandals on her feet, making her legs look ten miles long. Interacting with her as a grown-up fascinated him. Physical attraction to her aside, he'd been prepared to have complicated feelings about her. For one thing, she seemed to still be at war with the memory of the woman who'd been a pseudo mother to him. He understood that Daisy had had her problems, big ones. He also understood she hadn't been the best parent. But she also had most definitely not been the worst.

That honor went to his father.

But even if Lexi couldn't forgive the woman who'd saved Heath's life on more than one occasion, the woman had taken Ashley in as her own, raising her . . . Didn't that tell Lexi anything about her mom at all? That there had to be some innate goodness in her?

Maybe "complicated" was too mild a word for his feelings.

They drove through Sunrise Cove and . . . kept going. He glanced over at her, but she seemed disinclined to explain. She had her window down too, the wind in her hair, and she looked . . . relaxed.

When he realized they were driving around the lake, he began to relax too. For years, every waking—and sleeping—moment of his life had been consumed by work, by ambition, by what he'd thought had been love. He'd walked away from all of that, and now, being here, not worrying about where they were headed or what her mysterious errand was, felt like a luxury.

They'd been on the road for forty-five minutes, driving south around the lake, when he slid her a look. "Starting to wonder if I'm being kidnapped."

That earned him a half smile. "You're just now worrying about that?"

He shrugged. "I wanted some peace and quiet."

She gave him an incredulous look. "And you thought *I* could provide it?"

He grinned. "You're right. What was I thinking?"

She snorted, then glanced at him. "Can I ask you something?"

"Yes."

"Is this life here in Sunrise Cove enough for you?"

"If you mean being near and close to my family while living in what is not only one of the most gorgeous places in the world but also has a laid-back, easygoing vibe that lowers my blood pressure . . . yes."

She slid him another look. "You have a way of answering questions that seems designed to make me feel like I got a piece of your life but in reality tells me very little."

He chuckled. "You're one to talk."

"Do tell."

"You hide behind a razor-sharp tongue and a don't-get-too-close vibe."

With a snort, she cranked the music a little bit more. He didn't mind. He'd already figured out where they were going. What he didn't know was why.

Two hours from when they'd left Daisy's house, Lexi pulled down a quiet, slightly neglected street and parked. "Definitely not a grocery store," he murmured.

"Smart-ass."

"This is Margo Schutz's house," he said. "Where you and Ashley delivered envelope number one a couple of days ago."

"Yes. And no."

A woman came out of the house and, without glancing at them, got into an old RAV4 and drove off.

"Stay here." Lexi jumped out of the truck and started up the front path, a white envelope sticking out from her back jeans pocket.

"Well, that's too much to pass up," he said to no one, and followed, catching up with her bypassing the front door to head along the side yard to the back.

Where he found her letting herself in the back door. "B and E?"

She jumped, then glared at him. "It was unlocked," she hissed. "And what part of 'stay in the truck' did you miss?" She tiptoed into the kitchen, pulled the envelope from her back pocket, and leaned it up against the coffee maker on the counter.

"She wouldn't take the envelope," he guessed.

"I mean, who refuses a big fat check?"

"If I tried to hand you one from me, you'd most definitely refuse."

Her lips quirked, and he pointed at her. "I saw that. You *almost* gave me a smile."

"Because you're ridiculous."

"So you *would* take a check from me?"

"Hell no. But Daisy liked Margo. Liked her so much that she wanted us to give her money." She looked around at the cabin that was clearly in need of repairs and lifted her hands. "I don't get it."

"There's need," he said softly. "And then there's *need*."

Their gazes locked and held, and something that felt too uncomfortably real passed between them. "You do realize that there was a camera at the front door," he finally said.

"Which is why we're at the back door."

"Where there's one, there's always—"

"Hands where I can see them!" a man called out from behind them. "*Now!*"

With a sigh, Heath slowly lifted his hands and turned in unison with Lexi to face the cop on the stoop.

CHAPTER 7

H ours and hours later, after being hauled down to the Placer-ville police station for questioning and having to wait until Margo deigned to show up and begrudgingly corroborate Lexi's story, they were released.

But by that time, the truck had been impounded.

Heath ro-sham-bo'd with Lexi on which of them would have to call their respective sibling to come get them. To say that neither of them wanted to do any such thing felt like the under-statement of the year.

Luckily, he won.

"You're scum," Lexi told him as they stood on the sidewalk in front of the police station, watching Ashley drive up in an Audi. Lexi slid him a look. "Yours, I assume?"

He shrugged. The Audi had been a bonus from the law firm he'd worked for. He actually preferred his truck, but didn't like to lend it to Ashley since he enjoyed the lack of dings and dents all over it.

Ashley got out of the Audi and surveyed them standing on

the curb, thoughts unreadable. "I had to reschedule a drawing class I teach at the senior center."

"I'm sorry, I just wanted to get the envelope delivered," Lexi said, hands clasped, posture announcing that she was uncomfortable but trying hard and didn't know how to express it. It cracked something in Heath's chest.

"You should have told me," Ashley said.

"You'd mentioned you were done doing this with me."

Mentioned? More like yelled. They were so different. Ashley usually reacted with emotions, and not always in a good way. Lexi appeared to be the opposite of that, shoving things deep, wearing armor to protect herself. But even he could see that while she was struggling to do this, what Daisy had asked of her, she *was* doing it, whatever needed to be done. Whether that was for Ashley's sake or her own didn't really matter, not to him. Because he admired that while even though she could have walked away from all of it, she hadn't.

He looked to Ashley, ready to actually come to Lexi's defense, but Ashley held up a hand in the direction of his face. "I'm mad at you too."

"Don't be," Lexi said. "He thought we were going to the grocery store."

She'd defended *him*. Stunned, he turned to her.

She kept her gaze on Ashley. "I'm sorry for being rude earlier. I'm also sorry I didn't tell you what I was doing. I just wanted to help, and as I've already mentioned, you said—"

"I know what I said."

Lexi nodded. "I took your words at face value. Sorry you had to come all the way down here to save our asses."

Ashley blinked. "Are you just saying that because you want a ride home?"

Lexi grimaced. "Maybe it's ten percent that."

A little warmth came into Ashley's gaze. "I'm sorry too. I'm grateful you're here. I guess I'm just already sad that you'll be leaving again."

Lexi managed a smile. "Look at us. Being all grown-up and everything. What can I do to pay you back for coming all this way?"

Ashley smiled, and oh boy, Heath knew that smile. He'd fallen victim to it a million times.

"I teach a weekly class on drawing at the senior center," she said. "I could really use help."

"I don't know anything about drawing."

"Experience not required. My students will admire you for being so knowledgeable about art."

Heath was wondering if Ashley maybe had her sister confused with someone who cared what people thought, but then Lexi sighed. "So if I help you, you're going to forgive and forget? Really? It's that simple?"

Huh. She was actually considering falling on the sword of Ashley's charms.

"Of course," Ashley said. "Get in."

To his surprise, Lexi slid into the back seat. Heath started to open the driver door, but Ashley hit the locks. Right. His payment for being stupid was allowing her to drive his car. He walked around to the passenger side, and the doors unlocked. He'd barely slid into the seat when Ashley peeled out.

Thinking of his tires, he winced.

Ashley looked over at him. "Problem?"

He wasn't stupid. "Nope."

Ashley glanced at Lexi in the rearview mirror. "I get that you don't want to be here, with me, even if I'm literally your only relative, but—"

"It's not that," Lexi said.

"Then what?" Ashley softened her voice. "Talk to me, Lexi."

Heath had to clamp down on his urge to break in and try and defuse the tension. But they were actually talking, and talking was good.

Hopefully.

Lexi took a deep breath. "This is hard for me. It's going to sound selfish."

"Try me," Ashley said quietly. Willing to listen.

"I get that she wanted us to do this, but . . . what about what I asked of her? What about every birthday and holiday she flaked on me, and let's be clear, it was *all* of them. I never asked her to do anything for me, get anything for me . . . I wanted nothing other than to see her."

Heath hadn't known this. Probably because Ashley had been too young to see it, and Daisy too upset at her own failures to admit such things. All Daisy had told him was that she'd tried to reach out to her daughter many times, only to be rejected. He'd never thought to question Daisy, and wouldn't now, except . . . He could hear the very real emotion in Lexi's voice, how she was fighting for composure. Because she didn't want to lose Ashley? Or because her mom had disappointed her for so many years, until she'd finally decided she had enough and had stopped allowing Daisy access in order to protect herself?

And how often had she had to do that in her life?

He didn't know much about her dad, other than what Ashley had told him, that the man was stoic and hard. He'd taken Lexi for the sole reason that he hadn't trusted Daisy with her.

That was who had raised Lexi.

Thinking about it, thinking about some of the things they might have in common, things he wouldn't wish on anyone, made him ache for her.

Ashley pulled over and twisted to look at Lexi, her eyes sparkling with unshed tears. "Forgiven. Forgiven and forgotten." And with that, she put the car back in gear and drove them home.

When she pulled into the driveway, she looked at Heath. "Thanks for going with Lexi. For having her back. Also, for always having mine."

"Anytime."

She nodded, then looked at Lexi. "I made cookies." And with that olive branch, she got out and vanished inside the house.

Heath got behind the wheel just as Lexi slid out of the back seat, and he choked back a laugh.

She whirled back, giving him a flat stare. "What?"

He motioned for her to check her back pocket.

She reached back and . . . pulled out the damn envelope. Her mouth fell open as she sputtered with fury. "*Margo.*"

Seemed that Lexi had finally met her match.

A minute later, he let himself into his grandpa's house, wondering if the sisters might ever find their way to the kind of relationship he and Cole had. For them both, he hoped so.

Mayhem lifted his head from where he'd been asleep on the couch, blinking, trying to decide if Heath needed any emotional support or if he could just go back to sleep.

"You're not supposed to sleep on the couch," Heath said. "You've got a very cushy dog bed that cost me a hundred bucks at Costco."

Not caring, Mayhem yawned wide, stretched his entire body,

then trotted over, bumping his nose against Heath's thigh. Translation: *Missed you, love you, I got you, I always got you, and by any chance do you have a treat for me 'cuz I'm a good boy.*

Heath squatted down and gave the dog a one-armed hug. "You keep the house safe?"

Mayhem licked his ear.

"Good boy." Heath rose. "Grandpa?"

"Here!"

Heath followed the voice, heading through the house to the kitchen, Mayhem trotting along beside him, his faithful steed, whether he needed one or not. The back door was open, revealing his grandpa standing on the porch, smoke curling around him as he watched three deer happily munch on Heath's sunflowers against the side fence.

"We've got another fence panel down," the old man said, puffing away on a cigar. "So now you're feeding the deer."

"Did you ever think about waving your arms or yelling at them?" Heath snatched the cigar out of the old man's fingers and put it out. "And are you kidding me?"

"Hey, that was a gift from Frannie at the senior center."

"One, we've talked about Frannie being a terrible influence on you. Two, you aren't supposed to be smoking. And three—"

"Here we go . . ." his grandpa muttered.

"The entire kitchen smells like smoke."

"I didn't smoke in there, I smoked out here."

"Yes," Heath said. "With the door open."

"Whoops. My bad."

Heath resisted banging his head on the doorjamb. "Did you eat?"

"Do chips count?"

"You know they don't. Cole was supposed to bring you dinner."

Grandpa shrugged. "He called, said he was going to pick me up and bring me to his place. I don't mean to be rude, but his place is a zoo."

True story. "I'll put something together." In the kitchen, Heath went to the fridge, standing there with his hand on the door for a moment, seeking inner calm.

He missed his own place.

His own space . . .

There was nothing wrong with this house, except it wasn't his. Not to mention, it needed renovations and some serious TLC. But his grandpa had refused to allow Heath to change a thing. Nope, he wanted the house exactly as it'd been for the fifty years he'd lived here with his wife. Everything was outdated. The old electric stove had two burners that didn't work. There was not enough insulation in the walls, so it cost a fortune to heat. The linoleum was peeling up, but Heath's grandma had picked it out, so it stayed.

And so did Heath.

And therein lay the problem, but whining about it wouldn't make a difference. And he sure as hell didn't feel like cooking. So he called for takeout from the local diner. His grandpa loved the chili and corn bread from there, and because Heath had done some renovations for them, they knew about his grandpa and his dietary restrictions, so they used ground turkey instead of red meat. Twenty minutes later, it was delivered.

Cold.

Knowing his grandpa wouldn't eat unless it was piping hot, he was stirring it on the stovetop when he called Cole.

"Yo," Cole answered, the background sounding like he was standing in the middle of a crazy club.

"Thought you were taking care of Grandpa tonight."

"What?" Cole asked around a little person yelling "I do it 'self, I do it 'self!"

Heath didn't bother repeating himself. He heard Cole sigh and then move into a quieter room.

"Okay," his brother said. "I'm hiding in the pantry closet so I can hear you. What's up?"

"You tell me."

"It's been a day."

"It's my turn for the closet!" Misty yelled. There was a tussle and then she'd wrestled the phone from her husband. "Heath?"

"Hey, you. How's it going?"

"Well, my husband just told me he wanted a divorce, so—"

"That is *not* what I said," came Cole's voice. "My exact words were 'I think it'd be cool for the whole family to live in an RV and travel the country for a year.'"

"Same thing," Misty said.

Heath grimaced. "He never was the sharpest tool in the shed."

"Hey," Cole said.

"I'll pay you a million dollars to rescue me," Misty said to Heath.

"You don't have a million dollars. But even if you did, it's still a hell no. You're multiplying."

Misty sighed. "Okay, then maybe you can build me my very own escape closet."

"That I can do," he said. "What's all the ruckus in the background?"

"Matty's sobbing on the kitchen floor after your brother ignored my advice to cut his grilled cheese sandwich into triangles and not squares."

"Men," Heath said, and made her laugh. "What else is going on?"

He heard a rustle of what sounded like a bag of chips being opened. Sure enough, when she spoke, it was around a mouthful. "Earlier, Matty handed me a rock, patted my face, and said, 'Mommy, you're the best, here's a present for you.'"

"Sweet."

"The rock was a cat turd."

"Have kids, they said. It'll be fun, they said."

"This isn't funny, Heath. How did I end up living at, as your grandpa says, the zoo?"

"If it helps," he said, "this morning I took Grandpa to the store, where he proceeded to ask an elderly woman to pull his finger."

"Dear God. Did she?"

"Yep."

"And did he—"

"Fart loud enough that everyone in the aisle ran?" he asked. "Also yes."

Misty laughed. "I'm so sorry, your day was definitely worse than mine."

Actually, even though he'd spent five hours in the car and several more at the police station, the company had been . . . pretty damn great. So no, he wouldn't classify his day as bad. Not even close.

"Did you need Cole for something?" Misty asked. "Fair warning, if you do, Matty's also coming."

"Nope, we're all good here."

Misty laughed. "Coward."

Heath disconnected as Grandpa came inside, sniffing dramatically. "Is that your grandma's chili?"

"No, it's from the diner."

"Oh."

Heath glanced over at him. "You love their chili."

"It's not your grandma's."

"But you eat it every Saturday when we go out to lunch."

"It's Tuesday, not Saturday. Every Tuesday, your grandma always made me her chili."

Heath spooned a portion into a bowl and brought it to the table, pointing for his grandpa to sit. "You do realize no one's ever going to be able to make it like Grandma."

"You could if you set your mind to it, but that's the problem with your generation. You're all inherently lazy."

Heath got a bowl for himself and sat at the table. "You need a new song and dance."

His grandpa laughed. "I always did like you best."

"Uh-huh." He'd heard him say the same thing to Cole a million times. "Eat."

CHAPTER 8

I'm late, I'm late . . ." Lexi finally found a parking spot, jumped out of the truck, and ran up the block to the senior center building where Ashley taught her drawing class. The class Lexi had promised to help with.

It'd been a few days since the Margo Debacle, as she'd been calling it. True to her word, Ashley had appeared to move on from being angry and upset at Lexi.

Her sister was a far better person than she was.

She stifled a yawn. She hadn't slept well, trying to figure out how to get Margo to accept Daisy's money.

So far nothing had come to her.

Until today. When she'd lost her job, she'd been told that an internal investigation would be forthcoming. Being innocent shouldn't be this terrifying, but although there were no legal requirements in regards to becoming an appraiser, there were professional associations in the field. And each and every one of them required members to comply with an ethical standard called the Uniform Standards of Professional Appraisal Practice. In addition to the USPAP, members were required to pass tests and provide proof of continuing education, which she'd done faithfully.

But depending on the outcome with the investigation, she could face losing her good standing in the industry. For the most part, denial was her friend. But the worry and anxiety had a way of jumping out at her when she didn't expect it.

Like when she tried to fall asleep.

Or stay asleep.

Or every waking moment of the day . . .

She'd been applying for jobs back home, while also trying to connect with people looking for estate assessors—something she realized she could do here for the rest of her time in Sunrise Cove. Working for herself appealed to her far more than going to work for a big appraisal firm. Actually, it appealed to her more than anything she could think of.

She'd even taken a call earlier from a potential client that had gone shockingly well. She'd marvel over that later. Working for herself had been a secret dream of hers for a long time, one she hadn't quite had the nerve to seriously consider. But she wanted it now more than ever, to start up her own business, be her own boss, so that she'd never again have to put her security and future into someone else's hands.

But to do that, she'd need capital. A fact that put a whole bunch of pressure on her to finish this thing with Ashley and hope like hell that whatever money was left for them at the end would be more than ice cream money.

Which was getting ahead of herself.

She and Ashley had been spending the evenings going through Daisy's things. They had three piles going. One for donation, one for the garage sale Ashley planned to have when the whole house had been done, and another for the dump.

They'd spent that time steering clear of difficult subjects, sticking with what worked for them. Turned out that even as different as they were, they had things in common. Their guilty pleasure TV shows, deliciously smutty books, their love for tacos and ice cream. Full-fat, full-dairy ice cream. The difference there was that Lexi regularly gave in to her dairy ice cream cravings. Ashley was stronger.

They did have something else in common, something they'd mutually decided without a word to not discuss at this time. When Ashley was a toddler, her mom had peaced out and never returned, and with her dad having been killed in a car accident five years after he'd married Daisy, they were both effectively orphans.

Now, as she ran to the front doors of the senior center, she tried to catch her breath. She'd gotten a text from Ashley saying she had things to do before the class and that she'd meet Lexi there. She'd left the truck for her, which had been a surprise. If the situation had been reversed, would Lexi have been as thoughtful as Ashley?

The drive should have only taken her five minutes, but she'd hit every light in the entire town, all four of them, so Lexi entered the building fifteen minutes late, skidding to a stop at the reception area. "I'm looking for Ashley Fontaine. She's teaching a drawing class. I'm . . . her assistant."

"Oh, you must be her sister, Lexi," the woman at the desk said kindly. "She speaks so fondly of you. Down the hall to the left, dear. Class is full today. She's so popular here, everyone adores her. It's so kind of her to do this for free."

That Ashley could barely rub two pennies together and yet was giving away her time did not surprise Lexi in the slightest.

The art room was large, and indeed filled to the gills. Easels were set up in a semicircle, with a stool at each. Ashley was saying something about the eye of the beholder, but that wasn't what caught Lexi's attention. Nope, that went to the man standing at the center of the half circle, wearing a black T-shirt, faded Levi's, and battered work boots.

A woman on a stool directly in front of Lexi leaned close to the woman sitting next to her. "I give his butt a ten out of ten."

Lexi would've given the model a twelve out of ten, but she recognized that ass, and he already had enough of an ego. "Maybe an eight," she said.

The women turned to look at her.

So did Heath, his eyes filling with promised retribution.

"Eh, maybe even a six," she added, holding his gaze.

He gave a slow smile. "If it's only a six, why can't you stop staring at it?"

Damn. Note to self: not ready for prime time with Heath Bowman.

"Class, let's take five," Ashley called out.

"Excuse me, honey," one of the women said. "You're what, maybe . . . eighteen? But we're all old and need longer than five minutes to even get to the bathroom."

Ashley smiled. "I'm twenty-three, but thank you for making my day. Take all the time you need." Then she moved to Lexi's side. "You're late."

"Sorry, I got caught up with work . . ." She knew Ashley would assume Lexi meant the job she was supposedly telecommuting to. Probably, she'd tell Ashley the truth. Eventually. Maybe after she'd made a successful go at working for herself. "Hit all the lights too. Thanks for leaving me the truck, but you didn't have to do that."

"No worries, I got a ride with Heath. Last night, I had a dream you got a job here in Sunrise Cove and stayed." Ashley took in whatever Lexi's face was communicating, likely far more than she meant to show. "I'm manifesting it."

Lexi thought of the woman she'd met on the plane, Summer, the professional manifester. "Has that ever worked for you?"

Ashley smiled. "You're here, aren't you?"

Heath slid Lexi a look she didn't have to translate. *Don't break Ashley's heart.* Got it. These two were close friends, even family. And she wasn't. Not really. "I'll keep an open mind."

"All I can ask."

A few minutes later, people started to file back into class. Every single one of them stopped by their little group and struck up a conversation. With Ashley, with Heath, and also with Lexi. It surprised her, the easy acceptance, but what surprised her even more was that she'd indeed learned something from her world back east, and that was how to relate to people, draw them out. She listened as Mrs. Spencer regaled her with tales about some mysterious Mr. Chen—who turned out to be her cat. She listened to Mrs. Morales talk about her poor roses, and how Mr. Westmoreland had ruined them by getting drunk and peeing on them. This had greatly disappointed Mrs. Morales, who'd been dreaming of a man who opened doors for her but also smacked her ass as she walked through. Apparently a man who peed on her roses was out.

Oh, and she also heard all about Ashley's love life from Mrs. Jackson, who called herself a romantic at heart. "None of us know very many lesbians, but we've got a large network of wonderful people. We've simply got to help her find her HEA," she told Lexi. "She deserves the moon."

Lexi nodded in agreement. "She does."

Ashley blushed as Mrs. Jackson walked away. "You didn't have to say that."

"Why?" Lexi asked. "It's true. You deserve the moon. What do you need from me?"

Her sister blinked in surprise. "Besides you moving here? Maybe a little less assuming that we're going to fight over every little thing and a little more smiling?"

"I meant today in this class," Lexi said dryly. "But I'll work on it."

"Oh." Ashley smiled. "Sorry. I really just needed your presence and support. There's an empty easel. Mrs. Stonewell couldn't attend today. So if you could join the class and participate, that'd be great."

"You just want me to draw?"

"That's the definition of participating in my drawing class, yes."

So Lexi walked over to the only empty easel, which like all of the others had a direct view of Heath. She gamely sat down.

Ashley stood behind her. "Concentrate on his face."

Lexi forced herself to look at him. Those blue gray eyes shone with amusement—at her expense, of course. Given his tan, he'd been in the sun recently. He hadn't shaved today, probably not for several days. He could have no idea that she secretly loved the scruff, found it sexy as hell, but just in case, she rolled her eyes at him.

He smirked.

"Come on, really concentrate," Ashley said. "Not pretend concentrate. And if you keep rolling those eyeballs, they're going to fall out."

"Daisy used to say that."

"Yes, *Mom* did. Now, take in all the deets. His eyebrows, his eyes . . . Eyes are windows to the soul, you know."

Lexi usually did her best to avoid looking at his eyes, instead focusing right between them, or at his mouth. But his mouth was a problem because he had a really great one. She already knew he was a great kisser, damn him—

He winked at her, and she jumped, covering it up with a glare.

Thirty minutes or thirty days later, it was hard to tell, Ashley finally clapped her hands. "Class over, great job everyone."

Heath rolled his neck, then lifted his arms and stretched, and for a single beat, a strip of his stomach was revealed above the waistband of his jeans. Just an inch of taut, tanned abs, and her mouth watered like she was starving. She told herself that was because she *was* starving. For food.

But she was a liar.

Heath's gaze unerringly found hers. A beat went by where the air between them seemed electrified, and then he was prowling straight toward her. The closer he got, the more butterflies took flight in her belly. She tried to steady herself for the impact of his sexy energy, and how it made her feel ridiculously . . . female.

"No," she said. "No looking."

He smiled. "Oh, I'm going to look."

She blocked his view. She'd just spent the last half hour memorizing his face in every detail, his long dark lashes, how his eyes revealed more than she'd realized, and that his broad shoulders seemed capable of holding great weight. "I've never seen this side of you," she admitted. "You were good with the ladies, even when they objectified you. You knew them by name. You talked to each and every one of them."

"I like them," he said simply. "And you do too."

"What?"

"You charmed every single person in this room." He shifted closer, and her pulse kicked.

Um . . . "Wh-what are you doing?"

He leaned in, and she panicked. Was he about to kiss her, right here in the middle of this room where anyone could see? And why did he always smell so good? That wasn't fair at all. But then he shifted that last inch between them, and her eyes closed of their own will, and then . . .

Nothing.

She opened her eyes to find him peering over her shoulder to her drawing of him, biting his lower lip, clearly trying to hold in a laugh. "You're an ass."

"No doubt." He cocked his head and studied the sketch. "Interesting," he finally said.

She'd drawn that punk ten-year-old she'd known him as, and rudimentarily at best. "Are you making fun of my skills?"

He didn't shift away, just turned his head so his lips ghosted her earlobe when he spoke, giving her a full-body shiver, unfortunately in the best way possible, the jerk. "You wanted me to kiss you. Again."

"Did not!"

Ashley glanced over at them with a worried expression, and Lexi lowered her voice and spoke through her teeth. "I did *not* want you to kiss me again. I didn't like it the first time. Not even a little tiny bit." Okay, so she was a liar, liar, pants on fire, but no way was she going to admit it. "Things to do, see ya."

He caught her hand and put his mouth back to her ear. "By the way, when I do kiss you again, we won't have an audience, and I'll ask for permission first, which means you'll have to tell me it's what you want. With words, Lex."

"*You—*"

"And then you're going to tell me how much you liked it."

"Someone's quite full of himself—"

"Ash is waving at us to hurry."

And with that, he walked off.

One of these days, she was going to walk off first! "And I'm not going to tell you how much I liked it," she muttered to herself.

"What was that?" one of the ladies asked.

"Nothing. Sorry. Talking to myself about annoying men."

"Oh, honey, don't get me started."

A few minutes later, the three of them walked out of the building, Ashley beaming. "You guys! That was so much fun! Thank you so much for coming, Lexi."

"Of course. How long have you been doing this?"

"I took over when Mom died."

So a year. And Lexi hadn't any idea. Her fault, of course. Ashley worked hard to keep them connected, and Lexi was grateful for that, but she hadn't made it easy. What she didn't know was why. *Why hadn't she tried harder?*

Because she was jealous of the time Ashley had with Daisy, time Lexi hadn't had. The shame of that hit her like a one-two punch. She'd taken her frustrations about her mom out on Ashley, who hadn't deserved any of it. "It was a lot of fun," she said, and meant it.

"Why do you look so surprised?"

"I'm sorry," Lexi said. "I didn't mean to give you that impression."

"But it's still true. You're surprised you're having a good time while you're here."

"I'm sorry." Lexi shook her head. "I guess it's time that I make peace with my past."

Ashley nodded, then shook her head. "Why now?"

The question was valid. More than. And Ashley most definitely deserved the truth. But could she give it? "I guess I'm realizing I don't have a lot of family left. You're it."

Ashley took a step back like she'd just taken a hit. "So I'm what, the consolation prize? The poor little stepsister you're stuck with by default because there's no one else?"

"I didn't mean it like that. And you don't have anyone left either. I thought maybe we could have no one left . . . together." She was bungling this, of course. So much so that even Heath grimaced and took a few steps away, presumably to give them some semblance of privacy.

"Look, I don't know how to do this," Lexi admitted softly. "I don't know how to open up to people. I'm horrible at it."

"You really are."

Lexi let out a sound of frustration. "I'm trying. But there are things you don't know, things no one knows." Painfully aware of Heath far too close by, it felt hard to say what she wanted to, but she knew she had to try. "When my dad divorced Daisy, he moved on pretty quickly. His second wife was . . ." She swallowed hard, having never discussed this before, ever. "She started out nice, but it turned out to be fake nice. Her daughters, my *other* stepsisters, were worse. There was no faking with them, and it got . . ." She swallowed hard. "Ugly. But whenever I tried to tell my stepmom that they'd hurt me, she played it off as me looking for attention. I felt . . . very alone. I *was* very alone. And I got good at it."

Ashley let out a low sound of anguish. "Lexi . . . I'm so sorry."

Lexi shook her head. "No, I'm the one who's sorry. Those years are long gone, but I still suck at connecting with people, even when I want to." Her voice had to scrape past her raw throat, so it sounded a little thick. "I'm doing the best I can, Ash, I promise."

Her sister's eyes shimmered with emotion, so much that it was hard to maintain eye contact, but Lexi forced herself to, trying to forget she felt so exposed she might as well have been standing there naked.

Ashley took her hand. "You're here now. That's all that matters. And as for connecting, you might not be great at it, but I am." She squeezed her hand. "We've got this."

Lexi let out a rough laugh. "If you say so."

"I do." She paused, waiting until Lexi met her gaze. "And for what it's worth, I hate what happened to you. Mom should've put you first. I'm sorry she didn't. She wasn't perfect."

"Neither was I." Lexi's smile was grim. "I refused to look at her through anything but my ten-year-old's lens, and because of it, I never relented. Never stopped pushing her away. I push *everyone* away, including you."

Ashley gave her a very real smile. "I think you're better at opening up and connecting than you even knew." With that, she opened the passenger door of Heath's truck and got in. "See you at home."

Lexi walked to Daisy's truck and drove to the house on exhausted autopilot. She slid out from behind the wheel and nearly walked right into Heath.

That was when she registered that Ashley had clearly already gone inside and that Heath was clearly waiting for her. Too emotionally raw to talk, she just gave a dip of her chin and started to walk past.

Very gently, he took her hand.

"What?" she asked.

"Just wanted to make sure you're okay."

"I'm great."

His mouth quirked, but his eyes were solemn. "I didn't know any of that, about what you went through after your parents."

She tried to shrug it off. "Well, now you do."

"Yeah," he said quietly, holding her gaze. "Now I do."

"I know what you're thinking, and I'm not interested in your pity."

"You have no idea what I'm thinking. And I'm not looking at you with pity. I'm looking at you with awe at all you've been through and how strong you are." His voice was husky, low, and sincere, and nearly broke her. "If you ever want to talk about any of it—"

"I don't." Unable to handle the warmth and concern in his gaze, much preferring the sardonic tone he usually used with her, she took a step back. Then turned, heading to the house.

"I've been there."

That stopped her. She slowly pivoted back.

He didn't make a move to come any closer, just gave a very small smile and stuck his hands in his pockets. "My dad. He . . ." He shook his head.

And she knew. She knew without him saying another word. Just like she knew the sky was blue. Or that she hated bananas. She knew he'd been physically abused by his father, the way she had been by her stepsisters. Probably far worse, given the way he held her gaze, his own troubled, dark with painful memories.

"I'm sorry," she whispered.

He gave a single nod. "Right back at you."

She let her shoulders rise and fall in a casual, it's-all-good-now gesture, but she knew that he knew it wasn't all good, not in the least. She also knew that Heath, the one person she'd have bet her last dollar that she'd never relate to, understood her like no one else ever had.

CHAPTER 9

Heath thought about that conversation with Lexi far more than he wanted to over the next few days. And nights . . . Why hadn't he recognized her coping techniques—pushing people away—and suspected? Tried to reach her through understanding and kindness instead of baiting her like he was still that stupid ten-year-old kid?

Because she makes you feel things, and you're every bit as emotionally stunted as she is . . .

A terrible excuse, and he was angry at himself. He walked through the far left side of his grandpa's backyard, stopping at the fence line where he could take in the view down Daisy's side yard. The view being Lexi's jean-clad sweet ass, because her head was buried in the engine compartment of Daisy's old truck.

Smoke curled into the air, coming from the truck, and maybe also *Lexi* as she swore the early morning air blue.

It'd been a full week since she and Ashley had delivered—or attempted anyway—the first envelope. Today they would deliver envelope number two, which he had in his grasp. They also still had Margo's envelope, and at some point, the sisters would likely make another attempt. Hopefully a legal one.

Today's road trip wouldn't be easy. The sisters had to go nearly three hundred miles to Mendocino County for this one—five hours there, and five hours back. They'd decided to do a turn and burn instead of planning an overnight, probably not wanting to spend money on a hotel. He had offered to cover it, and when that hadn't worked, he'd said he could take it out of Daisy's trust if they preferred that. Because if the women had one thing in common, it was pride.

They'd still refused. But hey, at least they seemed to be making some headway on a relationship. After seeing how lonely Ashley had been this year, and now getting to know Lexi a little bit too, he wanted that for them, badly.

His grandpa sat on a twenty-year-old beach chair at the fence line. He refused to get a newer chair because "nobody makes nothing like they did in the good old days." He also refused to stop being nosy about what all their neighbors were doing. It'd gotten to the point where if anyone in the neighborhood wanted to know anything, they asked the old man.

"Whatcha looking at?" he asked Heath.

"Nothing."

His grandpa smiled. "Liar."

Heath shook his head at him and kept walking, stopping on the sidewalk near Lexi. "Hey, neighbor."

She jumped and bumped her head, swearing some more. "You need a damn bell."

He slid the envelope into his back pocket and cupped her face. While she sputtered at him like a pissed-off cat, he tilted her head down to get a good look at the top of it. "No blood."

He ran his fingers gently over where she'd connected. A slight bump. "I think you're going to live."

She shoved his hand away. "If my life hasn't killed me yet, a knock on the noggin certainly isn't going to," she muttered.

He didn't like thinking of all she'd been through, how alone she'd been, how utterly unprotected, although it explained so much about her. Her toughness. Her inner strength. The way she saw through bullshit, especially his own. "Take my car today," he said.

"Not necessary."

He peered into the smoking engine compartment of the truck. "The alternator's been threatening to go out for a month. If you take the Audi, I can change out the alternator for you while you're gone."

She went hands on hips. "You can change out the alternator?" she asked doubtfully.

"I can do a lot of things. If you don't believe me, feel free to pay someone."

She stared at him for a beat. "What are you doing?"

Honestly? He had no idea. None. When it came to Lexi, he had this strange mix of emotions going. She was equal parts frustrating and fascinating, hot and cold, sexy as hell and yet somehow clueless about that sexiness, but the kicker was that no matter what his body thought it was doing being so attracted to her, his brain knew better.

So did his heart. He'd fallen hard and fast for a woman before, only to get badly burned. Ever since, he'd been doing only the surface thing. And if that made him shallow, then so be it. At least his heart was safe. He'd had a near miss with Lexi five years ago after that holy-shit-balls-amazing kiss they'd shared, and it had scared him. He knew he could fall for her, but he also had known he'd get hurt. Self-preservation and all that . . . So he'd let her run scared. And the next time he'd seen her, he'd been casually dating someone who could never gain access to his heart. A much safer bet. He hadn't thought much about it, since Lexi hadn't expressed any interest in him that time, but now he worried.

Had he hurt her? If so, he hated himself for that.

"Dammit," she muttered, and kicked a tire, staring at the truck like it had personally offended her by breaking down. And when he felt something in his chest tighten at the same time that her expression made him want to laugh, he realized his heart wasn't anywhere close to safe.

Catching sight of her hand, he took it in his and studied her bloodied knuckles. "What happened?"

"I slipped checking the oil."

"I've got a first aid kit—"

"Not necessary." She wiped the blood on her jeans and turned away from him to scowl at the truck some more.

Oh yeah, he was screwed, because the tough-girl thing was really doing it for him. Pulling his keys from his pocket, he held them up and dangled them. "You can take my vehicle. Or . . . you could postpone until the truck's fixed. Which could be up to a week, I imagine." He was such a dick. "An *extra* week . . ."

Lexi tipped her head back and stared up at the sky.

"Looking for divine intervention?"

"No, I'm waiting for a storm to come along and rain on me, since that's the way this day is going." She sighed. "Ashley's excited about this one, and all packed ready to go. She even made a stupid sisters' road trip playlist."

He grinned. "Ah, yes, her road trip playlist."

Lexi's eyes narrowed. "Why? What's wrong with the road trip playlist?"

"It starts out with REO Speedwagon."

"*No.*"

"Oh yes. She's very much into seventies and eighties music. Got it from your mom."

Just then, Ashley practically skipped out of the house. "Let's do this!"

"Bad news," Lexi called to her. "Truck's broken down."

Ashley deflated. "What? No!"

"I can take you!" Grandpa Gus yelled from his perch against the fence.

Lexi looked at Heath, who groaned. "Normally, he just watches birds, but today he's chosen to drive me crazy instead. He can't take you. He had his license taken away in 1995."

"They didn't take it away!" Grandpa yelled. "They just never sent a replacement. There's a difference, you know!"

Heath shook his head. "Well your last car super disagrees with you, so . . ."

"Bah humbug," Grandpa said. "But I've got a better idea. You take them. I've got a hot date here tonight, and you'll just cramp my style."

"For the last time," Heath said, "Maria isn't your date. She's just a nice lady who brings you hot meals."

"That's our cover story."

Heath sighed and once again held out his keys to Lexi. When Ashley tried to snag them, he held them up higher where she couldn't reach.

"Hey," Ashley said, hands on hips. "You hardly ever let me drive the Audi."

At whatever horror hit his face, Lexi actually smiled. *At* him, but a smile was a smile. "Yes, Heath," she practically purred, the gorgeous witch. "Why can't Ashley drive?"

She was so mean. He loved it. "Better idea," he said. "If Cole or Misty can keep an eye on Grandpa, *I'll* drive."

"You'd come with us?" Ashley asked, and bounced up and down in excitement. "Yay! We won't get lost! Also, Lexi will probably veto my road trip playlist, but with you along, she'll be outvoted."

"I get three votes," Lexi said.

Ashley looked affronted. "Why do *you* get three votes?"

"I'll come up with a good reason, don't you worry."

Ashley just grinned wide. "This is going to be so much fun! Let's go!" And with that, she headed down the side yard, waving at Grandpa as she passed him on the way to where the Audi was parked.

Lexi looked at Heath, and tension crackled between them. "You don't have to do this, you know," she finally said. "We can rent a car or something."

"If you didn't want to get a hotel room, I know you don't want to rent a car. Let's just get this over with."

For a beat, Lexi didn't move. He could see her calculating all the reasons this was a bad idea, which he'd already done. Because it *was* a bad idea. A colossally bad idea. Not to mention he had a million things to do today. And yet he knew Lex would do all the driving, which would be a lot for anyone. If he went along, he could split it with her.

Music blasted from the direction of his car.

REO Speedwagon.

Lexi looked at him in horror. "You weren't kidding."

"I was not."

Which was how he found himself, after a quick call to

Misty—who'd gleefully made him repeat his story once she put him on speaker so Cole could listen, and laugh his ass off, before agreeing to watch Grandpa—driving down the highway. He was singing "Take It on the Run" because he couldn't seem to resist, while Ashley and Lexi laughed like actual sisters. He had no idea if Lexi even realized that Ashley was slowly slipping beneath her walls of steel, but he suspected by her smile that maybe she did. Either way, to hear her laugh and see that carefree smile on her face might just be worth enduring three hundred miles of Ashley's playlist.

CHAPTER 10

Five-plus hours later, Lexi's ears bleeding from Ashley's road trip playlist, she looked out the window as Heath pulled up to the address written on envelope number two. They were in a rural area, surrounded by ranches and farms. While the ranch house in front of them wasn't big, it was well taken care of. The same couldn't be said of the acreage around it. The overgrown wild grass danced in the warm wind as far as the eye could see.

Heath turned off the engine. "Go get 'em."

Lexi eyed the name on the envelope, then turned to Ashley. "Do you know this Judy Tyler?"

"I do."

Lexi waited for her to say more, but she didn't, clearly wanting Lexi to ask. Fine. "Are we up against another Margo?"

"Doubt it," Ashley said. "Judy was Mom's best friend. She moved out of Sunrise Cove to way out here a few years ago when her brother died and left her his rescue cat colony."

Lexi blinked. "Cat colony."

"She's got hundreds, and people keep dropping off more.

Mom brought her more than a few strays herself." Ashley got out of the car.

Lexi followed suit, then realized Heath hadn't moved, so she leaned in the window. "You're not coming?"

"No."

"Let me rephrase," she said. "You're coming."

And when he opened his mouth to refuse, she pointed at him. "If I fail at another envelope delivery because I can't find the right words to make someone take Daisy's money while you and that silver tongue of yours are sitting out here doing nothing, I'm going to be ticked off."

"Aren't you always ticked off?"

She narrowed her eyes, but before she could say anything, he got out of the car, all annoyingly, effortlessly sexy, laid-back attitude, like hey, nothing to see here.

She rolled her eyes and headed after Ashley.

HEATH HAD FIGURED he'd stay in the car on his laptop, working on the plans for Cole's kitchen remodel, but instead, he found himself standing at the front door of Daisy's best friend.

He blamed it on how Lexi had looked at him today, which didn't line up with the annoyed tone that came out of her mouth whenever she deigned to speak to him. And that hadn't even been the thing that made him get out of the car. It'd been his inability to ignore the nerves in her honeyed gaze—he'd caved like a cheap suitcase.

Judy was in her sixties, dressed in a flowy gauzy skirt and a T-shirt that said FLUFF YOU, YOU FLUFFING FLUFF FLUFF. She had a cat tucked under each arm. Another was wrapped around her neck like a scarf. "Hello?" she said when she first opened the door, then caught sight of Ashley and smiled. "Oh, hey there, honey." She winked at Heath. "And hey to you too, handsome. So great to see you both—" She took in Lexi, and after an initial start of surprise, she beamed. "And you! Oh, Lexi, I have always wanted to meet you! I've heard so much about you from your mom."

Lexi winced. "It's probably all true."

Judy laughed. "If even half of it's true, you and me are destined to be great friends. What are you all doing way out here?"

"We've got something for you," Ashley said. "From Mom."

"Aw, really? Well, come in, come in! Unfortunately, I don't have much time to sit, lots of stuff going on here today." She gestured them in past several dozen cats lounging in various poses on the furniture and cat stands and in windowsills . . .

They all sat. Lexi and Ashley on a couch, Heath on a chair facing them over a coffee table covered in cat hair, with Judy on a massive beanbag chair. Immediately all of them had at least one cat on them. Heath's was jet-black with bright blue eyes. The big guy turned in three tight circles and plopped down onto his lap. One heartbeat later, purring rumbled.

"That's Pablo," Judy told him. "He was actually a Daisy rescue. You know how she was, sometimes she'd vanish for a few days, which meant she was out there driving three states over, all to save a litter of unwanted kittens. She got Pablo and his siblings from somewhere in Nevada. I was able to get his brothers and sisters all adopted, but couldn't part with him."

Ashley was frowning. "I used to assume she was off gambling when she disappeared like that."

Judy nodded in understanding. "There were lots of times where that was definitely true. Especially in the beginning, all those years ago when you and your daddy first came into her life. But after she fell in love with him—*and* you—she worked hard to change. There were some setbacks, of course, and it nearly did her in when he died in that terrible car accident. I'm so sorry for your loss, honey."

"Thank you," Ashley said quietly. "I miss them both terribly."

Heath watched Lexi take this in, staring at her sister with empathy. No doubt she knew exactly what Ashley felt, belonging to no one, although the difference was that Ashley had grown up with parents who'd made her feel important, safe, and loved.

Had Lexi ever had that?

Ashley held out the envelope to Judy.

"Are you sure this is for me?" Judy asked. "It's been a year since—"

"She wanted it that way. We don't know why."

"Probably to make sure we were still thinking about her," Judy said on a grief-filled smile. "She did love attention."

Ashley let out a small laugh. "So true."

Judy was staring down at her letter. "Should I read it out loud?"

"Your call," Lexi said kindly.

Judy smiled, a little wobbly, clearly moved that Daisy had thought of her at all, and began to read out loud.

Dear Judy,

You know what you mean to me, but I'm not sure you know what you've actually done for me. By rescuing so many animals' lives, you inspired me to rescue my own. You taught me that everyone is worth saving, no matter how down and out. And we both know exactly how rock-bottom down and out I've been. But now it's my turn to do something for you. And, honey, it's about your social life. It needs a rescue. You always refused to take a single penny for all the animals I dropped off with you, so

I'm sending you a little something. Enclosed is a nonrefundable, nonexchangeable gift certificate to that nudist colony we visited in Boca Raton all those years ago, the one where you had a fling with the owner, Leaf. I checked, he's still there. So go and take your shot. Also included is a check that should cover a month of house-sitting for the fur babies. Fluff you, baby! Never stop being you!

> *Forever yours,*
> *Daisy*

The room was speechless.

Finally, Judy swiped at her damp eyes and sighed. "God, I miss that woman." She stood up. "Thank you. I so appreciate you driving all the way here to give this to me. It means everything. To honor Daisy, I'll try to figure out a way to take the trip, but for now, for right now, I've got three mamas in labor. Three! And no one to help me today, so—"

"We could help," Ashley said.

Heath nearly groaned. Ash would offer one of her own limbs if she thought someone could use it.

Judy was looking stunned. "Really?"

"Of course," Ashley said. "Anything."

Lexi barely squelched a grimace, and Heath had to bite back a laugh.

"You've *really* gotta teach your facial expressions how to use their inside voices," Ashley whispered to Lexi.

Judy, missing all of that, just beamed and said, "This way, kids."

And before any of them could second-guess things, Judy had

put Lexi in one room with a mama kitty in labor and Ashley in another. "And you," she said to Heath. "You're with me."

She led him outside. She had a barn and a bunch of animal pens, each with a shelter. She stopped in front of a massive cow under one of the shelters in the shade. "This is Caraid. It's Gaelic for 'friend.'"

"Moooooooooooooooooooooooo."

He stared at Caraid. "I can't help but notice that she doesn't look—or sound—like a cat."

Judy grinned. "Perceptive. And funny too. I bet women flock to you. You've really got that adorable nerd thing going."

He winced at the "adorable nerd" part, but didn't take his eyes off the cow, who looked to be pregnant with quadruplets. A Highland cow if her fluffiness—and adorable face—was anything to go by.

Judy opened the gate and nudged him in. Before he could say another word, she'd shut the gate behind him.

"I don't exactly have experience with this," he warned.

Judy waved off his concern. "I've got a vet coming to check on her. All you've got to do is pet her and talk to her. She's done this before. It's just that she thinks she's one of the cats, one of *my* cats, and doesn't understand she's a bit big to be a house pet. She requires a lot of love and attention, and when she doesn't get it, she—"

"Moooooooooooooooooooooooo."

"Does that," Judy said on a laugh. "I'll be back to check on you two long before any of the real work starts, so don't worry."

"Wait." It'd been a long time since he felt panic licking up his spine. "This is a bad idea—"

But she was gone.

Okay, then. He eyed Caraid.

She eyed him back. "Moooooooooooo."

Was she in pain? Then he realized how ridiculous that was. She was having a baby; of course she was in pain. Stepping closer, he eyed her carefully. Judy hadn't said if she'd ever trampled anyone, but Caraid's soft brown eyes seemed to beckon him closer. When he stroked a hand along her back, she pushed at him for more, nearly knocking him on his ass. A rough laugh escaped him. "Does that help?"

"Mooooooo."

He could tell when a contraction hit, because her entire belly tightened and she shifted restlessly. He took to rubbing his hands down her sides with each one, as it seemed to ease her. And then, just as Caraid's contractions appeared to be nonstop, leaving her panting and sweaty, Judy reappeared.

"Oh good," he said with huge relief. "I think she's getting close."

"Close and done," Judy said beaming.

Heath whipped around, and sure enough, Caraid's calf was fully out. "What do we do?" he whispered, awed.

"She's got it. And my vet is on her way now to check them both out." She clapped Heath on the shoulder. "I'd hire you on as a ranch hand anytime."

"I'll keep that in mind." He was surprised to find the sun setting as Judy led him back to the house.

He found Ashley and Lexi in the living room, each with a cat in their lap, sipping tea. None of them covered in God knew what, like he was.

Lexi gestured to his hair. "You've got a little something . . ."

He pulled several pieces of straw covered in sticky stuff he didn't want to think about from his hair.

"Thanks for having us today," Ashley said to Judy. "I'll definitely come back when the kittens are old enough to leave their mama. Can't wait to adopt one."

"Your mom would have loved that." She looked at Heath. "How about you, cowboy? Want to adopt a calf?"

"Not this time."

She grinned, then looked surprised when they all headed to the door. "I take it none of you have seen the news over the past few hours?"

They looked at each other and shook their heads. "Why?" Lexi asked.

"Fog moved in over the Summit and caused a twenty-car pileup. The Eighty is closed in both directions, and it's estimated it'll stay that way until morning."

Shit.

"Is there a hotel you recommend?" Lexi asked.

"Honey, the closest is a rinky-dink old motel, and that's fifty miles in the wrong direction. Plus, there are less bugs in my fields than there are in those beds. You can stay here." Her cell phone buzzed. "Excuse me a moment."

When she'd left the room, Lexi said one word. "No."

"But we could sleep with kittens!" Ashley exclaimed. "Judy's a saint for doing what she does." She glanced at Heath. "She told me she thinks you're—"

"An adorable nerd," he muttered. "Yeah, I know, she told me too."

Lexi snorted, but Ashley shook her head. "I was going to say steadfast, capable, and reliable, but adorable nerd works too."

He sank lower in his seat.

"At least she didn't say sexy," Ashley said. "Sexy nerds are in right now."

This didn't make him feel any better.

"I'm betting it's the nerd part that's getting him," Lexi said.

It didn't escape him that she took pleasure in his pain.

"But the nerd part is the part that's true," Ashley said.

Lexi actually laughed at that, and he turned to her, unable to keep himself from enjoying that smile on her face, even if it was at his expense. "Let me guess," he said. "You've got a better description."

"Oh, I have several."

"And?"

Her smile turned feline, but before she could respond, Judy came back into the room, arms full. "I've got a two-man tent left over from my music festival days, along with a few sleeping bags. Plus there's the couch. Feel free to divvy it up however you'd like."

Ashley clasped her hands together beneath her chin and looked beseechingly at Lexi and Heath. "Camping! I love camping! We're staying, right?"

Heath looked at Lexi, certain she'd put a swift end to the insanity and agree with him that they should get on the road, go as far as they could, and take their chances at finding a hotel at the base of the Summit. A hotel with each of them ensconced in their own room.

Not sharing a tent or a couch in far too close quarters.

But Lexi just stared at Ashley, an expression on her face he'd never seen before—soft and . . . *yearning*. Was there also dread? Most definitely. But Ashley clearly wanted to stay, and just as clearly, Lexi didn't want to disappoint her.

And he knew they weren't going anywhere.

Ashley threw her arms around Lexi and hugged her hard. Lexi stilled for a beat, then her arms came up and patted Ashley awkwardly on the back. "I mean, it's just sleep. It's not like I gave you a car or anything."

"No, it's better than a car!"

Lexi shook her head, but a smile peeked through. "You have got to get out more."

Heath didn't have the heart to veto the stay, not when he hadn't seen Ashley look this excited at anything since Daisy's death. Well, except for when Lexi had shown up, but Ashley had been down for a while. He wouldn't take this from her, even if the thought of staying overnight with a thousand cats—one of them with a sharp mouth and sharper honey-brown eyes that saw so much more than he wanted her to—made him want to run screaming into the night.

"I've left some things out in the bathroom for you," Judy said. "Extra towels and a stack of some spare clothes left behind from other guests over the years. Help yourselves. I'd suggest the tent and camping out under the stars in the back. It's going to be a beautiful warm night."

The three of them went outside and decided on the wild grass patch at the edge of the property, overlooking a small meadow that had a creek running through it. Heath spread out a tarp and started to put the tent together, looking over in surprise when Lexi dropped to her knees at his side and helped.

"What?" she muttered when he stared at her. "I'm handy too."

And helpful. He was starting to get that it wasn't that she didn't care. No, it was the exact opposite. She cared, too much, much more than made her comfortable.

When they were done, they all looked at the tent, smaller than he'd imagined it might be. Still, it brought him back to long-ago nights when he and Cole would escape their angry household—i.e., their drunk father—and go as deep into the woods as they dared to camp out.

At the time, life had felt . . . hard.

But they hadn't a clue, not really. Because life being hard, really hard, had come later.

He gave a grand gesture for them to inspect inside.

Ashley sneezed three times in a row. "Ruh-roh. I think I'm allergic to the wild grass."

Lexi crossed her arms. "Really."

"Yes, and . . ." Ashley clasped her hands together over her heart. "Okay, so the truth is I wanna sleep with the kittens. You guys don't mind if I take the couch, right?"

Lexi opened her mouth, but Ashley hurried on. "Tonight's going to be epic! And you know what would make it better? Group hug."

"I don't hug liars," Lexi said, but Ashley just laughed and pulled her in tight, along with Heath.

He was completely unprepared for the sensation of having Lexi against him. If Ashley had caught sudden allergies, he'd most definitely caught something far worse—feelings. Feelings he had no idea what to do with, because he knew Lexi wouldn't be open to them.

And was he? Open to them?

More than he wanted to admit.

"Thank you," Ashley whispered, kissing them both on the cheek. "Thank you for doing this for me. It's going to be so fun."

"Fun," Lexi repeated with a forced smile.

She was so full of shit that he very nearly laughed, but she was doing this, trying hard, for her sister, and it sent another feeling through him. Pride. But he couldn't resist teasing her, just a little. "*Fun?*" he mouthed over Ashley's head.

She glared at him, made him grin as he crawled inside the tent to unzip the two windows to get some air flowing, since it had the faint scent of . . . summer festivals.

When he backed out of the tent, Lexi stood there alone, and he was pretty sure she'd been staring at his ass. "You were staring at my ass."

"Of course I wasn't. That would be sexist and rude."

"Uh-huh. Should I go back in and then come out again so you can stare for longer?"

"You're such an ass."

"Or . . . you *like* my ass."

She rolled her eyes. "How do you get through any doorways with that big fat head?"

He laughed. "I manage. So, you ready to be all outdoorsy?"

"I'm not outdoorsy. I'm . . ." She waved a hand, clearly looking for the right word. "Outsidey. Do I want to sleep in a tent? Absolutely not. Do I want to stare up at the gorgeous night sky before going home to a real bed? Sure. Bathe in an icy stream? Nope, no thank you. But roast a marshmallow? Yes, please."

"Maybe Judy has marshmallows."

She looked around them uneasily. "Do you think she also has bears?"

He eyed the open land, the green meadow, the rushing creek, the pines soaring toward the sky, all framed by the rocky hills in the distance that probably held caves for a multitude of wild animals, including bears, mountain lions, bobcats, deer, coyotes . . . "I think there are a lot of things out here."

She bit her lower lip. "Things that eat people?"

"Depends on how you taste."

She gave him a shove, and he grinned at her. But when she moved ahead of him to go back to the house, he let his grin fade. In order to keep people at arm's length, in order to protect a heart he wasn't sure even worked anymore, he'd worn an easygoing façade for a long time. So long that he wasn't even sure he could let it go. Not even when he wanted to. It'd been forever since he'd even thought about it, but he was thinking now. Thinking far too much—specifically how, now that he was starting to know her, he could see the cracks in her own armor. Cracks and glimpses of the real her that made him want to let her see the real him in return.

Apparently they had far more in common than he'd ever realized, and he wasn't sure that was a good thing.

The three of them took turns showering in a bathroom so small, his elbows kept bumping into the walls. He went last, which meant he got sixty seconds of hot water before it got icy, turning him into a soprano. Pushing the shower curtain aside to climb out of the tub, he nearly tripped over no less than *five* cats staring up at him, judging him as he dried off.

Lexi had helped Judy make a stack of grilled cheese sandwiches for dinner. Judy grabbed one for herself and waved it at them. "Well, kiddos, I'm off to meet my friends to discuss how I can get some time away and use Daisy's gift. You all be good, now. Don't do anything I wouldn't do!"

And then she was gone.

Ashley finished her sandwich, then stood and stretched, yawning wide. "I'm exhausted. Gonna hit the couch and get some sleep. Night."

"And you're sure you don't want to sleep in the tent?" Lexi asked.

"And miss out on my top bucket list item of sleeping with a colony of kittens?"

"Uh-huh," Lexi said dryly. "I thought your top bucket list item was to sleep with Margot Robbie."

"The kittens and Margot are tied for first." Ash smiled. "You two have fun, now."

And then she was gone.

Lexi stood still, face solemn. Worried. He knew he could rile her up without trying, which he'd always done just to watch her come to life. But annoying her was no longer his objective. No, he wanted something else entirely and was smart enough to understand he needed to come at her in a different, softer way if he wanted her to really see him.

And he did want that . . .

No matter how bad an idea it might turn out to be.

Lexi was still watching the doorway where Ashley had vanished. "You do realize what she's up to, right?" she asked.

He nodded. "Classic Ashley."

"She's set you up before?"

Heath washed the pan she'd used to make the sandwiches. "She thinks she's got a degree in Matchmaking 101."

"Hate to break it to her, but her plan, whatever it is, even combined with your sexy charm and killer smile, won't work on me."

He arched a brow. "You think I have sexy charm and a killer smile?"

"*Everyone* thinks that, including yourself." She took in his smile and pointed at it. "But neither are going to work on me." And with that, she grabbed one of the sleeping bags and let herself out the back door.

CHAPTER 11

Grateful that dusk seemed to go on forever this warm June night, Lexi didn't waste her phone battery on her flashlight. At least not until she'd neared the tent and heard a soft rustling in the trees off to her right. She froze for a beat, then hit the app, but the beam of light didn't cut through the purple sky.

A breeze brushed over her face, and she relaxed. "Just the wind dancing through the trees," she said out loud, wanting any wild animals within hearing range to decide she might taste as bitter as she sounded.

Crawling into the tent, she sat back on her heels and eyed the space as small as Judy's bathroom.

Maybe smaller.

And she and Heath would be sharing it . . . That morning when she'd realized he'd be coming on this trip, she'd wanted to argue that his presence wasn't necessary. But a part of her, an annoying part, had settled and calmed at the thought of him being here for them.

Gah. Her emotions were giving her whiplash.

Suddenly, she registered the utter lack of sound. No cars, no sirens, no city noises. Nothing. A little unnerved, she once again pulled out her phone, pleasantly surprised to see she had enough service to stream something. She picked *Bake Wars*, a show she had a love-hate relationship with. Love, because she had some weird obsession with judging the bakers who competed. Hate, because despite having watched the show for years, she sucked at baking.

Ten minutes in, she was stretched out on her sleeping bag, staring at her screen. "What are you doing? You can't just dip the walnut whirl into the tempered chocolate. You've got to carefully drizzle it over the top to achieve the characteristic wobble of the coffee ganache, Parisian café–style!"

She heard a short laugh just outside the tent. The calm energy told her exactly who it was, but her heart still leapt inside her chest. "Password required," she called out.

Heath's shadow on the other side of the zipped tent made him look ten feet tall and broad as a mountain. "Are you really streaming a show in there?"

"Nope, sorry, that's not the password."

"Your sister's peeking out the curtains, spying to see if you're going to let me in."

"It's not that either."

His shadowy stance—feet spread, hands on hips, the tilt of his head—suggested irritation. Good. He could join her damn club. *How were they going to share this tiny tent without killing each other?*

"I brought dessert," he said.

"Ding, ding, ding, we have a winner."

With a low laugh, he crouched and reached for the zipper, but stopped. "Are you . . . changing?" he asked.

"I've tried, but it never takes."

That got her another brief chuckle, but he still didn't move. After a few beats of silence, he quietly spoke without an ounce of his usual dry wit or sarcasm. "It's okay, Lex. I can sleep out here."

And even though he couldn't see her, she nodded. Definitely, that would be the safe route, and she watched, silent, as he stood and walked away. But then she remembered the bears, coyotes, mountain lions, oh my, and scrunched up her face. "Heath!"

His shadow reappeared, said nothing.

On her knees now, her show paused and forgotten, holding her breath, she tried to figure out what she thought she was doing. "I don't want you to get eaten. I mean, it'd make a big mess and all."

The tent's zipper slowly rose, and then there he was, hunkered low, balanced on the balls of his feet, his hooded gaze holding hers prisoner. Whenever she tried to hold that pose, she tended to fall over. Heath didn't. He seemed perfectly comfortable and . . . damn. Sexy as all get-out.

He flicked a gaze to the show still paused on her phone screen. "Do you bake?"

"Only if I want to burn a kitchen to the ground."

He snorted, and she rolled her eyes. "Hurry, you're letting bugs in."

He did not, in fact, hurry. Instead, he remained still. "Are you comfortable with this?"

"I think it's fair to say I'm comfortable with almost nothing these days."

He didn't smile. He merely grabbed the sleeping bag he'd brought out of the house.

"Stay," she whispered.

His eyes held hers. "You're sure?"

"I mean . . . I have some rules." She half expected him to smirk or make a joke.

He just nodded. "Whatever you need to feel comfortable and safe."

This took some of the starch out of her righteousness. How did he know that she rarely, if ever, felt truly safe? "First . . ." She tossed him a bug spray, which she'd gotten from the supplies left out for them and had already used.

"I'm surprised you don't have bear spray."

"Oh, I have that too," she said. "Judy is, thankfully, well prepared. Second—there's only one pillow, so we'll have to thumb wrestle for it."

His mouth quirked. "You can have the pillow, Lex."

Whenever he shortened her name in that low timbre of his, she melted—every single time—even if she had no intention of following up on that feeling.

Ever.

"Anything else?" he asked.

The question caught her off guard. He wasn't mocking her, or even teasing. Rules had been an important part of her life. Rules kept her sane. But the truth was, she was overwhelmingly tired of making them, tired of letting them keep her from things that might've turned out to be good for her.

Not that Heath was going to turn out to be good for her. She wasn't that naïve. But . . . maybe sometimes she needed to step outside her comfort zone and just let things happen. "Not right now," she finally said.

He nodded. "If that changes, just say the word."

Control. He was giving her all the control, which she appreciated, more than he could ever know. Returning the nod, she scooted back, making room for him to crawl in. "Now hurry."

"Is that actual concern for me, or are you worried that if I get eaten, I won't be able to share my body heat?"

She rolled her eyes so hard, she saw her own brain.

Chuckling, Heath climbed in, and suddenly the tent felt even tinier. There would be no moving around without bumping into each other, which would make things . . . interesting, to say the least.

He looked around, then unrolled his sleeping bag. "Going to be tight in here."

Extremely.

He looked at her and cocked his head slightly, clearly taking in her lingering tension. "Seriously. Say the word, and I go. I'll be fine out there."

She shook her head. "I want you to stay." True story.

"Okay, but you should know, I like to be the small spoon."

She snickered as he kicked off his shoes and stretched that delectable body out on his back as much as he could, his long legs bending at the knees to fit. At ease as always, he laced his hands behind his head and stared up at the night sky through the decent-size hole in the canvas above them. "Hope it doesn't rain."

"Do you want to adjust your sleeping bag so you're going corner to corner?" she asked. "It'd give you more legroom."

"Aw, you worry about me."

"I'm worried you'll get a leg cramp in the middle of the night and wake me up."

A pleased laugh escaped him. His smile was pure bad boy. "Liar."

"Just . . . stay on your side."

"Of course."

She was stuffed into her sleeping bag, but he was still on top of his. "Aren't you going to be cold?"

"Nah. I run hot."

No kidding . . . She shivered at the thoughts flitting through her brain, thoughts that had nothing to do with survival and everything to do with scooting close enough to climb him like a tree. Or better yet, ride him like a bronco.

And kissing him. Again. Because . . . and this was no news flash . . . no matter what she'd said about him being a bad kisser, he was the absolute best kisser on the planet.

He laughed softly and her gaze flew to his, horrified as she wondered if he could read her dirty mind. "What?"

Still smiling, he shook his head.

"Tell me."

"Do you have any idea how expressive you are?"

"I am not."

"Hey, that wasn't a diss. I like it." He met her gaze, his tone teasing as he murmured, "You want me. You want me bad."

Stomach flipping over itself in anticipation, she threw the sole pillow at him, nailing him in the face. "You wish!"

He slid the pillow beneath his head. "I do."

This shut her up, because there was nothing teasing in his gaze now, only a barely banked fire, scorching and direct. The kind that ignited white-hot flames deep inside. Too chicken to face it, she closed her eyes and pretended to settle in. Pretended, because her heartbeat thundered in her ears, the opposite of settling in. Same with her thoughts. She tossed and turned for a few minutes, but couldn't get comfortable.

Silently, he pushed the pillow back over to her. Gratefully, she tucked it beneath her head. After a few minutes, she whispered, "I have no idea what to do with you."

It took him almost as long to respond. "If you ever figure it out, let me know."

Would he be shocked to know how much that appealed? Giving in to this crazy attraction? Appealed and . . . terrified. She could hear crickets and a hoot of an owl. And some sort of rustling that she didn't think was wind this time. Maybe a coyote. Maybe a whole band of coyotes.

"Breathe, Lex."

She sucked in some air and turned on her side to face him. He was already facing her, and suddenly she realized how close they actually were. How . . . intimate the space suddenly felt.

"You're shivering," he murmured, and zipped her sleeping bag up for her. "And still holding your breath."

Dammit.

He took a steady but deep inhale through his nose, and then slowly let it out through his mouth. Then again.

And she found herself mimicking the cadence, until her heart slowed down and her shoulders lowered from her ears. He kept at it, a quiet, calm presence, never indicating any impatience as he waited for her to get it together, no snark to be found. His quiet attentiveness unnerved her, mostly because it felt . . . comfortable. Easy. She hadn't felt pressure to plaster on a smile, or pretend to be anything other than who she was—contrary, and also maybe a little angry.

Okay, not angry. Not when she was this close to him, stirred by his closeness, and how that closeness made her . . . feel things she didn't want to feel.

No, that was a lie. She *wanted* to feel. She wanted to feel *him*. Far too much.

"You know," he said softly, as if talking to a deer in the headlights—which she absolutely was. "We can either ignore this thing between us, or we could talk about it, maybe even see where it goes."

"There's no thing." She said it too quickly, she knew she did by the almost smile that crossed his mouth. "And even if there was . . . a thing . . . all evidence points to this being a bad idea."

He nodded. "Because you aren't attracted to me? Or because you're leaving as soon as the envelopes are delivered? Or maybe . . . maybe you're afraid."

She stared at his mouth and bit her lower lip. "It's a twofold answer."

His eyes lit with the humor she'd gotten accustomed to seeing. "Do tell."

"I *am* leaving when the envelopes are delivered, but that doesn't fall into play here, since I'm a terrible long-term bet anyway."

"Agree to disagree about you being a terrible long-term bet," he said. "What else?"

"As far as not being attracted to you . . ." She gave him a wry look. "You have mirrors in your house, right?"

He rolled his eyes for a change. "So we're down to option number three. You're afraid."

Dammit. "Maybe." She flopped to her back again. "We've tried this before. I kissed you. You were . . . horrified."

"Not horrified." He drew a deep breath. "Maybe . . . maybe just as scared as you."

Her heart started to race. "The next time I came here, you were dating someone."

He shrugged. "No law against that. And I had no idea you were coming, or I'd have warned you. It wasn't anything deep, and it didn't last."

She wasn't sure what to say to that, so she just stared up. Night had consumed dusk. The stars she could see through the hole above astounded her with their brilliance. So many, many stars, like diamonds on a blanket of black velvet. "How did I forget how gorgeous the night skies are out here?" she whispered.

"You didn't forget. You were ripped away—cruelly, in fact. I'm guessing you put all of it, good and bad, in a box and locked the memories away."

Uncomfortably right on the nose. "Do you ever think about that time when we were kids? When I was such a . . . brat?"

He was quiet a moment, and once again she turned her head to look at him, in profile now, as he was also looking up at the stars. "When we were in school," he finally said. "Competing with you, being challenged by you, I could be whoever I wanted to be. And what I wanted to be was your friend. You were smart, and a smart-ass. You were brave and stubborn, and never backed down. You weren't a girlie girl—not that there's anything wrong with being a girlie girl—but you didn't care to put on any sort of show. For anyone. You just wanted to be who you wanted to be. And I . . ." He took a deep breath, still not looking at her. Maybe it was easier to talk if he didn't. "I envied that," he said. "I envied it so much, because in my house, I didn't get to be who I wanted to be. I had to be strong, fast, and smart as hell to keep my younger brother safe."

Utterly drawn in by his words, by the emotion in his voice, by the feelings he'd revealed, she swallowed a sudden lump in her throat. "I'm sorry. No kid should have to go through what you did."

"Or you. And agreed. But all that was a long time ago, and we've both grown up. I admire who you grew up to be."

Unbearably moved, she swallowed hard. "Right back at you."

He ran a hand over his jaw, the several days' worth of growth making a rough sound in the silence. His wavy, sun-kissed brown hair had fallen over his forehead, and she entangled her fingers together so she wouldn't accidentally reach out and brush it off his face. Her heart hurt—burned, really—with fury. For him. For his brother. "What about your mom? You don't talk about her," she asked softly.

"She died when I was ten."

She squeezed her eyes shut, picturing him as what she'd always thought had been a cocky, annoying boy who wanted to always be in competition with her.

But in reality, that had been her. She'd been the annoying one who always started their fierce rivalry. She'd had some weird obsession with being the best. No doubt, it'd been about needing attention, and when she'd gone east with her dad, she'd kept it up. It'd been a pattern, contesting with the men in her life, none of whom had tended to like it. Including her dad.

She thought of how she'd spent so much of her life in survival mode, and now she knew Heath had done the same. Maybe by always wanting to be in her orbit, he'd just been looking for an escape, or a friend. "I admire you as well," she whispered. She didn't even realize she'd said the words out loud until she felt him shift. When she looked over, he'd propped his head up on a hand.

"I hate that you were hurting too," she said. "Sometimes I feel like all I've done is fail. Fail the people I care about, and fail myself."

"Lex." A big, warm hand reached out and gently cupped her jaw. "You never failed me. In fact, there were some days where trying to beat you at whatever we were doing was all I had." He gave her a small smile, and she managed one in return.

"Yeah?"

He nodded. "Yeah."

She realized he'd never once asked her to cool it, back down, or give up. Actually, in hindsight, even now, he always seemed to take great pleasure when she'd make him work for it. When she showed him her unapologetic true self.

"What else?" he asked, watching her quietly.

"I didn't get Margo to keep her envelope."

"That's not all on you, but I'm sure you'll find a way to get her to keep it," he said with utter confidence. In her.

Certainly more than she'd ever had in herself.

"Is this about Ashley?" he asked. "Is being here bringing back memories of how she got to stay and live with Daisy when you didn't?"

She turned her head to stare out at the stars again.

"No one would blame you for those feelings, Lex. No one. Not even Ashley."

How had he hit a nerve, when she'd thought she'd hidden them all? A memory came to her then, an early call with Daisy shortly after she'd moved east. Daisy had asked to speak to her dad, and she'd overheard him tell Daisy how difficult Lexi was and how he had no idea how to love her.

She felt the weight of Heath's gaze and turned to look at him. There was something in his expression that assured her he wasn't judging her. That he genuinely wanted to understand. So she swallowed hard and drew a deep breath for courage. "What's hard is hearing how everyone idolized Daisy, when I never got to see that side of her. She flaked on me so many times, usually when I needed her the most. But then I hear all these stories from perfect strangers who loved her, and I can't . . . I can't reconcile who that woman is with the woman I knew." She sucked in a breath. "I know my dad was right, that I was difficult. I can't imagine why he wanted me to go with him."

"You were the child, not your parents. And all children are

difficult. They're still to be protected, at all costs. Maybe your dad thought you'd be better off with him, maybe he didn't realize what you were going through. Which is not an excuse. He should have known." He paused, and she knew he was giving thought to what she'd said, taking her seriously. "I think Daisy had a lot of regrets and heartache over her failures when it came to her relationship with you. Her failures, Lexi. Not yours. No matter what you said to her, or how you asked her to stay away."

"I wish I hadn't."

Reaching out, he took her hand in his, squeezing gently. She could feel calluses on his palms and the rough pads of his fingers, and she wondered how he'd gotten them.

"A kid can only take so much rejection from a parent who never actually showed up."

She drew a shaky breath. She'd never actually spoken to anyone about this. Whenever she and Ashley had tried, it ended in awkwardly hurt feelings. Her dad had never wanted to hear about Daisy at all. And as recently as an hour ago, she'd have said there was no way she'd have a conversation with Heath about her either, mostly because it was obvious they'd been close, very close, and he wouldn't want to hear anything negative about her.

"I'm sorry about everything that happened to you," Heath said, gently squeezing her fingers. "No kid should go through that."

It took her a moment to gather herself, because for some reason, his words touched a spot deep in her chest that she'd not accessed in a long time. "Right back at you." It helped that they weren't looking at each other. In fact, she'd closed her eyes, which made it easier to say things she'd normally never say out loud. "Maybe it made us who we are, for better or worse."

He bumped a broad shoulder to hers. "For what it's worth, you're not so bad."

And there, in the dark, out of time and place, she smiled. "A compliment. Wow. You better be careful or I'll start to think you've gone soft."

"I've given you plenty of compliments," he said. "I told you only a few minutes ago how smart you are."

"Smart *and* a smart-ass," she reminded him.

"Smart-ass is also a compliment."

That made her laugh, even as that spot in her chest warmed further. "You didn't grow up to be who I thought you would."

"Is that your way of saying I'm not so bad either?"

She smiled. "Maybe." Opening her eyes and turning her head to his, she found him studying her face. "What?"

Those blue gray eyes pulled in the moon and starlight, nearly glowing. Not cold, but warm. Amused. Affectionate . . . "I like when you glare at me, but I love your smile. Your laugh." He shook his head as if marveling. "They're contagious."

A matching affection spread through her, but she gave him an eye roll. "You *like* when I glare at you?" she repeated in disbelief.

"I like when you call me out on my shit."

His voice was husky and seductive, and wove through every nerve ending in her body, but she found a laugh. "You need help."

"No doubt. You've stopped shivering."

She had, clearly thanks to the delicious body heat he put out, not to mention how she felt with him. Fear and anxiety seemed to vanish. She'd even forgotten to worry about the wild animals watching and waiting for their chance to have her for dinner. Something about Heath made her feel stronger, secure, and something else, something completely alien.

Safe.

And given the unexpected heat and carefully banked desire in those blue gray eyes, maybe also . . . wanted.

Dangerous. He was dangerous as hell, to both her heart and soul, and she should probably try to remember that, but in the moment, she couldn't.

CHAPTER 12

Lying in that tent, Lexi should've been worried and anxious about whether spiders liked to camp or what would happen when she had to walk all the way back to the house to pee. Would she risk being eaten by a coyote, or . . . take the bigger risk and wake up Heath to walk with her?

Instead, all she could think about was how the night sounds— wind in the trees, the gentle hoot of an owl—somehow calmed her brain so that her thoughts didn't race fifty million miles an hour per usual. She could just . . . be.

All while being incredibly aware of the deliciously warm man lying next to her, not quite touching, but not out of range either. Was sharing air, sharing space, startlingly intimate? Yes. But was she, in a rare change of pace, perfectly content? Also yes.

She wished she knew what was going through Heath's head. Was he wondering how the hell he'd managed to get stuck out here with her? Was he counting sheep? Was he, like her, thinking about what would happen if they turned to each other and gave in to this crazy addicting chemistry she couldn't stop thinking about, even when she wanted to kick him?

She had no clue, because in perhaps one of the nicest things he'd done, he was letting the silence lie there between them, more comfortable than she could've imagined. Especially since she was also wondering if that natural, effortless sexiness he exuded extended to certain skills . . .

She'd never just slept with someone out of basic hunger for intimacy. Never. She needed to be comfortable with that person. And while she was getting there—shockingly—with Heath, she wasn't in a headspace to start something.

Not that this stopped the sensual desire for him from sweeping through her, firing all her nerve endings. "I don't know very much about you," she said into the relaxed silence.

"You know more than most."

"But not enough."

He glanced over at her, his eyes asking, *Enough for what?*

She knew she'd broadcast at least some of her feelings when he paused, then said, "What you see is what you get."

"I doubt that."

He smiled. "Do you?"

"Come on, tell me something. Something real."

"Such as?"

"Such as . . ." Where to start? "Why are you single?"

A half smile quirked at his lips. "You looking to apply?"

"Deflection." She jabbed a finger into his chest. "Which I know because I'm the queen of deflection." She jabbed him again. "An open book, remember?"

He exhaled a long breath. "I'm single by choice. I thought I'd found the One once, back when I was a trial attorney working eighty hours a week. When I left that job, I learned she was more interested in the lifestyle I was able to provide her while she lived on the other side of the globe from me. Let's just say,

I'm not cut out to live my life any differently than how I do right now, nor does a long-distance relationship work for me."

She stared at him, knowing they were both very aware that if they started something up, it'd be a long-distance relationship.

He hesitated. "And in the name of transparency, I haven't been in any kind of a relationship, long distance or otherwise, in a while. By choice."

Unease filled her, which was ridiculous. She didn't want a relationship right now. And maybe, after her last one, not ever again. "Good thing we don't like each other very much."

"Good thing." But there was no tease or taunt behind the words.

In fact, she couldn't read him at all in the moment. "I'm . . . sorry you got hurt."

He shrugged again. "Happens, right?"

She could have ignored that, or even changed the subject, but he'd opened up to her. And she got the sense he didn't do that easily, no matter how laid-back he was. And she was starting to think maybe that was just a front to keep people at arm's length.

Something she knew a little bit about.

Either way, he'd managed to hide in plain sight. Most everything she knew about him was something she could see. He was strong, inside and out. Smart as hell. Brave. Wildly sexy. Fun. Physically and emotionally agile. As for anything deeper, like his hopes and dreams . . . she had no idea. But she knew it was her turn, so . . .

"I got played," she said quietly. "In my last relationship. We worked together, and I really thought it was real." She shook her head. "Turns out it wasn't. And to be honest, I let it . . . destroy me, and my life. I'm on a break from the job." Okay, so that part was a bit of a fib, but there was being honest and then there was baring her soul. "I'm on a break from everything, mostly because I don't know how to come back from it, how to trust or believe again." She shrugged. "So until then, I'm on a moratorium from connections."

His eyes softened. "Explains the claws."

She gave a mirthless laugh. "Yeah."

"I thought you were working remotely while you were here."

Shit. Caught in a web of her own deceit. "It's . . . not working out. The job requires me to determine the monetary value of a client's personal property. In person. Hard to do from nearly three thousand miles away. But I've put out feelers. I hope to be able to pick up some independent work while I'm here." She faked a smile. "Gotta pay the bills."

His eyes warmed. "You'll be great."

And that was that, just quiet, unwavering, easy support.

"Do you miss your life back east?" he asked.

"I miss the job itself." Not a fib. "I realize that the work I do might seem cold and calculating, but honestly, that's why I'm good at it."

"You'd be good at anything you put your mind to." He gave a slow shake of his head. "But the cold and calculating part? I think that's just a mask."

Not much surprised her, and she'd long ago lowered her expectations when it came to being understood. But Heath Bowman . . . he did surprise her.

"I'm sorry you got hurt," he said. "If you ever want to talk about it . . ."

And reveal just how stupid and gullible she'd been? How she'd lost not just her belief in herself, but her job as well? No thank you. She could barely face the humiliation of just *her own* knowledge of what had happened. So she just nodded noncommittally.

He ran a finger along her temple, nudging a stray strand from her face. "You okay?"

"I'm always okay."

That got her another little smile. "So . . . we both know what we don't want."

She snorted. "I guess the question is, do we know what we *do* want?"

Heath nodded. Then shook his head, and they both laughed a little.

"How about a truth for a truth?" he asked.

Her stomach jangled. "A dare seems like a better idea."

"All right." He smiled. "I dare you to tell me a truth."

She grimaced. "This is a terrible idea."

"Even if what happens in this tent stays in this tent?"

She gnawed on her lower lip for a beat, unable to deny she wanted to do this, if only to hear a truth from him. "A truth . . ." She paused. "I have no idea what I'm doing with my life."

No pity on his face, no judgment, just an easy understanding that didn't make her want to curl up and die. "Is that why you agreed to come out here?" he asked.

"That's what I told myself," she admitted. "I thought maybe all I needed was a break. A week-long break. And then I got here, and . . ."

Heath was watching her think too hard. "And . . . ?"

"And . . . I think I agreed to stay for a few reasons."

"Ashley."

"She's one of them, yes." Her gaze dropped to his mouth. She hadn't felt much of anything for a long, long time now, but suddenly she was feeling plenty, not the least of which was a warmth heating her from the inside out.

"What else?"

She bit her lower lip. "I'm not entirely sure."

His head propped up by his hand, he gave a small smile. "Thought we agreed to a truth."

And maybe it was that his gaze had landed on her mouth as well. Or maybe she felt tired of not living her life. Either way, she shifted closer without making any conscious decision about it. "I didn't expect you." There. That was as close to a real truth as she could get.

Heath nodded, holding her gaze. "My truth. I didn't expect you either." He ran his fingers up her arm, then around the back of her neck, sliding them into her hair, the slow, purposeful touch waking up her entire body.

"Truth," she whispered. "I lied about you being a bad kisser."

He smiled. "Truth. I already knew that."

She swallowed hard and looked at the sky, at the dark tent around them, at everything and anything other than those mesmerizing eyes that made her ache to do something stupid here tonight. "What do we do now?"

He leaned in to press a kiss to her temple before brushing his mouth along her jaw, stopping at the sensitive spot just beneath her ear.

Her eyes drifted shut in pleasure. So much for not doing something stupid. "What are you doing?"

"Giving you a good night kiss."

"You missed my lips."

"I was waiting for permission."

Her eyes fluttered open. It was definitely very dark now, but the stars provided a silvery glow. Heath's five-o'clock shadow had a five-o'clock shadow, and it seemed dangerously alluring on him. "Do you want it in writing?"

He smiled. "*There's* the smart-ass."

Tilting her head slightly, she lined up their mouths a fraction of an inch from each other. "Yes, I want you to kiss me good night," she whispered. "And you?"

"One hundred percent, yes—"

He hadn't finished his sentence before she closed the gap and kissed him. Immediately, a very low, very male sound of pleasure rumbled from his chest, igniting her own pleasure. As did the way he wrapped his arms around her, drawing her in tight. With a teasing nip of his teeth, he coaxed her lips apart so they could taste each other, an exploration of mutual fascination that just might've made her rethink her stance on men—if she could have thought.

She couldn't. Not with his mouth on hers, sweet, sexy, and entirely unexpected.

When they finally broke apart, her heart thundered in her ears and at each pulse point. She blinked a few times, and his lips tilted into a satisfied smile. "I've spent the better part of the past week and a half thinking about what that might be like," he said, voice low and husky.

Pulse still racing, she bit the inside of her cheek to keep from begging for more, but when she realized his heart was drumming as fast as hers, she nearly started purring. "That was very . . . nice."

He choked. "Nice?"

"I said very. *Very* nice."

His eyes narrowed. "We really going to do this again?"

"Do what?" she asked innocently.

"I can do better," he said.

"Really?" Because any better, and her clothes would melt off.

At the slight tone of doubt she'd put in her voice, he gave a rough laugh and hauled her into him again. "Just so we're clear," he murmured. "I know you're baiting me. Just as you know I'm using it as an excuse to kiss you again."

"Well, as long as we both know—"

His mouth came down on hers, and she might've moaned a little. At the sound, his careful control seemed to shatter like glass. His hands tunneled in her hair, holding her to him, kissing her like he wanted the very air she breathed. Arching her back, she struggled to get even closer, needing to eliminate every inch of space between them. And when she was as close as she could get, she touched everything she could reach, quite happy to hear the hitch in his breathing, the low groan that rumbled from deep in his throat.

The sound gave her a delicious full-body shiver. He had one hand fisted in her hair, the other beneath her shirt, driving her crazy. The highly skilled groping had her panting as he toyed with the clasp of her bra, but didn't unhook it. She opened her mouth to encourage him, but before she could, he ended the kiss, his hands slow to fall away from her body, as if he didn't want to let go at all.

The whole encounter had only been a minute, tops, but it'd been so sensual that she quivered as she drew in a deep breath. "What . . . why?"

He kissed her again, quick this time, but no less devastating for it, before flopping to his back. "Because if we're going to be stupid enough to do this, it's not going to be in someone else's tent, in someone else's field, with a rock digging into my ass."

"Stupid enough?" she repeated, brows up.

He grinned, then he pulled her over the top of him and kissed her again.

"I thought you had a rock digging into your ass," she managed breathlessly. "I thought we were stopping."

"We are." With a groan of frustration, he shifted them to their sides, her back pressed to his front. Drawing one of the sleeping bags over the top of them, he whispered, "Sleep."

And shockingly, or maybe not so shockingly given that he was still stroking her body, not to arouse now, but to quiet and soothe, for the first time in her life, she followed a command and went to sleep.

CHAPTER 13

Lexi spent the next few days attempting to put that night in the tent beneath the stars with Heath out of her head, trying to forget the warm connection they'd made, the fun they'd had, the way his kisses had awakened her body, making her hungry in ways she'd forgotten about.

She and Ashley spent a lot of hours slowly making their way through the garage, which had decades of stuff packed into it. They found a lot of junky furniture that Ashley got excited about restoring and selling. And then a pair of end tables that, if they'd been in prime condition, might've fetched them a mint. Even a little dinged up and worse for wear though, Lexi thought they could still get a grand apiece for them.

"Look at these," Ashley said, holding up a pair of gaudy brass and gold salt and pepper shakers. "Definitely toss pile, right?"

Lexi looked them over. "These are from Liberace's collection, and they're worth several thousand dollars."

"But . . . *why?*"

Lexi laughed. Trust Daisy to have shoved things of incredible value in with things that were solely sentimental and treated them all the same.

And then there'd been the highly collectible ceramic Dickens village pieces still in their original boxes on the shelves lining one wall. Not worth what they once had been, but worth selling.

"Pretty!" Ashley said. "Let's set up the village!"

"This whole set is probably worth thousands."

Ashley bit her lower lip, and Lexi knew they weren't selling. They hadn't unearthed anything else of monetary value, but Ashley didn't seem to mind. She said she was just excited to be hanging out.

Lexi had to admit, it had been nice. More than nice. It'd been the best time she'd had in . . . well, she couldn't even remember. They laughed over silly stuff, ate each other's food, jokingly critiquing whether healthy or junk food served them best.

Turned out, it was a tie.

Making everything even better, she now had two new clients. Each a family estate that needed to be gone through and evaluated, one in South Shore, and the other right here in Sunrise Cove, both of which would provide her several weeks of work.

All in all, she was no longer resenting every moment in Sunrise Cove.

Four nights after Tent-Gate, as she was calling it, she looked at the bedside clock. Two in the morning, and she was no closer to sleep than she had been hours ago. Giving up, she slid out of bed and went to the window, staring out at the part of the yard that Ashley had taken over with her large garden. The rest of the land was overgrown and neglected. They still had to talk about whether to sell or not, but either way, they'd have a lot to clean up. Beyond their yard, she could see the vague outline of the back of Heath's grandpa's house. It was dark—except for the single light burning through the night.

Someone else couldn't sleep.

Huh. Maybe she needed some fresh air. *Uh-huh, and the Easter Bunny is real . . .*

She pulled a pair of thick, baggy sweats over her pj's, stepped into her fake Uggs, and slipped out the kitchen door.

For that fresh air.

To prove to herself that was all she needed, she sat on the top porch step. Sunrise Cove sat at high altitude, 6,300 feet, which meant they usually had a drastic temperature drop in the evenings, even in summer. Tonight she found herself shivering in the forty-two-degree temp, and thought about going back inside for a coat.

Then decided to walk instead.

She'd just go to the end of the yard and pick an apple from the tree. Yep, and she also had some swampland to sell herself . . . At the base of the tree, she reached up and grabbed two apples, shoving them into her sweatpants pocket.

Then stared at the lone light still burning from that small side door window of the garage. A tall, built shadow moved inside, and she could've sworn she heard something. The rev of a power tool, maybe. So either a serial killer . . . or Heath.

She didn't realize she'd moved until she climbed through the break in the fence between their yards. Maybe it was Gus. Maybe Heath wasn't even home and his grandpa needed something. Maybe he was hurt. She sped up. Just to make sure everything was okay, of course.

When she got to the door, she peered in the window, getting a front-row view of Heath, a sander in hand, bent over a piece of furniture that looked like it might be a bathroom vanity. An old one.

He wore no shirt, just a pair of low-slung sweatpants cupping an A-plus ass as he leaned into the task, sawdust spinning in the air all around him, lit up like tiny specks of gold in the light hanging from the rafters above. The smooth muscle and sinew of his back, shoulders, and arms bunched and released as he moved with easy grace, and her eyes ate him up.

Stupid eyes.

Mayhem lay a few feet from Heath, snoozing. Lexi lifted her hand to give a light knock, but before she could, both dog and man turned, four sharp eyes unerringly landing on her.

Mayhem yipped with joy at the sight of their unexpected guest. Much more muted, Heath set the sander down and headed to the door, meeting her gaze with absolutely no in- dication of how he felt about his middle-of-the-night visitor.

HE HAD NO idea why he was so surprised to see her. Lexi had been surprising nearly all their lives. He took in the oversize sweats and boots, hair loose and a little bit wild, and nearly smiled at the adorably sexy vision. Nearly, but not, because in the days since that night in the tent, he'd almost managed to convince himself that he'd dodged a bullet.

But looking into her pretty eyes, he knew he was full of shit. It made him feel like he'd stepped onto a Tilt-A-Whirl—upside down and inside out.

"Hey." She gave him a little wave, then grimaced. "I saw the light and just wanted to make sure everything's okay."

He found his voice. "I should be asking you that question. It's the middle of the night. Why aren't you asleep?"

"Why aren't you?" she countered.

"I needed to get some stuff done. Is everything okay? Sorry, Mayhem has zero chill."

The dog had turned into a wriggle worm, his tail knocking against the doorframe, fussing over their guest, trying to lick her to death.

"Mayhem. Calm."

Mayhem did the opposite, getting the zoomies, racing around the garage like the Tasmanian Devil. Cutting a corner too tight, he skidded and careered into a shelving unit, immediately leaping up to begin again, ears flopping, a wide smile on his face, tongue lolling out.

"I think your dog's broken," Lexi said.

"I blame his previous master."

The dog, having finally let go of all his pent-up energy, trotted back and sat at his feet. "Good boy." Heath rested an affectionate hand on his head as they both looked at Lexi. "You're okay?"

"Yes."

But she didn't sound sure. Worried, he stepped back, gesturing for her to come in.

She didn't move.

He studied her face. "Something's wrong."

"Um . . . no." She shook her head. "I mean . . . Not really."

"Okaaaaay." He tried to read her mind and failed. "Do you want to stay standing in the doorway, or . . ."

She eyed the garage beyond him, but still paused, and he felt his lips twitch. "You've come this far."

She rolled her eyes, though he wasn't sure if it was for him or her. But she did finally step past his ferocious guard dog, who let her through for the price of scratching behind his ears and a belly rub.

Just inside, she stopped.

Mayhem stared sweetly up into her eyes, leaning so hard on her that she nearly toppled over.

"I'm sorry." Heath turned to the ridiculous dog. "She doesn't need support right now, buddy."

Mayhem just leaned on Lexi, thumbing his nose at his fearless leader.

Lexi laughed and bent to pet him some more before looking around, taking in the space that Heath had claimed as his own.

He'd pretty much turned it into a woodshop filled with tools and other projects waiting their turn.

"Looks like I'm interrupting something important," she said.

"I'm restoring a bathroom vanity for a friend of my grandpa's." Post stroke, Mrs. Cromwell was now in a wheelchair and couldn't afford to make her home more accessible. His grandpa had offered Heath's services. Ironic, the man who wanted Heath to slow down was also the one who kept bringing him work, but Heath knew Mrs. Cromwell. She'd been one of his English teachers back in middle school and was one of the few to actually give a shit about him and Cole, so agreeing had been a no-brainer.

"You're busy," Lexi said quietly. "I shouldn't keep you."

Keep me . . . And where that thought came from, he had no idea. "It's okay, I'm done working for the night."

She cocked her head. "I wasn't aware you worked these days."

The Heath of just a few weeks ago would've offered her a mocking smile and made a joke to deter her, but he couldn't stomach the game anymore. The game where it amused him to let her think the worst of him. They'd begun opening up to each other, going from adversaries to friends to . . . well, factoring in their chemistry and those off-the-charts kisses they'd shared, also far more. A terrifying thought. "You never asked."

She just blinked. "I did."

He gave a slow headshake.

She stared at him some more, and a flush rose to her cheeks. "Oh my God. You're right. I didn't. At the airport, you joked about not being a nine-to-fiver, and later Ashley, and also your grandpa, teased you about being a man of leisure. I . . . I made assumptions, and I shouldn't have." She paused. "A part of me knew I had to be missing something. I'm sorry." She gave a tentative smile. "Is it too late to ask now?"

If he was smart, he'd scare her off with a resounding *yes*. But apparently he wasn't nearly as smart as he thought he was. "Would you like something to drink?"

"Sure." She eyed the open bottle on the workbench next to him. "Whatever you're having."

He grabbed the bottle and poured some into the tumbler next to it and then handed it over. "Whiskey."

She took the shot, then sucked in a wheezy breath and held out the tumbler for more.

He poured another shot. "Don't go too hard. I'm so tired, I'm not sure I can carry you home."

With a snort, she tossed it back and then looked at him expectantly.

Right. She wanted to hear about him. He held out his hand for the glass and poured himself another.

"You're stalling," she said.

"I don't stall."

"No, apparently you just let people assume the worst of you." She looked like she was mad at herself. And maybe him too, but instead of saying so, she raised her eyebrows.

"I never said I *didn't* work, you know. You just assumed."

She sank to one of the two long workbenches lining the side walls. "And you let me."

He dropped onto the opposite bench from her. "You know I was a trial attorney. I dealt with high-powered clients, brutally long hours, and all the soul-crunching stress that came with it. During that time, I had zero life. Hell, I barely managed to get a few hours of sleep a night."

She hadn't taken her eyes off his. "Something happened."

He leaned back against the wall. "A few things, actually."

She didn't say anything, but her silence wasn't cold. In fact, it felt the opposite. Even though she sat a good five feet away, he could feel her genuine interest and care. "I started getting chest pains."

She sucked in a breath.

"I thought it was just indigestion, so I took over-the-counter meds and ignored it. Until I couldn't." Hell, this was harder than he'd thought. Besides Cole, he hadn't told anyone this story. Ever. "One day in the middle of a hellish eighty-hour workweek, I collapsed in the middle of a big meeting with our most important clients, who'd flown in from all over the globe."

"Oh my God, Heath." She had a hand over her mouth. "A heart attack?"

"It felt like it. I've never experienced pain like that. I couldn't breathe, couldn't so much as get up off the floor." He closed his eyes and shook his head. "Thought I was a dead man. But after an embarrassing ambulance ride and a barrage of medical tests, it turned out to be an anxiety attack. The first of . . . well, many."

"It must have been terrifying."

He was startled to realize she'd come to sit at his side, turning on the bench to face him. Her hands reached for his, gently squeezing. When he lifted his gaze to hers, he braced himself for pity, in which case, this story would be over.

But all he found was an understanding. A warm, easy understanding.

"What did you do?" she asked softly.

"I did everything that was suggested. I got meds, I got a thera-pist, but neither really helped. And then the perfect storm came." He drew a deep breath. "I've got a house not too far from here. I bought it my first year as an attorney, but I've never spent any significant time in it. I was living and working in San Francisco. At least, until Cole had a health scare—much worse than mine."

Cole had been in remission for years at that point, but he'd found a swollen lymph node. It turned out to be nothing, thankfully . . . He closed his eyes for a beat, remembering Misty's and his own co-terror—that Cole's childhood cancer had come back. "And right on the heels of that, my grandpa fell in the shower and broke his hip. He couldn't take care of himself, but we all knew he'd wither and die in assisted living. Cole and Misty wanted to take him in, but he wanted to be here, in this house, where he'd spent fifty-plus years with his wife, and I could hardly blame him for that. So . . ." He lifted a shoulder. "I quit my job and came home. I'd hoped to talk him into living at my place, but you've met him. He's stubborn as hell."

Her eyes had warmed as he talked, but at his last sentence, she let out a low laugh. "Apple. Tree . . ."

A wry smile curved his mouth. "Yeah."

"Do you miss it?"

"Being on the hamster wheel?" He shook his head. "No. My point is that for a while, I was exactly who you thought, a lazy bum—"

"I didn't think that—"

He gave her a look, and she bit her lower lip. "It had nothing to do with you, Heath. I wanted to hate you. I was a hot-as-hell mess." She paused. "Still am."

She had the hot-as-hell part right. "You're not a mess, not any more than the rest of us, anyway."

She seemed amused by that notion.

"As for what I'm doing now . . ." He realized he was covered in sawdust and brushed a hand over his arms and chest, which only dispelled some of it. He needed a shower. "Turns out, doing nothing wasn't the answer either."

"So you've been . . ." She lifted her gaze from his chest, looking a little dazed—flattering—and then she eyed the garage around them. "Building stuff?"

He shrugged. "Back in high school and college, I worked as a laborer for a general contractor. Learned a lot, not the least of which was that working with my hands fulfilled me more than anything had up to that point. But I was dead set on never going back to being poor, so I went against my instincts and did the attorney thing. It wasn't until I came back here that I remembered how restoring and renovating old stuff into something beautiful again made me feel. It's not lucrative," he said wryly. "But having worked myself half into the grave for years, with little to no free time, I've got enough money socked away to live on."

"Ashley has mentioned restoring old furniture."

He nodded. "I got her into it. She comes over and uses my tools and this space whenever she likes."

"That's sweet of you."

"She does plenty for me too, like watching my grandpa when I can't."

Lexi smiled. A real one, and he felt his shoulders slightly lower from his ears. She had a way of lightening his load by just looking at him. He knew all too well what was missing from his life. Connections. Intimate connections. He also knew he could fall for Lexi, and fall hard. They'd have a good time. Hell, a great time. And it would work.

Until it didn't.

Because she was leaving. No if, ands, or buts about it. She was leaving as soon as she could.

Which was fine.

Absolutely fine.

And maybe if he kept repeating that to himself, he'd learn to accept it.

"So what happened after you came here?" she asked. "Did the panic attacks stop?"

"No." He laughed roughly, and why he felt like tugging her close and burying his face in her hair, he had zero idea. Well, other than she smelled amazing, and he thought he might find his own little slice of that heaven if he leaned forward and fell into her arms. "I felt like I was drowning. Dying. But it was Daisy who told me it was okay to fall apart sometimes. She said s'mores fall apart, and we still love them."

She smiled, but it didn't quite meet her eyes. "True. But a panic attack isn't nearly as much fun as a s'more."

"You know what they're like," he said quietly. "Anxiety attacks. Firsthand."

"Oh yeah. In fact, I had no less than two on the plane here. And then another when I realized I was going to stay for six weeks."

"I'm sorry." He brought their joined hands up to his mouth and kissed her knuckles. "I know how bad they suck, how helpless you feel."

"Helpless, and furious," she agreed. "But mine don't manifest externally, like yours. They're all internal. If you didn't know what to look for, I don't think you'd be able to tell I was having one." Her mouth twisted in a grim smile. "I'm good at pretending. *Really* good." She knocked her shoulder into his. "Seems like we're both pretty good at hiding behind the person we want the world to see."

"Or maybe it's just that if you keep up the pretense for long enough, you become that person."

She nodded and turned away, but not before he caught a flash of tears. "Lex," he said softly, pained.

Her shoulders had bowed inward a little. "Ignore me."

As if that were even possible. Gently, slowly, he pulled her into him. "You don't have to hide. Not here. Not with me."

"I hurt people with my pretending," she whispered into his chest.

He lifted her face. "If you're talking about Ashley, she's good. She's just happy you're here now."

Her gaze turned earnest. She wanted to believe him, believe she and Ashley would be okay, and he was again struck by how he'd misjudged her aloofness. She cared. She cared deeply, even if she didn't always show it. He knew it drove Ashley crazy that Lexi called her mom Daisy, and not Mom. But Lexi hadn't gotten the same Daisy as Ashley had. Her life had been hard, unfamiliar, and cruel.

And Daisy had let it happen. Granted, she'd had serious issues, but all that ten-year-old Lexi had understood was that her mom hadn't fought to keep her.

Heath remembered enough about his own beautiful, wonderful mom to know that he'd have been devastated beyond consolation if she hadn't fought for him.

Lexi pulled free and got to her feet to leave. She was so fast, he barely managed to catch her at the door. "Lex?"

"I should get back."

He turned her to face him, her spine pressed into the door. "What just happened?" he asked.

Her eyes slid closed. "I don't want you to feel sorry for me."

"I absolutely do not feel sorry for you. I mean, I'd like to go back in time and hurt anyone who hurt you, but that's not pity. That's just me understanding how a sucky past can shape the here and now. You deserved better." He paused. "Daisy broke your heart."

She gave a little shrug, like it no longer mattered, but he knew it did.

"It happened again with the men in your life," he said.

Her gaze flickered away. A confirmation. And he knew right then and there that he wouldn't ever risk doing the same.

"I really should go," she said softly, her eyes telling him that if he said *stay*, if he took her hand and pulled her into him again, she'd meet him halfway.

But he couldn't do that, not to her. "I'll walk you," he managed to say.

Surprise hit her, then a flash of embarrassment. "No, it's okay." She shook her head. "I'm good." And then she slipped out the door as quickly as she'd slipped past his inner walls, the darkness swallowing her up.

Hating himself, he stepped out into the chilly night, quietly following to make sure she got inside safely, before going back to his cold bed, alone with his regrets.

CHAPTER 14

B oy, you work too much. Did you forget what happened to you last time?"

Heath didn't glance at his grandpa, keeping his gaze on his laptop. "I'm working for *you*, at the moment. Do you have any idea how much paperwork you generate? Bills, insurance claims, general accounting . . . the list goes on and on."

"Huh. I should double your salary."

Heath snorted. "Double zero is still zero." He was on the back porch swing, enjoying the last of a warm summer day. Or as much as he could while trying to keep up with everything his grandpa and the house required.

"You're going to get old and gray," his grandpa said.

When Heath turned his head to look at the old man, his neck creaked like a ninety-year-old's, and he winced. "You might be right."

"I'm always right. I'm also hungry."

Heath glanced at the time. "I'll put in a takeout order. Preferences?"

"Anything."

"Soup and salad."

"No," his grandpa said.

"Tacos."

"No."

A headache began to form between his eyes. "Okay, so then what does 'anything' look like to you?"

"Fish-and-chips. And beer."

"You're not supposed to have deep-fried or alcohol," Heath reminded him.

Grandpa dramatically tossed his hands up. "Why don't you just kill me?"

"I mean, I keep trying."

His grandpa cackled. "You were always my favorite."

"Yeah, yeah, you say that now. But wait until I order you a salad." Heath stood and stretched. His phone buzzed with an incoming text from Ashley.

> You can run but you can't hide.

It'd been a few days since he'd slept in that tent with Lexi, since she opened up to him, since he'd had his mouth on hers, his hands on those delicious curves, since he'd slept with her hair in his face, the scent and feel of her lulling him into the best sleep of his life, even with the rock pressing into his ass.

And last night she'd found him working in the garage, where they'd come far too close to giving in to temptation.

And Ashley had been hounding him ever since, the nosy busybody. He loved her, but he wasn't going to crack, which he made clear in his return text.

> I'm not hiding. I'm working. You should try it.

His grandpa plopped down at his side. "That doesn't look like my bills."

"Because I lied."

The old man laughed. "You never lie."

"Fine, I evaded. I *was* doing all your paperwork, and now I'm on to something else. Kaley Johnson from the ski and bike shop has a customer threatening to sue her. She asked me to read through the emails to see if she needs an attorney. She's coming by in a bit to go over everything."

His grandpa grinned.

"What?"

The man lifted his hands. "Hey, you could do worse. Kaley is pretty and smart, and on the hunt for a man. Last I looked, you were one of those. Though you wouldn't know it by your social life."

"I don't mix business and pleasure."

"You sure about that?"

Heath tilted his head. "What does that mean?"

"It means Ashley thinks you and her sister would be a good fit. And I'm assuming you think so too, given how you slept with her already."

"I didn't—" He gave a purposeful exhale and then pointed at him. "You're fishing."

"And you nearly took the bait." His grandpa smiled and tapped his own temple. "And you thought I was starting to lose it. I'm sharp as a tack, boy."

"I've never doubted that. Tell Ashley her intel's faulty."

"She said you'd say that. But she knows without a doubt that you and Lexi—"

"I will pay you not to finish that sentence." Heath paused. "Did Lexi tell Ash that?"

His grandpa grinned. "Nope. You just did." He pulled out his cell phone.

"What the hell are you doing?"

"Reporting in."

"Are you serious?"

"Hey," his grandpa said. "She bribed me with promises of homemade meals and freshly baked cookies. I'm not stupid."

"I feed you every single day, whatever you want."

"Not whatever I want. And anyway, Ashley's cuter than you." His grandpa cackled. "So what kind of a moment did you two have?"

"Why, do you get extra goodies if you provide details?"

"Yep."

"Unbelievable."

"So that's a hard no on the details?"

Heath gave him a look that had his grandpa grinning un- abashedly, but he at least had the good sense to go back in the house and leave Heath alone.

Ten minutes later, Kaley came by. They'd gone out twice in high school, nothing serious. He'd been in her shop a few months ago looking at a new bike for himself. She'd flirted, and maybe he'd flirted back. As he was leaving the store, she'd asked him out, but he'd been too busy at the time. He hadn't even con- sidered that she might have an ulterior motive with her request for help.

Their meeting lasted five minutes. He gave her his advice— yes, she needed an attorney, and no, unfortunately he couldn't be that attorney, since he didn't work in law anymore—and she'd nodded and thanked him.

And then asked if he was less busy now, maybe they could catch a meal together.

He declined, and maybe last week he would've said he didn't know why. But he knew exactly, and it had everything to do with a beautiful honey-brunette who had somehow gotten past his defenses.

Who he'd turned down last night out of fear of hurting her.

And maybe also because he didn't want to be hurt either.

When Kaley left, Heath went back to work. It was some-time later when he heard his grandpa laughing inside the house. Shutting down his laptop, Heath headed into the kitchen, then blinked in surprise to find Lexi sitting at the dining room table laughing too. She wore a gauzy sundress that hugged her to the waist and then fell loose around her long legs. Her hair had been pulled back in a ponytail, her eyes were shiny with good humor, and her mouth . . . the one that had been starring in his nightly fantasies . . . didn't stop smiling when she took in the sight of Heath.

"And then," his grandpa said, wiping tears of mirth from his eyes, "Cole goaded Heath into a polar plunge competition. He said whoever went in first won a week of the other having to do all the chores. So Heath jumped in." He grinned. "Cole didn't. Instead, he stole Heath's clothes, leaving him to make the walk back home bare-ass naked. Cole always was brilliant. Not sure what happened with this guy here . . ."

"Thanks, Grandpa."

"Just sayin'."

"Maybe you could say less." Heath said this with zero atti-tude, because seeing his grandpa laugh was . . . well, everything.

The doorbell rang. "That's the food," his grandpa said. "I'll get it." He pushed to his feet, then took a moment to steady himself. "One day you're jumping out of swings without a care in the world," he told Lexi, "and the next you're leaning against a wall to put on your pants." He gestured for her to stay seated. "I ordered plenty. Call Ashley, see if she's hungry."

"Please," Heath said. "You mean call Ashley, *please*."

Grandpa rolled his eyes. "I said please."

"You absolutely did not. You never say please."

"It's okay," Lexi said. "Ashley's out on a date."

"I hope she's nicer than her last girlfriend," Grandpa said. "'Cuz that one stole from her and then left town so that even the cops can't track her down."

Lexi blinked in shock as Gus left the kitchen to get the front door.

"You didn't know," Heath said.

Looking distraught, she shook her head. "She's so . . . cheerful all the time. I guess it's an act."

"It's not. She says she's processing things just fine, but that it takes far less energy to be positive than negative.

"I . . . I didn't know she'd been hurt." Lexi closed her eyes and shook her head. "What kind of a sister does that make me?"

"Hey," he said quietly. "You're here now. And for what it's worth, she's happier than I've seen her in a long time."

"I just wish . . ." She trailed off.

"That you could do more?"

She nodded, and he slid a hand over hers. "Trust me, I get it. But you're doing so much more than you think. Do you know that this is the first time I've heard my grandpa laugh, like, genuinely laugh, in . . . I don't even know how long. Ever since my grandma passed away two years ago, he's been down, always grumpy and irritable. Cole and I try, but we're not who he wants, not really."

Her eyes softened. "I like him."

"He likes you too. I'm glad you're here. Did you need help with something?"

She looked at him strangely. "Do people only come to see you when they need your assistance?"

"Mostly."

"You deserve better," she said.

Something loosened in his chest at her repeating his words back at him. She cared about him, and after a few years of not letting much emotion get through his thick skin, and certainly not caring what others thought, it was an alien feeling. And he couldn't say he didn't like it.

"I'm here because Ashley said you needed to talk to me," Lexi said.

"Did she, now."

"Yes," she said slowly, clearly figuring out Ashley had pulled a fast one on them both. "But when I got here, I saw you were busy with . . . someone on your patio. Your grandpa said he'd get you, but I asked him not to interrupt in case it was your girl-friend or something."

She didn't look at him as she said it. Her hands were clasped, one thumbnail picking at the other like she did when she seemed to feel the most. He crouched at her side. "Lex."

He waited until she tipped her head up to his. "If I had a girlfriend, I'd never have kissed you."

She stared at him for a long beat, then nodded.

Okay, so she wasn't completely on board with the trust-Heath program, and hell, he got that. "Whatever we're doing, whatever this is, you never owe me anything you're not ready to give. But I'd like you to know, I'm not built to be kissing one woman and dating another. That won't ever be me."

She opened her mouth, but before she could speak, his grandpa picked that exact moment to come back into the room, a bag of food hanging off either arm.

He stopped short, a mischievous smile crossing his face. "Am I interrupting something?"

"No," Lexi said, just as Heath said, "Yes."

His grandpa snorted and set the food on the table. "I'm hoping I did. I tease him," he said to Lexi, "but he's smart as hell. Has two or three college degrees. Takes care of everyone in his orbit, opening his veins for us so that we're always in a good place. But does he do it for himself? No. He thinks he doesn't deserve a pretty young woman looking at him like maybe he rose the sun and the moon." He winked at Lexi.

Who promptly covered her red cheeks. "I-I'm looking at the food, that's all."

"Good." Grandpa nodded in approval. "Don't show him all your cards, make him show his hand first."

Heath rolled his eyes. "You're the biggest interfering nosybody I've ever met." He looked at Lexi. "Ignore him. He's messing with you."

"Actually, I'm messing with *you*." The old man turned back to Lexi. "You see what I have to work with? He's all barking alpha—Grandpa, you gotta exercise, Grandpa, you gotta eat better—when the whole time, he's ignoring his own needs. I think it's because his dad was an asshole. It's like he's worried he's got those bad genes in him and doesn't deserve love."

Heath piled a plate with food and thrust it at his grandpa. "Take this to another room."

The old man grinned at him. "Hit a nerve, did I?"

"More like you ran it over, backed up, and then hit it again."

His grandpa cackled with pleasure and then . . . sat at the

scarred table in one of the six mismatched chairs. It squeaked in protest. "This one needs to be fixed," he said to Heath.

"The whole set needs to be refurbished or dumped."

His grandpa looked at Lexi as he jabbed a thumb Heath's way. "This guy doesn't appreciate anything old."

"I absolutely do appreciate old. I love old," Heath said. "What I don't love is living in an overstuffed house and watching you trip over things. You're going to get hurt. Pass the wings that you weren't supposed to get."

Grandpa smiled at Lexi. "My wife picked every piece of furniture in this place . . ." He passed her the wings instead of Heath. "At first I hated everything, plus it was way too expensive. We got in a huge fight over most of it, but like in all things, she always won. Mostly because I loved seeing her happy." He took the wings back from Lexi and dumped all the rest onto his plate."

Heath sighed.

His grandpa jabbed a fork in his direction. "I think the real question is, why doesn't he believe he's worthy of a woman as great as his grandma? Especially when there's one sitting right here at this table. He's book smart, I'll give him that, but he don't seem to know much."

Heath stood and went to the freezer for the bottle of vodka his brother kept there.

Lexi laughed, and even though it was aimed at him, the sweet musical sound made him smile as well.

CHAPTER 15

Lexi knew she should be beyond irritated at Ashley for manipulating her to come to Heath's, but . . . she was actually having a good time. She'd never had a grandparent's presence in her life. As a kid, she'd met some of her friends' extended family, and she'd envied them. But as time had gone on and she'd grown up, she hadn't given much thought to what she'd missed.

Heath's grandpa was wonderful. *And* obviously a meddling troublemaker. But even though he clearly loved giving Heath a hard time, there was an undeniable loving undertone to it that she could feel all the way to the corners of her own cold heart.

She'd gone a whole bunch of years being mostly on her own, and she'd gotten pretty good at it. Okay, maybe not good, but hey, she was breathing, and that counted for something. But somehow, sitting here, she . . . wanted more for herself. Unnerving thought.

They'd finished eating but hadn't left the table when Gus looked around the kitchen. "I know an upgrade would be good, but I really love this old place. Maybe we could paint, if we use the same color."

Heath nodded. "We could do that. And maybe a new dining set."

"That would just be throwing money away, as I like this one." Heath sighed.

Gus smiled at Lexi. "We were pretty poor when this guy was little. Didn't have two pennies to rub together." His smile faded. "I got injured in a car wreck and couldn't help out my daughter much—Heath's mama. She'd married an asshole—pardon my French. He couldn't keep a job. The boys wore hand-me-downs and never had enough food. The memories keep me from wanting to spend money frivolously."

The look on Heath's face, regret, guilt, grief . . . slayed her. When they were kids, all Lexi had seen when she looked at him was the cocky, annoying, competitive boy who'd gotten beneath her skin embarrassingly easily. She'd had no idea he'd been hungry for more than just challenging her at everything. Hungry, and abused. It made her heart ache.

As for Heath, he looked like he was pretty sure there wasn't enough vodka left for this conversation. "Oh, good, we're going to keep talking about me," he muttered.

"Hey, I'm trying to give the girl a leg up. Seeing as I'm willing to bet you've been hiding in plain sight." He winked at Lexi from the same blue gray eyes Heath had. "Thought you might appreciate a peek inside that hard head of his."

"I absolutely do," she said in a light tone, knowing how much Heath would hate a show of sympathy. "Since he's locked up so tight he squeaks when he walks."

His grandpa laughed so hard he spilled his drink.

Heath just looked at her, brows up.

"When we were little, we didn't get along much," she told his grandpa while still smiling at Heath. "He was a know-it-all, and all I wanted was to beat him at something."

Some of the shadows left Heath's gaze, replaced by a small smile at the memories she'd invoked.

"Hard to beat him at anything," his grandpa said. "He's sharp and quick and sneaky—motivated, of course, by never wanting to be poor again. Well, that and the fact that when Cole got so sick and we had shit insurance, he had to take on a second job while in college to cover the medical bills. Let me suggest flat-out cheating when you want to beat him at something. That's what I do."

"Good to know."

Heath lowered his head to the table to knock it against the wood a few times.

Lexi laughed with Gus. "I take it he doesn't know you cheat."

"Oh, I always know." Heath lifted his head. "I once had to bail him out of jail after he got caught cheating at a casino."

"False charges," his grandpa said with a shrug.

"They had you on video, and you got a lifetime ban."

"Bah humbug. And you and Lexi nearly got yourselves tossed in jail not all that long ago. Pot, meet Kettle."

Heath looked at Lexi for the first time since his grandpa had revealed some of his secrets, a guarded expression on his face that she hated to see. "What?"

"You're looking at me different," he said.

"How?"

"Like you feel sorry for me or, worse, like I'm perfect."

She choked on her tea, which nearly came out her nose.

With a chuckle, his grandpa handed her a napkin. "Don't you worry, darlin', he's not even close to perfect." He started ticking the reasons why off on his fingers. "He's bullheaded to a fault, he can't admit when he's wrong, thinks he doesn't need anyone or anything, and don't even get me started on what a know-it-all he is."

"Thanks, Grandpa," Heath said dryly. "But don't worry. Lexi's fully aware of my faults."

His grandpa slid her a look. "Good. Because women tend to throw themselves at him. Don't be one of them. Make him work for it."

"Don't you worry," Lexi said. "I have no intention of throwing myself at him." Because she already had, in that tent, the memory of which made all her good parts tingle, something they absolutely should *not* be doing.

Gus's phone alarm went off, and he glanced at the screen, then at Heath. "Really? You set an alarm for me to take my meds?"

"Yes, so you can't pretend to forget."

"For your information, I was just about to take them." Gus rose from the table. Stopped. Scratched his head. "Where are the meds again?"

"On your bathroom counter."

"I knew that."

In the ensuing silence of his absence, Lexi searched for something to say. She didn't often think about her childhood, because it made her feel sorry for herself. But Heath had had it far worse than she, only instead of burying the memories deep, he'd processed them and moved on, growing up to make something of his life. It touched a part of her she didn't know could be touched, but also . . . Heath had been there for his family.

Unlike her, who'd not been there for hers. Not once.

"Sorry Ashley manipulated you into stopping by yet?"

She laughed softly. "No, but I bet you are." Getting to her feet, she collected some of the dishes, moving to the sink.

"I'm not."

Their gazes held for a beat as Heath got the rest of the dishes. Setting them in the sink, he gently nudged her aside. "Guests don't do dishes."

"But, as it turns out, I'm not a guest, because you didn't invite me here. I'll load." She opened the dishwasher and looked at him. "Unless you're anal about how it's done?"

"Anal?"

She laughed. "It's a yes or no."

He stared at her, then snorted and shook his head. "I think you enjoy driving me insane."

"Very, *very* much."

He chuckled and once more tried to nudge her aside, but she refused, instead taking the dish from his hands and setting it inside the dishwasher.

When she caught him staring at her, she sighed. "See, you are anal."

He laughed. "No. I just didn't know there was a wrong way to load it."

"According to Ashley, there most definitely is."

He shook his head. "I love your sister, but sometimes she's an old lady in a twenty-three-year-old body."

Lexi laughed, and they worked in companionable silence for a moment. "Can I ask you a personal question?" she finally drummed up the courage to ask.

"Sure."

"What was wrong with your brother?"

He didn't take his gaze off the dish he was rinsing. "Leukemia. Years ago. He was fourteen."

She stared at him in shock, but he was rinsing another dish with incredible attention to detail. "He got better though, right?"

"After a bone marrow transplant."

She did some math. Heath would've been a freshman in college. "You gave him your bone marrow."

"No." He allowed her to take the dish and load it into the dishwasher. "I wasn't a match."

"But you would have, if you could."

"He's family," he said, lifting shoulders capable of holding such weight. "It's what family does."

She slowly shook her head. "Not all families are like yours."

"I know." He paused. "I saw how you looked at me when my grandpa wouldn't stop flapping his lips. I'm not defined by having a shit dad, probably because I had a great mom and grandparents, and Cole. *Those* were the relationships that molded me, that made me who I am." He turned to face her. "I'm sorry you didn't have any of that."

She shrugged. "I had my mom until I was ten. And my dad . . . He wasn't a bad guy. Not really. He just . . . had other important things to concentrate on."

His gaze said he disagreed with that. She busied herself fussing with the silverware, setting the pieces carefully into the dishwasher to give her hands something to do. "Plus, I watched lots of TV. Movies. I understand that plenty of families stick together above all else. It just hasn't been that way for me."

"Do you want that life, the family life you never really had?"

"I'm not sure I'm up to the risk of going all in on something without a guarantee, and who gets a guarantee? No one."

"Maybe it'd be worth the risk."

She didn't know if she'd ever be brave enough for what she saw in his eyes, no matter how much she thought she might come to want it. "I think . . . I should go." Before he could stop her, she poked her head into the living room to wave at his grandpa. "Good night."

"Come back anytime. You're more fun than this one . . ." He jerked his head at Heath.

Heath pinched the bridge of his nose like he might be getting a headache, and his grandpa grinned.

Lexi smothered her laugh and moved to the back door.

Heath stepped outside with her, a frown on his face.

"Maybe you really do need a nip of vodka."

"Smart-ass," he murmured, but it sounded affectionate. "What I actually need is to keep my wits about me when you're around."

She stopped and looked at him.

"It's not an insult." His smile was wry. "It's a statement about my inability to think clearly when you're around."

She blinked, absorbing the meaning behind the words. Decided she liked it way too much. "And that's a bad thing?"

"The worst."

She grinned. "Right back at you." She stepped off the porch. "Night."

"I'm walking you home."

Bad idea. Very, very bad idea, because she was feeling weak enough to pull him into her childhood bedroom and do things to him beneath the NSYNC poster. "Not necessary."

"I'm walking you home," he repeated.

"I can literally see Daisy's house from here, even in the dark."

"This week alone we've had a band of coyotes hunting wild rabbits, a teenage bear hunting our trash, and rumors of two bobcats looking for trouble."

She stopped short, her stomach jangling uncomfortably at the thought of meeting any of those things on her walk back. "And if we run into anything like that, you're going to what, exactly? Throw yourself in front of me, risking life and limb?"

He chuckled, a disembodied sound in the dark as he took her hand and they started walking. The feel of his palm warm and callused against hers, grounded her. "How about if we just keep talking and making plenty of noise so that we don't have to offer anyone up as a sacrifice."

"Well, if you're going to be all logical," she muttered.

They had only a sliver of a moon tonight, the sky glowing as the stars twinkled like jewels. She didn't realize she'd stopped just short of Daisy's back porch until Heath turned her to him, studying her face. "You okay?"

Was she? She wanted something, yearned for something . . . but it felt out of reach. They stood toe to toe in between the two yards, out of time and place, barely an inch separating them, reminding her of that night in the tent under a different but similar sky, and her traitorous gaze dropped to his mouth.

Which slowly curved. "You want me to kiss you again," he murmured, not a question, but a statement as he dipped his head closer to hers.

No. Yes. "*Gah.*" She glared at him. "This is all your fault."

"I'm sure it is, but maybe you could be more specific."

"Making me want this." And then she fisted her hands in his shirt, went on tiptoes, and kissed *him.*

And it was like coming home. She heard the needy sound that escaped her throat, one that made him groan and haul her in even closer. But then, far before she was ready, he pulled free.

At least he was *also* breathing hard. "We're not in a tent," she said, as casually as she could. "With a rock under your ass."

"No, but your sister's watching us out the window."

She looked, and sure enough, the light she'd left on in Daisy's kitchen was now off, and in the window she could see the very faint outline of her sister's face.

Relief and frustration warred within her. Relief because they weren't going to make a terrible decision and sleep together—at least right now. Frustration because they weren't going to make a terrible decision and sleep together right now.

And judging by Heath's smirk, he knew *exactly* where her thoughts had gone.

But he didn't know this: Both times he'd been able to let go of her far too easily, a terrible, ongoing theme in her life. So it was that more than anything else that allowed her to step free and jab a finger into his chest. "We're finished here."

Another slight dip of his head. "Whatever you say."

Ugh. She turned to go inside.

"Lexi."

She stopped but didn't turn back.

"To be clear, this wasn't me not wanting you. This was me acknowledging you're in the driver's seat. What, if anything, happens, the ball's in your court. Always."

"And what, you're good either way?"

Something passed over his face, an emotion that came and went too fast for her to get a bead on it. "What I'm good with," he said, "is this being your choice."

She tried to translate that. Thought about what she'd learned about him. He rarely, if ever, put himself first when it came to the people he cared about. And given how he'd grown up, having lost his mom, his dad's treatment of him . . . maybe he didn't believe what he wanted mattered. "And what would be *your* choice?" she asked very softly.

His eyes tracked to her mouth, and she could almost see the

answer in his eyes . . . *You*. But he didn't say it. Didn't say anything, just took his bottom lip between his teeth, maybe to keep himself from spilling his thoughts. They were inches from one another now, the air still thick and charged between them, her heart beating like a drum.

He finally drew a deep breath. "You're not the only one scarred by previous relationships. My grandpa loves to yank my chain, but the things he told you tonight . . . He's not wrong about me. I put bars around my heart a long time ago. It's still incarcerated."

"You . . . put your heart in jail?"

"Yes."

Hard to blame him. And maybe this was a good thing. Maybe it put this thing between them, the thing they hadn't labeled, on notice. "So we're on the same page, the page where we're ridiculously attracted to each other, but neither of us is ready for . . . more."

He slid his hands into his pockets as he held her gaze, but didn't use any actual words. Neither of them seemed able or willing to step into the ring.

Good to know.

"Good night, Heath," she whispered.

He gave a slow nod, still not giving anything away, so she had no idea if he even felt disappointed. Which, in turn, disappointed *her*. Shaking her head at the both of them, she turned and walked through the yard and into Daisy's house.

At least Ashley was smart enough not to wait for her in the kitchen.

Lexi strode straight to the drawer where her sister kept a bunch of vitamins she usually forgot, and pulled out the box of cookies she'd stashed behind them. Then she took herself and the cookies to bed.

The cookies did not show her a good time. All that happened was indigestion. Restless, staring up at the ceiling, she decided that maybe Heath was onto something. As of this moment, her own heart would also be incarcerated.

CHAPTER 16

The next day, Lexi borrowed the truck and drove into town to begin work with her first official client. Cassidy Tyler and her three siblings had inherited a large piece of property from their parents, and while the will was perfectly clear and for once there was no dispute between the benefactors, the five-thousand-square-foot house was filled from forty years of living. The parents had passed several years before, and because there'd been no issues between the remaining family and no one had wanted to rush into anything, the estate had never been evaluated. But now, for whatever reason, Cassidy and her siblings were looking to get everything evaluated so they could decide what to sell and what to keep.

When Lexi had first gotten into the business, it'd been unexpectedly more difficult than she'd imagined, entering homes where someone had died, where the property needed to be thoroughly gone through without any emotional attachment, putting what essentially came to a dollar amount on the deceased and the life they'd lived.

But she'd quickly found that the beauty in honoring those

lives was actually in doing just that. Not to mention the undeniable thrill she got handling antiques and antiquities alike,
feeling the power of history thrum through her, loving the sense
that each item had a story to tell.

She'd already met with the family after her and Ashley's trip
delivering Judy's envelope, so she dove right in, spending the
day happily lost to the work. She liked that it kept any errant
thoughts at bay. Especially since she had a lot of them.

The good news was that when she finished up here in a few
days, she had that second client in South Shore. After that, if
no other jobs came through, well, then she'd probably be waiting tables to keep herself afloat. There were far worse things,
but she'd been a waitress for several years while working herself through college. People sucked when it came to treating
servers right, not to mention that the job was vastly underpaid
to begin with, so the thought of going back to it, working so
damn hard that her entire body hurt after every shift, made
her want to cry.

But she'd given up crying. Given up feeling sorry for herself too.
As always, she'd find a way.

That night, she slept better than she expected. She woke up
to a text from Cassidy that the painters they'd hired had shown
up a week early, so she suggested Lexi give them a day or two
before going back to finish the job.

Her day suddenly free, Lexi opened her laptop to check email.
Nothing. No new clients, and no responses to applications she'd
submitted back home. To distract herself from that, she ended
up scrolling through Instagram, stopping cold when she came to
a post from Elaine, her work friend.

Or her used-to-be work friend. Elaine and a group of others from the office were at a restaurant, all squished into a pic,

smiling broadly. In the center was Dean, her ex, a birthday hat on his head, his arms spread wide as he hugged the people on either side of him.

They'd all gone on with their lives without any concern for the fact that hers had been destroyed.

For something she hadn't even done.

She was so intently staring at the screen that she nearly screamed when Ashley poked her head over Lexi's shoulder. "Who are they?"

"Coworkers," she somehow managed to say evenly.

"How great is it that they're letting you work remotely for these six weeks?"

So great. She smiled noncommittally.

"I know you probably have to get to it, but I was hoping we could go through more of Mom's stuff when you're free. What time will you be done for the day?"

"How about now?" Lexi stood and looked out the window. Rainy and chilly. "Though the garage will be freezing."

"So let's get started on Mom's bedroom. When it's done, one of us could move in there, since it's the biggest room, with a bathroom."

"It's all yours," Lexi said.

They walked into the room together. Lexi sucked in a breath and turned in a slow circle. Every last corner was an ode to the seventies—Daisy's self-proclaimed favorite decade. A lot of orange and green and brown. And paisley prints. Oh, and a disco ball overhead instead of a light.

"She loved that thing," Ashley said, staring up at it. "She got it for ten bucks at a garage sale."

"She was ripped off." Lexi shook her head. "It looks the same in here as it did when I was little."

"That's because it *is*. She loved it just like this, never wanted to change a thing." Ashley's smile faded. "After . . ." She swallowed hard. "After she was gone, I couldn't bring myself to touch anything. But you're here now. You can make sure we don't toss out anything of value."

They started with the closet. Within two minutes, Lexi had three piles going. One for the local thrift shop, another for trash, and the third for things Ashley wanted to keep. That pile was the biggest, and looking at it, her sister sighed. "I know, I know. But so many things in here have a memory of Mom attached to them."

Lexi picked up a gaudy peace sign necklace made of plastic and wood beads, then eyed Ashley with doubt.

Her sister smiled. "I made that for her. Yes, it's god-awful, and don't get me started on my questionable color choices, but she wore it proudly." She lifted a brow. "No pile for you?"

Nothing in this room held any emotional attachment for her, but to say that would only hurt Ashley. "Haven't found the right thing to keep yet, is all."

Ashley nodded thoughtfully. "You will."

Onward they worked, with Lexi feeling oddly and annoyingly emotional. She hadn't realized how different it would feel doing this for Daisy rather than for a job. And she sure as hell hadn't expected the warm sense of nostalgia that hit her, the ease and comfort of doing this with her sister and not by herself.

"You okay?" Ashley asked.

"Yeah." She paused, then admitted, "It's not as hard as I thought it'd be. Doing this with you, spending time, it's . . . nice."

Ashley bumped her shoulder to Lexi's. "You don't have to look so surprised."

Lexi folded a tie-dye sweatshirt that had seen better days at least four decades ago and set it into the thrift store pile. "You're right. I shouldn't be surprised at all. You've never been anything other than sweet and amazing to me." She paused. "And . . . *meddling*."

Ashley turned her back to go through another box. "I have no idea what you're talking about."

"Uh-huh. Let me submit the evidence. One, when we delivered the second envelope to Judy, you maneuvered it so that Heath and I would be alone in the tent."

"Because I wanted to sleep with the kittens."

"Uh-huh. And two, the other night you sent me over to Gus's house, saying Heath wanted to talk to me."

Ashley winced. "Okay, yes. I did those things. But you were just staring at your phone, like you were waiting for a friend, or anyone, to text or call. And I know that in all the time we've spent together since you got here, no one has. *And*," she quickly added when Lexi opened her mouth, "I also know it's none of my business. But I recognize loneliness, Lexi. I recognize it hard, and I knew I could help."

Lexi's heart tightened. Because Ashley didn't have much more of a social life than she did, which made her ache—for the both of them.

"And I know what I promised," Ashley went on. "But there's something between you and Heath. And I guess I worried that if I didn't . . . nudge, you'd both ignore it."

"Which is our right."

Her sister sighed. "I know."

"Ash, I don't need you to fix anything for me."

"What? *No*." Ashley shook her head vehemently. "I'm not trying to fix you. I like you just as you are."

The warm fuzzies she felt at that surprised her. "Really?"

"Really."

"I like you too," Lexi said. "You're clever, creative. You're not a pushover, but you're sweet enough to make time for anyone and everyone who needs it. It's an amazing and rare balance, and it makes you special."

Ashley smiled, her cheeks going a little red. "Aw. Thanks." She went back to her box.

Lexi waited, but Ash said nothing. "Aaaand . . . ?" Lexi prompted.

"And what?"

"I thought maybe you'd say what you like about me."

"Truth?"

Oh boy. "You know what? Never mind—"

"*Everything*," Ashley said. "I like everything. You're smart and fierce and strong, inside and out. I just really want you to be happy."

Undone, Lexi had to clear her throat. "Thank you." The two words didn't seem adequate enough. "That truly means a lot. But if your plan is for Heath to be the one to make me happy, you should know that we're not . . . compatible."

"Well, that's a lie."

Fine. So parts of them were *extremely* compatible—like their mouths . . . "Neither of us want this—"

"*Another* lie."

"Maybe I need to add shrewd to your list."

Ashley laughed. "Don't even try to change the subject. When you two are in the same vicinity, the air sparks from all your chemistry."

"Okay, so I admit, there's *some* attraction—"

"Or a lot."

Lexi had to laugh wryly. "Or a lot. But, Ash, that's *all* there is."

"No, I can tell it's more! Look, I know you're all about working hard and making your own way, but Heath is the same."

"Ash—"

"All I'm saying is don't take him at surface value, okay? There's a lot more to him beneath all that effortless, laid-back charisma. He doesn't even realize his own worth. The way he grew up was hard. And his grandpa, wonderful and amazing as he is, he's from a generation that doesn't know how to be emotionally available. There were no I-love-yous. Heath had to learn to speak a different language. It's made him kind of empathetic to people who are closed off."

Lexi blinked. "You mean me. I'm closed off."

Ashley's smile was sheepish, and also full of understanding. "They say knowing your faults is half the battle."

"Ha ha. And if the next thing you're about to say is that Heath's an onion and I should peel back his layers, please don't. There will be no peeling."

"All I'm saying is that he's like . . ." She waved a hand in the air, looking for a word. "An antique. Priceless and worthy."

"An antique," Lexi repeated, brow raised.

"Well, he turned thirty this year, so . . ." Ashley laughed when Lexi choked. "All I'm trying to say is don't make the same mistake that others have by taking him at face value. Yes, the package is pretty, but he's also a hard worker and has the biggest heart of anyone I know. He gives free legal consulting to those who can't afford it. He repurposes old furniture, making it new again for the people who lost everything in the wildfires last year. Right now he's renovating old Mrs. Cromwell's house, making it accessible for the wheelchair she's now confined to. He'd hate me telling you this, like, *hate it*, hate it, because he thinks his worth hinges on people being able to depend on him, all while he never needs to depend on anyone else. Never allows himself to be cared for."

"Look, I know he's a good guy." More than. "That's not the issue."

"Right, because the issue is that neither of you think you can be enough for someone."

Lexi sighed. "Are you sure you're not the older, wiser sister?"

"Wiser, for sure." Ashley's lips twitched. "But you're also nearly thirty. Ancient." Her smile vanished. "How about this. I'll stop meddling, if—"

"Aha! So you admit that you *are* a world-class meddler!"

"Of course, I'm a world-class meddler. And I'll stop, *if* you stop trying to be an island of one."

"I could say the same thing to you."

"What does that mean?"

"You were in a relationship, and you got hurt."

Ashley's eyes shuttered. "Grandpa Gus gossips like a teen-age boy." She turned away. "And I didn't get hurt, not really. We'd only dated a few times. I was stupid enough to catch early feelings that I thought were reciprocated. I made a bad call to have her stay here at the house one night. When I woke up, she was gone. And so was my laptop, phone, tablet, and other stuff. Thousands of dollars—poof—gone, because I was too stupid to understand you can't find a relationship through a hookup app." She shrugged. "I filed a police report, changed the locks, dumped all the dating apps, and learned a painful lesson about taking things slower and smarter. Period. End of story."

Lexi wanted that to be true, but she knew from experience what betrayal felt like, how it felt like maybe you'd never be okay ever again. "I'm so sorry."

"I don't need pity."

"It's not pity. It's understanding." She paused. "I wish you didn't have to pretend to be okay, not with me."

Ashley met her gaze with a small smile. "I'm not pretending, I *am* okay. I mean, did I make a stupid mistake? Yes. Will I let it change my outlook on life? No. Live and learn, right?"

"Yeah." Lexi returned the smile. "See? Definitely the wiser sister."

"That's right, I am. So you should listen to me when I beg you to consider staying. Here, with me. And you already even have friends. Heath and his grandpa, and trust me, you're going to love Cole and Misty too . . ."

The yearning in Ashley's eyes made Lexi swallow hard as she realized that she wasn't the only lonely one. Driven by an emotion she hadn't experienced in a long time, she stepped close and took Ashley's hand. "Let me make you a promise."

"But you never make promises."

"I know." Lexi squeezed tight. "Which is how you know you can believe me. I promise I'll do better at this sister thing. I won't let us fall by the wayside again."

Her sister, eyes shiny, nodded. "And Heath?"

She let out a breath. "I don't want to disappoint you, but I don't think we're going there."

"Because you don't want to?"

"Because *neither* of us are ready for it."

Ashley stared at her for a long beat. "Dammit."

"What?"

"That wasn't a lie."

Lexi gave her a grim smile. "It wasn't." No matter how much she secretly wished it was.

"I just don't get it. When you guys are near each other, I swear

I hear the air crackling. It started that day when we delivered Judy's envelope. I *know* something happened."

Lexi couldn't help it, she felt her face heat.

Ashley's mouth fell open, then she squealed and jumped up and down. "Oh my God, I was right!"

Lexi looked around for alcohol, but they'd split the last bottle of wine the night before. Just in case, she stalked to the kitchen and opened the freezer, hoping against hope that Ashley stocked it like Heath did at his grandpa's. But nope, no vodka.

Ashley was right there when Lexi turned from the freezer. Like, *right* there. Grinning. "So you two—"

"*No!*" Lexi lowered her voice with effort. "We didn't . . . We just kissed."

"Again, you mean. You kissed again. Just like I saw five years ago. That one felt different than last night. Last night's kiss looked hot enough to melt the polar caps, if they weren't already melting."

Lexi shook her head. "We need to get you a new hobby. Spying on me is getting old."

Ashley waved this off. "Just so I understand. You're not in the market for a guy, but if you were . . . what would you be looking for?"

"I'm not."

"But if you were."

Lexi sighed and tried to be flip. "Smelling good is a must."

Ashley didn't look impressed. "Dig deeper. What would you feel when you see him?"

She racked her brain. "Um . . . happier than I felt before I saw him, I guess?"

"You've just described a cookie."

"Okay, yes, but think about it. Cookies are everything."

Ashley sighed. "I think it's time to break into my top-secret emergency stash of wine in the attic."

"Why the attic?"

"So that I'd only go after it if I was desperate. There're spiders up there. I volunteer you as tribute."

Thirty minutes later, they were halfway to hammered and still working in Daisy's bedroom. Lexi was deep in a small dresser inside the closet, which had been painted white with a bunch of flowers all over it, lending it a sweet charm. "This is cute. Doesn't fit with the rest of the furniture, but I like it."

"Yeah?" Ashley beamed. "I found it at a garage sale with Mom when I was a teen. The wood stain was long gone, and it was all scratched up, but I got it for ten bucks. One of my favorite memories of Mom is from that day. She bought me some paint. The flowers were my idea. They're not very good, but she claimed to love it." Ashley looked at her almost shyly. "Do you have a favorite memory of her?"

"Uh . . ." Lexi actively thought about it—something she'd purposefully not allowed herself to do. "I guess I was somewhere around five. We made our own pizza, and she let me use whatever toppings I wanted. I picked M&M's. They melted in the oven, of course. And the pizza was . . ." She shook her head with a laugh. "Disgusting. But one thing she could always do was make me laugh."

Ashley looked so happy at the story that Lexi felt bad for not sharing more. She tried to think of something else. "She used to take me bowling. The place we went to played only seventies rock. She would dance her way to the aisle before releasing her bowling ball. It was pretty cute."

Ash grinned. "She could always make me laugh too. Even at the end. Which is my worst memory, by the way. Being with her at the end. She hadn't told anyone she was sick, not a soul. So to me it all happened quickly, so quickly. It was . . ." She shook her head. "A shock."

Lexi swallowed. "I'm sorry. I'm so sorry I wasn't here."

Ashley shook her head again. "It's not on you. Like I said, she didn't want anyone to know, including us. She'd have hated a big fuss. She went out as she lived, hard and fast." Her eyes were suspiciously shiny again. "Can I hear your worst memory of her?"

Lexi felt the air leave her lungs. "I don't think that's a good idea," she said gently.

"Please? I want to understand more about you. I've always wanted to know, but never wanted to push."

"All right." She had to draw a deep breath because she'd buried most of her worst memories. "I think I was . . . eight? Nine? One day after school, she didn't show up in the pickup line. I stood there in the pouring rain waiting. And waiting."

"Wasn't there an aide to make sure everyone got picked up?"

Lexi shrugged. "I must've slipped through the cracks somehow." One thing about trying to be invisible was that it often worked. "Turned out, she was at one of the casinos at Stateline and lost track of time."

Ashley let out a pained sound that had the potential to completely undo Lexi, so she swallowed the lump in her throat and busied herself with pulling a stack of shoeboxes down from the shelves above the dresser.

"How did you get home?" Ashley asked.

"I walked. Well, actually, I started out walking, but some older boys came along and . . ." The memory made her heart pump way too hard. "I ended up running through the woods. Fell and ruined my clothes. So yeah. Definitely one of my worst memories."

"I'm so sorry."

Lexi waved a hand. "It was a long time ago."

"I'm starting to get it."

"Get what?"

Ashley's eyes were sad. "Why you didn't keep in touch. I wouldn't have wanted to either."

Lexi shook her head. "I was wrong not to." She turned to face Ashley. "I want you to know how much it always meant to me, you making the effort to call and text and keep in touch . . . You were the one who kept us together, and I'm not proud of that." The words felt like glass scraping over her raw throat. She hadn't had to fight tears for a very long time. But here in Sunrise Cove, it seemed like every day she felt far too much. "When I first left here, things weren't exactly easy for me, living with my dad. My stepsisters took one look at a sullen, introverted kid, and it was instant dislike. My dad worked, a lot, and they were stuck with me. They weren't kind."

"I'm sorry," her sister whispered.

Lexi waved that off, knowing she had to admit the truth, her bitter truth, even if it meant possibly alienating Ashley. "I was angry and hurt. And . . ." She grimaced. "Jealous. Jealous as hell that Mom got clean for you and not me."

Regret crossed Ash's face.

"No, please don't feel bad. You were a kid too. It had nothing to do with you, and I shouldn't have let it affect our relationship. And I hope you don't mind, but I need to talk about something else now. Anything else." She pulled a pair of go-go boots from the closet that were so used, the heels were gone. She tossed them into the trash pile, then laughed a little when Ashley snatched them and put them into her pile. "You do realize you're doing the opposite of downsizing."

"I know." Ash swallowed hard. "It's just that she really loved these."

And Ashley had loved Daisy. She'd loved her as if she'd been her birth mom. To her shame, Lexi wasn't sure she'd really understood until that very moment. "I meant what I said, I *am* going to try harder. To be sisters. Real sisters."

Ashley sniffled. "Yes, please."

Lexi went into the adjoining bathroom and came out with a roll of toilet paper, which she tossed to Ashley, who was now sitting on the bed. Taking the spot next to her, she nudged her knee into her sister's. "I didn't know it when I decided to come here, but I needed this. I needed you." She gave a small smile. "But you have to stop crying. We're out of tissues, and at this rate, we'll be out of toilet paper too."

"No, we won't," Ashley said soggily. "You just bought us a year's supply when you went to Costco."

"Hey, it was on sale."

Ashley laughed soggily. "I'd like to propose a pact. It's just us now, we're all we've got. And we're all right. So we each let go of our guilt. Period. End of story."

The second Lexi nodded, Ashley wrapped her arms around her. "Let's hold on to that."

"Okay," Lexi managed to squeak out, her air supply cut off by how tight Ashley held her. "But you mean emotionally, right? Not physically."

With a snort, Ashley just tightened her grip and . . . kissed her face all over.

"Ew! Gross! Foul!"

With a laugh, Ashley kissed her some more.

CHAPTER 17

L exi."

"No."

"Lex."

"Shh," she mumbled, burrowing deeper into her bed. "She's sleeping. And turn off the light."

"Wake up, Sleeping Beauty."

Heath's husky male voice finally penetrated, and she froze. In direct contradiction with her suddenly pounding heart, she let her tone drip with sarcasm. "My, Ashley, how your voice has changed."

But nothing. No more words. She cracked open an eye, and yep, found the last person on the planet she expected to see. "Why is it still dark?" she groaned, rolling to her belly, hiding her head beneath her pillow.

"Ashley got a late-night email. She sold a set of her saw blades, but the woman needs them today for her husband's birthday, so Ash offered to deliver them to San Francisco. She left a few hours ago, before dawn, so she wouldn't hit work traffic. Didn't she tell you?"

Lexi lifted her head. "She sold what?"

"She hunts down big saw blades that are discarded from over-use, and then paints Tahoe landscapes on them, turning them into wall art. She uses the back corner of my grandpa's garage. She sells a bunch of stuff on Etsy and other places. Don't you two ever talk?"

"Hey, Mr. Judgy-ass, I'll have you know—" She rolled to her back and . . . fell right off her childhood twin bed to the hard-wood floor. Staring up at the ceiling, she sighed.

Heath came around the bed and crouched low, offering her a hand. "You okay?"

Instead of answering or taking his hand, she grabbed the pillow that had fallen with her and covered her face. "Just leave me here."

He tossed the pillow aside, then studied her, from her no-doubt-flushed face, to her bedhead hair, then southward. His frown vanished, replaced by an almost smile.

Which was when she remembered that her pj's were nothing but a T-shirt that said NOPE, NOT TODAY . . . and a pair of itty-bitty bikini undies. "Well, this is embarrassing."

He grabbed the blanket off the bed and tossed it over her. "That's not what I'm feeling. And you have no idea, do you."

"About what?"

"How beautiful you are."

With a snort, she staggered upright, wrapping herself in the blanket. "I need at least an hour to even approach almost pretty. And at the risk of repeating myself, why is it still dark outside? Why are you here? Why don't I have caffeine?"

"It's dark outside because it's five a.m., and I'm here because I'm your partner in crime for the third envelope delivery today. You don't have caffeine because I'm a very stupid man who woke you up before making coffee. I'll go rectify that right now. But first . . ." He scooped her up like she weighed next to nothing—which was most definitely *not* the case—and set her on her feet, holding on to her hips for a second until she was steady.

Their gazes locked. The second turned into a bunch of seconds as the air seemed to do that crackle thing again. "Static electricity," she said.

He gave a slow shake of his head.

His hair was damp, probably from a very recent shower if the citrusy, woodsy scent wafting off him meant anything, so tempting that she nearly buried her face in the crook of his neck to get a better whiff. But he was . . . shaking? She pulled back. "Are you . . . *You're laughing at me.*"

He reined in the amusement, but the smile remained. "Cute."

She narrowed her eyes. "You did hear the part where I'm not caffeinated yet, right? Laughing at me in this state is dangerous to your health. So is calling me *cute.*"

He outright grinned at her now. "I'm laughing at *us,*" he said. "We don't want to want this, we don't want to want each other, and yet you just inhaled me like I was your first coffee of the year and I'm—"

"Still touching me."

They both looked down at his hands, most definitely still on her, her barely dressed, him in jeans and a button-down, sleeves shoved up past his elbows. Standing there in almost nothing, with him fully dressed, made her quiver in a ridiculous way. In a ridiculously good way. *Way* too good.

"Shit." Yanking his hands from her, he strode to the other side of the bed.

Her mouth twitched. "You think that's far enough?"

"You don't want to know what I think."

Actually, she did, she really, really did, but that wouldn't do either of them any good. Ugh. "Just give me today's envelope and get out."

"Trust me, I'd love to get out, but Ashley's got the truck."

She stared at him, then shook her head. "Whatever. I'll take a rideshare."

"We're going to Santa Barbara. It's a seven-hour trip. That's fourteen hours on the road, not counting however much time is spent with the recipient."

Seriously? What was up with her karma? "Fine," she said. "I'll just wait until tomorrow."

"Ashley's giving a three-day workshop at the city college starting tomorrow."

Lexi crossed her arms, not wanting to delay that long, not wanting a reason for having to stay a day past six weeks. "This is ridiculous. Daisy's gone. We could be mailing these, she'd never know."

He at least looked sympathetic as he said, "It's not what she wanted. She wanted contact made in person."

"Fine. Can I borrow your car?"

"No."

"Okay, I'll rent one." Her credit card would cry, but so be it. She wasn't willing to postpone doing this, because that would extend her stay even further. And she was starting to worry that every day she stayed was another little string from her heart to Sunrise Cove.

And the people in it.

"You don't need to rent a car," one of those very people said.

She raised a brow. "Why not?"

"Two people make the deliveries, always, for safety reasons."

"Oh come on," she said. "Daisy really dictated that?"

"No, I did. Daisy knew these people, but we don't. We're try-ing to follow her wishes by delivering in person without advance notice, as she asked, by spreading them out with a week be-tween, like she asked, but I'm not willing to send either of you out there alone."

"We're grown-ups, Heath. If I want to go alone, I can go alone."

"I understand that," he said. "But there's no reason for you to when I'm willing to go with you. Get ready. We need to leave in the next fifteen minutes to avoid traffic on the Eighty."

And then he was gone.

Ugh. She took a shower, blew her hair dry, and dressed with more care than she had in . . . She didn't know how long. Hell, she even put on mascara.

Her armor.

But also, she wanted to drive him crazy, wanted him to know what he was missing out on. Childish? Yes. But there was some-thing about Heath, about his easy calm in any situation that made her want to ruffle his feathers. She wanted to see what he had beneath his own personal armor.

She found him outside, leaning up against his car as he thumbed through his phone. "That was thirty minutes" was all he said as he pushed off the car and slid behind the wheel.

She flipped him off behind his back.

"I saw that," he said, and hit the gas.

A few minutes later, she saw the post office up ahead. "Stop!"

He pulled over and glanced over, but she was already hop-ping out of the car and dropping an envelope into the big blue mailbox on the sidewalk. When she slid back into the passenger seat, he raised an eyebrow.

"Margo's check."

"You . . . mailed it."

"I did." She lifted her chin. "I put a stamp on it yesterday. We've already made contact, so I didn't break any rules." She stared at him, waiting for him to object.

He put the car in drive, pulled away from the curb, and said with impressive sarcasm, "As long as you didn't break any rules."

"I actually like rules." She liked order. "And you?"

"Rules were made to be broken."

She had no idea why that scraped at something low in her belly. They spent the next half hour in silence. Her feeling a little discouraged, not exactly knowing why. Him in his driving zone, dark sunglasses and no expression on his face, cool and calm, thoroughly ignoring her.

Which only made it all the more confusing when he pulled into a drive-thru and ordered himself coffee and a breakfast bagel. He glanced her way.

Word hoarder.

But she caved because she wasn't stupid, and she absolutely was hungry. "Same," she said. See? He wasn't the only one who could hoard words, thank you very much.

Thirty minutes later she'd eaten her bagel and finished her coffee. She had to pee, but she planned to drown in it before admitting any such thing. Instead, she was on her phone, scrolling through Instagram when she stilled in disbelief and irritation.

Heath glanced over.

He still hadn't spoken, and she absolutely hadn't wanted to be the first one to crack, but . . . "Ashley's not in San Francisco. At least not anymore."

Another glance.

She just met his gaze and raised a brow. If he wanted to know, he was going to have to use words.

Playing hardball earned her a blink-and-you'll-miss-it quirk on one side of his mouth. "Where is she, then?"

Aha! Four whole words! "She's in Berkeley, at an aerial acrobatics camp! She just posted some pics. What the actual hell?"

She couldn't say she'd ever seen him surprised, but his eyes widened slightly. "Maybe it's an old post."

"Her caption says 'GUYS! THIS CLASS IS THE BEST!' all in caps. She posted it an hour ago."

Heath just kept driving, going ten miles per hour over the speed limit, probably to get there faster and avoid any extra minutes with her. She hoped he got a ticket. "No comment?"

He lifted a shoulder. "Well played."

"Why aren't you angry?"

Another shrug. "Anger is an unproductive emotion and a waste of energy."

"So you're smug on top of being a know-it-all?"

He nearly smiled, she could tell. Then he said, "If you want to know what she's up to so badly, why she saddled us with each other today, just ask her."

"You know what? I will." She called Ashley on speaker.

"Hi, this isn't Ashley's phone. You've reached Sisters' Anonymous, a gentle help service that brings sisters back together, especially when one sister's wrong—cough, *you*, cough—and the other sister's just trying to bring joy to her older sister's life. Don't blame her, because—"

"Ash," Lexi said with an eye roll. "I know you're not delivering saw blades, you big, fancy liar. You're at some air aerobics camp."

"It was a gift card, and it was going to expire!"

"Ash, what are you doing?" Lexi asked softly. "We're supposed to handle this together, and you keep bailing on me. Plus we talked about this, about the meddling—"

"This isn't meddling," Ashley said sincerely. "You're trying to learn how to open up your heart, and I'm trying to help you."

Lexi tipped her head back and stared out Heath's sunroof. "You need to stop worrying about the state of my heart. We have a task."

"And we are on task."

"We?" she asked in disbelief.

"Look, I'm sorry. The last thing I want to do is let you down. But that's why I did this. After we talked, I realized how bad it really was for you when you were a kid. With . . . Daisy."

It was the first time Ashley had called their mom by her given name, and Lexi's throat went tight. She turned away from Heath to stare out her side window. "This isn't really the time—"

"It's not okay that she did things like forget to pick you up from elementary school because she was at the casino, leaving you in the pouring rain waiting on no one, that you somehow slipped through the cracks and no adult even noticed. I couldn't sleep, thinking about what could have happened to you on that long walk home, when those boys chased you."

Why had she made this call on speaker? She fumbled with her phone, taking the call to private so hard she broke a nail. Great, and now she was sweating in places she hated to sweat. "Ashley—"

"No, I need to say this. I know that was only one of a bunch of different ways she failed you. And how in the world can I expect to have a hope at convincing you to stay, or even come back once in a while, if we don't replace those old memories with better ones? I know you have a very full life back east, so I wanted to show you what you could have here, because I know I won't be enough—"

"You're more than enough." Why had she lied about having a life? "Please, can we talk about this later—"

"Yes, of course." Ashley let out a shaky breath. "I just want to say this one last thing. When my dad married Mom, I was too young to understand the feeling in my chest when I realized you weren't going to get to live with us. I couldn't put a name to the emotion until I was older. But it was guilt. Guilt that I had her and you didn't. You deserved better, Lex."

Shaking her head even though her sister couldn't see her, Lexi kept her voice soft, hating the tears she heard in Ashley's. "You have nothing to feel guilty for. *Nothing.* I'm okay, you're okay, we're all okay." She forced some badly needed levity into her voice. "But no more shirking your sister duties to deliver these envelopes with me, okay? I just—" She suddenly realized Heath had pulled the car over, that they were no longer moving, that he'd once again parked on the side of the highway. "I want to get this done, okay?"

"And I want you to be okay."

"I am. I promise."

"I feel like I owe you as much family as I can give you."

Lexi found a smile. "And you think constantly pushing me on a man who doesn't want a relationship any more than I do is going to do that?" She felt Heath shift in his seat, but nope, still not gonna look at him. "We'll be home super late, so I'll see you in the morning. I stashed some ice cream in the freezer, the full-dairy kind. You'd better leave me some."

Ashley laughed softly, but didn't speak, and then out of the corner of the eye she was absolutely not looking at Heath with, she saw him check his phone.

"Yes," Ashley finally said. "But you should spend the night somewhere. You can't possibly mean to drive straight through."

"Goodbye, Ash."

"But—"

"Love you." Lexi disconnected. *Love you?* Where the hell had that come from? But then her phone lit up with a text that said *LOVE YOU TOO* with a bunch of exclamation points and hearts of every color. Letting out a slow exhale, she turned to Heath. "What did she text you?"

"An apology." Those see-all eyes weren't giving much away. "I didn't know about Daisy forgetting to pick you up."

"Oh, so *now* you have words?" she asked in what she'd intended to be a teasing tone. He didn't smile, and she sighed. "Why would you have heard about it? You were a little kid then too. And anyway, we're not going to talk about it."

"Fair." With a nod, he pulled back onto the road. At first the silence felt . . . awkward. But then he turned up the radio and Cher came on. "Do you believe in life after love . . ." he started singing. Loudly.

And off-key.

And damn, there was something incredibly attractive, not to mention endearing, about a man so secure with himself—not cocky, there was a definite difference, as she knew all too well— just confident.

So she sang too, liking the smile he flashed at her way too much. So she'd had a rough childhood, lots of people did. She needed to work on putting aside her fear of letting people in.

Maybe she could even practice with her sister and Heath— neither of whom, for whatever reason, seemed inclined to turn their back on her.

She believed Ashley when she said she wanted Lexi in her life.

As for Heath, well, she wasn't quite exactly sure what he wanted. His mouth said he wasn't interested in a relationship. But his actions didn't quite match up with that. He'd been there for her, no questions asked. Even when she hadn't known she'd needed him. Like today. And there was more. He didn't look at her as he looked at Ashley, whom he clearly considered a younger sister.

Nope, there was nothing fraternal in how he looked at Lexi.

And now here he was, trying to make her laugh by singing at the top of his lungs, suggesting that she couldn't scare him off, not when she made mistakes, not when she let herself be vulnerable, not even when she didn't know how to ask for, much less receive and accept, help . . . He was here, having pushed off whatever his plans were for the day, to back her up. Just the two of them . . .

No Ashley as the buffer.

She didn't know if she had the words to express the comfort she felt in knowing that both of them accepted her as she was. Yes, they teased her, but made sure she was in on the joke. But even more boggling, much as she pushed, neither turned their back on her.

He was still singing, his low baritone purposefully missing the notes. He even let that well-toned body move to the beat, stymied by the seat belt, but no less sexy for it, damn him. He could dance. "We should have a dancing contest," she said. "Since you can't dance and all."

The corners of his mouth tugged. "Is that a challenge, Lexi?"

A jolt went through her core at the way he said her name. "Is it?" she asked, and was that really her voice, all breathless?

"I accept." He slid her a look so hot she had to look down to make sure she was still dressed, that her clothes hadn't melted off. "Bring your moves," he dared her.

"You think you can handle it?"

He just smiled, and her pulse skipped a few beats. This was a very bad idea. Terrible, horrible, no good, *very* bad idea. And still, she couldn't tear her gaze off him, the way he moved, how he had no problem being ridiculously silly . . . and why that was so ridiculously sexy, she had no idea. She reached out to pick a song, but he nudged her hand clear.

"Driver picks the tunes," he said, and then the jerk turned it up.

Oh, game on. "Pull over."

"What?"

"Pull over." And then to make him comply, she pretended to gag and covered her mouth.

He whipped the car to the side of the road so fast her head spun. She hopped out and he was at her side in a moment, hand on her back. "Are you okay—"

She ran around the car and hopped into the driver's seat. Then she honked at him. "Hurry up."

He stood there, hands on hips, head tilted to the side, studying her with a small smile. "You won't leave me here on the side of the road in the middle of nowhere."

So he was cocky after all. "Try me." She revved the engine.

"Shit." But he got into the car.

CHAPTER 18

Heath had barely gotten his seat belt on before Lexi hit the gas, flattening him against the back of his seat like they were heading for space. "Hey, *easy*."

"Things to do, places to be."

She sounded . . . happy? And he couldn't take his eyes off her as she pulled onto the highway again and fiddled around with the music. Two seconds later, "Walk Like an Egyptian" came on. She grinned and started singing.

And here was the thing about Lexi. Unlike him, she could really sing. Clearly, she was using the music to relax and get out of her own head, and enjoying herself while she was at it. And he couldn't take his eyes off her. He could watch her move like that all day long.

"What are you staring at?" she asked, not taking her eyes off the road. "Never seen a girl sing before?"

"Not this girl." And what made him smile his ass off was how she held her cell phone like a microphone, even adding choreography, in spite of her seat belt. He hadn't expected to laugh today. Nope, he'd expected one battle after another, but she cracked him up for three songs straight.

"Someone Like You" came on.

She slowed to match the beat. She could move even better than she could sing, and that was saying something.

So was how those moves affected him.

When the song ended, she grabbed her drink and sucked it down, waving a hand in front of her face.

He nearly did the same thing. "You have a pretty voice."

"My dad's wife had a karaoke machine. It was pretty much my babysitter. By the time I was a teen, I could sing just about anything." She glanced over. "You didn't mention my dancing."

He felt a small smile curve his lips. "I'm not trying to get kicked out of my own car."

"That bad, huh?"

"That good."

She laughed, and while he had no idea what he thought he was doing, encouraging anything between them when it couldn't happen, he laughed too.

They hit the coast and headed south. Rocky cliffs and blue surf to their right, rolling green hills dotted with oaks to their left. Several hours later, they stopped for gas and snacks. While he got to the pump first, she also got out and climbed onto the bumper to clean bugs off the windows. She was in a little summer dress that showed off her long legs, a fitted, cropped jean jacket, wedge sandals on her feet, and she stood on his bumper cleaning his window. No clue that she looked like a walking wet dream.

He was no stranger to having a woman in his car. But he couldn't remember a single time he'd ever stopped for gas, or anything, when he didn't handle everything.

But Lexi . . . she didn't need him, not for a damn thing, and for a guy who considered himself a fixer, who was pretty sure his only value was in helping others, Lexi *not* needing him was attractive as hell. "You don't have to do that," he said.

She leveled him with those knock-'em-dead, drown-in-me eyes. "Why not? You're filling us up with gas, and I can help."

"You'll get dirty."

She laughed. *Laughed.* "You do realize you're just as bad as I am at letting people care about you, right?" She finished and hopped off the bumper. "It's like you don't feel you have the right to ask people to care at all."

And how she'd figured that out about him, he had no idea, but he was left feeling stripped bare, naked to the soul.

It was early afternoon when they pulled into Santa Barbara. The region's geography stretched from the foothills of the Santa Ynez Mountains to wide swaths of south-facing beaches.

He'd taken over driving after their last stop, and Lexi had fallen asleep hard. So hard he wondered if she'd been sleeping poorly. Given what he'd overheard today—which, for the record, he'd like to go back in time and hurt anyone who'd ever hurt her—he had no doubt that being in Sunrise Cove had her revisiting all sorts of not-great memories.

He could relate.

He parked on the street in front of a very small but well cared for house, and took the pulse of the place. The property had a mix of pines and oaks, contrasted by an abundance of grassland.

Lexi hadn't budged, her breathing deep and slow. When he gave her a few minutes and still nothing happened, he said her name softly.

She nearly jumped out of her skin, turning to stare at him from eyes that were not entirely with the program. "What the—"

He lifted his hands. "Just wanted to give you a minute to gather yourself before we go in. You okay?"

"Fine."

"You sure?"

She didn't bother to answer, instead pulling down the visor to look at herself in the mirror. With a grimace, she ran her fingers through her hair, then searched her purse, coming up with some lip gloss. When she caught sight of the time on her phone, she gasped. "What the— You let me sleep for three hours?"

"You seemed tired."

"I said I was fine."

"Noted." He met her gaze. "Also noted is that you're grumpy when you wake up."

"I'm always grumpy."

"No, you're not." He looked at her for a long beat. "And you're also not cold and calculating, like you want people to think."

"Oh, so you've got me all figured out, do you?"

"Some." His mouth curved slightly. "You're wary. Pragmatic. Tough. You've had to be. It's your armor, your defensive mechanism."

"Like recognizes like."

He smiled even though he knew she didn't mean it as a compliment. "It does."

She frowned and put her hand on the passenger door handle. "I'll be back."

"*Two* people," he reminded her. "We both go."

"Which of us is the muscle? Let me guess. It's you, because you've got the penis?"

He choked. She raised a challenging brow, and he couldn't help but laugh.

The way she looked at him called to something deep inside his chest.

"I get to be the muscle," she said.

"Hey, if you want to protect my ass, by all means."

She snorted. "I mean, I can't have anything happening to it. It's a good ass."

He tried not to let that go to his head and failed. "Maybe that's not even my best part."

It was her turn to choke on a laugh as he got out of the car with her, reaching for her hand, pulling her around to face him on the sidewalk. "And for the record? I prefer your road trip playlist over Ashley's."

"That's not saying much." She gave him a nudge with her shoulder that was probably more of a shove. "And don't think I don't know what you're doing. You're bullying me out of my bad mood."

"I don't bully."

"No? What would you call it, then?"

"Cajoling," he said. "I cajoled you out of your bad mood with my wit and charm. *And* my great ass."

And that won him another laugh. Then she was heading up the walk ahead of him. His eyes took her in, and while *she* was the one with the spectacular ass, that wasn't what caught his attention. She was still smiling a little, relaxed for once, and maybe even enjoying herself. He realized he was seeing her, all of her, the real her.

And liking what he saw.

He matched his stride to hers, but she picked up the speed. "Are we seriously racing to be the first to the door?" he asked.

"Aren't we always racing?"

He could think of one situation where he most definitely wouldn't want to hurry with her.

Lexi was staring at his face. "What's that look?"

"What look?" He leaned in to knock, but she stopped him.

"You know what look." She stepped in front of him, eyes on his. "Tell me."

He met her gaze, a challenge in his. "Bad idea."

"I'll just bug you until you're so sick of me you'll cave."

"I don't cave."

"Everyone caves eventually, Heath."

"Not me." Tugging free, he knocked on the door, staring at it while he felt the weight of her gaze on his profile, thinking, *Open, open, open*—

"You have no idea how stubborn I can be," Lexi said.

"Oh, I think I do." Because if anyone could outstubborn him, it was her.

"Tell me."

He just shook his head. Nope, taking that one to the grave.

Still staring at him, like she was running their conversation back through her head, her eyes suddenly widened. "You . . . *Oh*," she breathed.

He knocked again. "I don't think she's home." He turned away from the door, wondering how he could avoid this conversation for the long drive home.

"Oh my God, you meant in bed. You would like to *not* be in a rush while in bed. With me."

Of course that's when the front door opened.

"I never answer my door," the elderly woman said in a smoked-for-decades rasp. "Especially during *Jeopardy!*. But your conversation was too good to pass up." She eyed Heath. "Mostly

I wanted to see if you could back up what you were putting down."

"He can't," Lexi said.

Heath arched a brow at her.

The woman sighed. "Well, don't that beat all. I mean, look at him. You'd think being that ridiculously handsome, he'd have some game."

Lexi laughed, a sweet, genuinely amused sound as she held out her hand, effortlessly charming. "Are you Suzie Anderson?"

"Sure am, honey. And you're Lexi, Daisy's daughter. You probably don't remember me, but we met once or twice."

Lexi cocked her head. "It's been a while."

"It sure has. What can I do you for?"

"This is Heath Bowman," Lexi said, introducing him. "The two of us have got something for you. Could we come in?"

Two minutes later, they were seated at an old Formica table in a small but neat kitchen, their asses all stuck to small vinyl-padded chairs.

"So." Suzie set a plate of cookies on the table. "To what do I owe this pleasure?"

Lexi pulled the envelope from her back pocket and slid it across to Suzie. "This is for you."

Suzie stared down at the envelope and swallowed hard. It took Heath a minute to realize she recognized Daisy's writing and it was emotion shining from her eyes. "What is it?"

Lexi shook her head. "All I know is that she left instructions for it to be delivered to you a year after her passing."

Suzie nodded, then shook her head. "I lost my glasses this morning."

Lexi gave her a gentle smile, one Heath had never seen, and gently pulled a pair of readers off the top of Suzie's head.

"Oh." Suzie grinned. "Right." She opened the envelope and read out loud.

Dear Suzie,

I'm going to keep this short because your ADD means you're only going to read the first paragraph. This isn't a monetary payback because we both know you wouldn't take it. But I am going to express my gratitude for you sticking by my side all these years. We both lost the loves of our lives at the same time. You chose to give up on men. But life's too short to go it alone, Suze. It's also too short to go without a man-made orgasm. So I'm sending you on an all-expenses paid, first-class singles cruise. Find yourself that Italian stallion you always wanted. They're supposedly hung. Don't disappoint me, I'll be watching from above. Or below. I'm not sure, but please do this. Not for me, but for you.

Love,
Daisy

Suzie blinked at the letter in her hands while Heath and Lexi gave her a moment, pretending not to notice that she was fighting tears. "Damn, I miss that bitch," she finally said. "Thank you for delivering this to me in person."

Lexi nodded. "That's how she wanted it. And for the first time, I get why."

Suzie smiled. "Thank you for honoring her wishes. You're a good girl."

That made Lexi laugh. "I don't think anyone's ever said that to me before."

Suzie's eyes filled with genuine affection. "Honey, that's a reflection on the people in your life, not you." She paused, tilted her head. "The last time I saw you was right before you moved with your dad. You'd just gotten in trouble for tripping another kid at school. You said he'd cut in line to beat you to the last cupcake."

Lexi turned to glare at Heath. "True story."

Heath grinned. "I still remember how good that cupcake was too."

"Aw." Suzie put a hand to her heart. "You two really have something. Daisy would be so pleased."

"Oh, we're not . . ." Lexi squirmed on the chair. She looked at Heath, then bit her lower lip. "We're not."

He had zero idea why that disappointed him. Zero.

"You sure?" Suzie asked.

"Very."

"Well, that's disappointing."

It was entirely his own fault, but Heath had to agree. Disappointing.

"Well, I'm so glad to see you," Suzie said, reaching out for Lexi's hand. "Your mom would be so happy you're doing this for her. She always worried so much about you. She . . ." Suzie's eyes went solemn. "She was all too aware of how badly she'd messed up with you."

Lexi swallowed hard and Heath felt his heart squeeze for her.

"I still miss her," Suzie said. "I miss her so much. And . . ." She hesitated. Wrung her fingers together. "There's something I need to tell you. I promised your mom I never would, but now that she's gone and you're here, I can't keep it to myself any longer and let you continue to think the worst of her."

Lexi shook her head. "I don't think the worst of her."

"But you don't think the best of her either. And I get why. I do. And I don't blame you. I just want you to know that when she was . . . healthy . . . She was the kindest, most generous person I knew. Years and years ago now, I found out I had breast cancer. My husband, God rest his soul, had just lost his job. We didn't have medical insurance." She drew a deep breath. "Your mom paid off my medical bills."

Lexi's face softened. "I love that she did that for you. Let me guess, with one of her big windfalls?"

"No, honey." Suzie reached for Lexi's hand. "With your college fund. The one your grandma set up for you when you were still a small girl, with your mom in charge of the trust."

Lexi stilled. Hell, Heath wasn't sure she was even breathing. He wasn't sure *he* was breathing. He'd had no idea that Daisy had taken Lexi's college fund.

Suzie swiped another tear away. "Your mom was sick about it. I didn't know until later what she'd done, and it's made me feel terribly guilty all these years."

Lexi shook her head, dismissing that. "All that matters is that she saved your life."

Heath tried to imagine what it must feel like after all these years to hear this story. There hadn't been many secrets in his family. Nope, they'd much preferred to put it all out there. Loudly.

"I wish she would've told me." Lexi had her arms crossed across her chest, a self-soothing gesture Heath recognized. She was feeling too much, so that she had to hug her heart to herself to keep it from cracking open. "I'd have understood."

Suzie handed Lexi a box of tissues. "You'd asked her for space," she said gently. "I think she was trying to respect that."

Lexi looked startled to realize she had tears on her cheeks. "I did ask her for space. Actually, I demanded it. I was . . . angry. Young and stupid and so very angry."

"You were young, yes," Suzie agreed. "But she'd hurt you. She knew that. She understood. She did. I think— No, I *believe* she honestly thought she'd win the money back and replace it before you needed it."

Lexi drew a ragged breath and nodded, and Heath was viscerally reminded that her relationship with Daisy was not even close to what Ashley's had been. More than that, his own perception of Lexi as an adult had been through Ashley's eyes. Ashley, the caretaker, and . . . Daisy's excuse maker.

That wasn't what Lexi was. She didn't make excuses, not for herself, and not for others, and for the first time he grasped the enormity of the difference between the sisters. Lexi didn't deal with life in the same way as Ashley. Lexi's wounds weren't "let's just put up a colorful curtain so we can't see the problem, it'll be fine." Lexi didn't sugarcoat anything. If something was wrong, she fixed it. And it didn't escape him that she didn't know how to fix her tumultuous and complicated feelings about her mom.

He put a hand on her knee. He meant only to give her a squeeze of comfort because he knew she hated crying, hated feeling vulnerable every bit as much as he did. But she surprised him by setting her hand over his, and when he turned his palm up, she entwined their fingers and held on.

Suzie caught the gesture and smiled to herself, but was thankfully wise enough not to comment. He turned his attention back to Lexi. She was struggling to reconcile her feelings for Daisy, while also forging a relationship with Ashley, and it did something to him. Lexi definitely had a guard up, but he knew her now, or was starting to. He recognized her inner loneliness, understood it at a core level.

They weren't all that different after all.

"You remind me of your mom, you know," Suzie said.

Lexi grimaced a little, and Suzie gave her one of those quiet smiles. "Daisy came from a broken family. Her dad walked away from her and her mother. Left when she was very young, so she didn't recall much. But what she did remember was her dad's addiction to alcohol. She always said she'd raised herself, she'd had to, and her prize for that was you."

Lexi had gone utterly still, her face a mask of quiet devastation. "She never talked about her family or childhood."

"It was hard for her. She'd hoped to do better by you. Failing you was her biggest regret."

Abruptly, Lexi stood, pulling her hand free from Heath's. "I'm sorry. Excuse me a moment." She left the room, and a beat later, the front door opened and closed.

CHAPTER 19

When Lexi heard a set of easy, unhurried footsteps heading her way, she didn't move from her perch on the front bumper of Heath's car, eyes closed, face tilted up to the light rain now coming down, cooling off her overheated face. The afternoon sky was muted.

She was not. She'd hoped the misty air would chase away the heat of regret burning her from the inside out.

So.

Much.

Regret.

But it didn't. Only a few weeks ago, she'd have sworn that her heart had long ago withered and died inside her chest. But if it was dead, then why did it hurt so bad?

The footsteps stopped at her side.

She didn't look over at Heath. Nor did she have any idea what she expected, but it wasn't for him to perch his previously noted very fine ass on the bumper next to her. From her peripheral, she saw him mimic her posture, slightly slouched, face tilted up to the rain. It only made the still breathing, hurting thing that beat inside her chest ache more that he'd sit out here with her, not speaking, just letting her be. "I'm not going to talk," she warned.

"That's okay, I like the quiet." He shifted and then something came around her shoulders.

His windbreaker.

"You'll get all wet," she said.

He shrugged. "I also like the rain."

And then, in possibly her favorite thing he'd ever done, he went on to just sit there with her while she felt the warm tears continue to stream down her face, mixing with the chilly raindrops.

Everything Suzie had told her was playing on repeat in her head. So much of what Lexi had gone through, Daisy had also gone through. Her mom had been more like her than she could have ever thought, and wasn't that a terrifyingly vulnerable thing to realize? "How come she never told me, about any of it?"

He didn't have to ask her what she meant. He knew. He always seemed to know. "Maybe it was too painful."

She nodded, then shook her head. Never once had she realistically analyzed why her past hurt so much, why *this* hurt so much. On the one hand, it was a brutal reminder that she was her mother's daughter, which . . . gah. She hated. But on the other, it personalized her mom in a way that she could absolutely relate to. "Before these damn envelopes, I never pictured her as . . . generous. And *beloved*." But she should have, she should have remembered the good parts of her mom. "I didn't realize how hard she tried, in spite of her own demons." She closed her eyes. "I don't know what to do. I feel . . . stuck."

"Maybe you do what you've always done. Put one foot in front of the other."

"That simple?" Opening her eyes, she looked at him, taking in the raindrops in his hair, on his jaw, his eyelashes. Eyed the way that, without his windbreaker, his T-shirt now clung to every line and lean muscle of his shoulders, chest, and annoyingly flat stomach.

"That simple," he said.

How did he do it, somehow cut through all the BS, allowing her to see things more deeply than felt comfortable? And why in the world was that the best thing anyone had ever done for her, even if it also meant that she suddenly felt even more emotionally connected to him? Terrifying in its own right. "Thank you."

Very gently, he reached out and stroked a wet strand of hair from her face, tucking it behind her ear. "For what?"

She lifted a shoulder. "For not hating me when I tried to push you away from the moment I got here. For supporting me and Ash through this. For being here today, even when I thought I wanted to be alone."

His eyes were dark and solemn, serious on hers. "Never. Always. And anytime."

She nodded, then shook her head, overwhelmed and confused. But she knew that his presence somehow lightened the weight.

"Lex . . ." He slid a hand into her hair, gently gliding his thumb over her jaw, which was so tight she could feel her muscles straining and bunching. "You're holding on to so much. It's okay to let it out. Let it go."

No. It wasn't okay because she didn't have anyone to catch her. Never had. Yes, Heath was right there, literally holding her upright from sliding to the ground, but that was temporary.

She was temporary.

It all made her chest ache, ache so much she could hardly

stand it. "I should try to be more like Ashley. Eternally chipper. Maybe I should sign up for aerial aerobics . . ."

He let out that low, sexy laugh of his and shook his head. "Please don't ever try to be anything other than exactly who you are, Lexi Clark."

She stared at him, a hand pressed to her own chest to hold the pain in. "I . . . at the moment, I'm not really even sure who Lexi Clark is."

"Well, until you figure it out, let me tell you who I see when I look at you. A woman who's fiery and fierce, strong inside and out, smart, resilient, caring, and amazing . . ." His gaze dropped to her mouth, then he lowered his voice to a rough timbre. "And a whole bunch of other things that don't have a place in this moment."

She blinked, really, *really* wanting to know. "Name one."

That mouth of his curved. "Sexy as all hell."

She shivered, but not from the rain or the cold.

He nudged more of her wet hair from her face, then shoved those hands through his own hair, pushing it off his forehead. His shirt had become a second skin, but if he was cold, he didn't say a word. She knew he'd sit here in the rain as long as she wanted or needed. They should get in the car, but she was afraid if they moved, the intimacy bubble would pop and vanish. But even as she thought it, the sky opened up, and big fat raindrops began to pelt their skin now, startling them out of their cocoon.

Heath grabbed her hand and pulled her off the bumper. She let her momentum knock her body into his, and as she knew he would, he caught her, nudging her toward the passenger side. It took him a moment to find the key fob, mostly because it was in the pocket of his jacket, which was on her. Just as he pulled it out, she accidentally knocked it from his hand. By the time he got the door open for her, they were both swearing and laughing.

But the laughter died in her throat when Heath slid behind the wheel and turned to her, the heat in his eyes stoking the smoldering fire inside her.

"You're shaking." He cranked the heater, aiming the vents at her.

Only it wasn't the cold making her tremble. Okay, maybe it was a little bit because of the cold, but it was mostly him.

"You need a hot shower and dry clothes," he said.

"Actually . . ." She swiveled in the seat to face him. "Neither of those are at the top of my list."

Holding her gaze, he stretched his arm across the back of her seat, a finger running along the outer shell of her ear. "No?"

"No." She tried to give him her best, hottest suggestive gaze, but since she was woefully out of practice, she didn't know if she pulled it off. So she tried again.

His smile faded. "You okay? Your eye's twitching."

She groaned at her lame attempt at seduction, and he looked even more concerned. "What is it?" he asked.

"Nothing!" When he just raised a brow, she sighed. "I was trying to give you a look. *The* look."

He stilled, but not before she saw the quick flare of surprise. "Lex—"

"No!" *Shit*. "It's totally just an eye twitch."

He didn't say anything, but one of his hands slid into her wet, tangled hair and gently tightened. His other dropped to her thigh, the warmth seeping through her drenched jeans.

"I mean . . . it's a terrible idea." She nodded, determined to be a grown-up. "It's okay to just, like . . . let the moment pass. Totally one hundred percent okay. Even two hundred percent okay." She bit her tongue to shut herself up. *Two hundred percent okay?* She'd completely lost control of her mouth.

His eyes lit with amusement now, which meant she was going to have to kill him, but then he said her name again and waited until she looked at him. "We're not going to let the moment pass," he said.

Her heart skipped a beat. "We're not?"

"No. But—"

"Oh great." She butted the back of her head to the seat rest. "A 'but' . . ."

"*But*," he repeated, his voice a low, sexy rasp, as if the mental images of what he wanted to do to her were already playing like a movie in his head. "We're in a car, and even with the windows fogging up, we're too visible."

"First a tent, and now a car. The universe hates me."

With a laugh, he slid a hand to the nape of her neck, his fingers tunneling in her hair. "The car is far too limiting for my best moves."

Desperate, she looked around at the car's interior. "Are you sure?"

Still grinning, he put the car in gear.

"Where are we going?"

"To find a hot shower and a warm, dry bed."

"Are you sure you can make your best moves in a warm, dry bed? Because I'm starting to doubt you—"

"Let's go find out."

Challenge apparently accepted.

It took them two tries to find a hotel, since the storm had driven a lot of people off the roads in search of shelter. On their third try, the front desk clerk smiled and welcomed them. "One room or two?"

"Two," Heath said, and when she looked at him in surprise, he pulled her a few feet away from the check-in desk. "I'm trying to not be presumptuous," he said in a low voice.

"You do remember that this was my idea, right?"

His smile stopped her heart. "Trust me, Lex, I've been thinking about this since far before you ever stopped glaring at me. But . . ." He squeezed her hand. "Whatever happens, whatever *doesn't* happen, it's your choice. Always. And to make sure of that, I want you to have a space to retreat to if you need it."

She smiled, hoping to tease away the serious and earnest expression on his face. "Why? Do you plan to be bad at it?"

His eyes dilated. "Lex, I plan to be so amazing that you forget you have choices at all."

She burst out laughing. "Good to know you're still cocky as hell." She stepped back to the clerk. "*One* room, please. King bed."

They barely made it inside the room. The elevator had been an exercise in self-control, but the minute Heath hit the key card against the lock and the door opened, they lunged at each other.

She forgot about being icy cold or that their clothes were wet, at least until she struggled to get his soaked shirt off him. It'd suctioned itself to his skin. He had to help, but that might've also been because the sight of him made her mouth dry. They laughed breathlessly when he had the same trouble with her shirt, but only until his hands slid around her waist and pulled the hem of her T-shirt out of her jeans. Her hunger and need made her quiver, and intensified as he wrangled her out of the rest of her clothes and gave a rough, heartfelt groan at the sight of her. Until that moment, his eyes had been soft, making her all . . . melty. It was the only word she could think of. But now that she was completely bared to him, his gaze turned pure fire and heat and erotic desire.

And she wanted *everything* that look promised.

"I don't know exactly what you're thinking," he murmured, voice low and raspy. "But I encourage you to act on those thoughts."

She laughed, pressing her body into his.

"Shower or bed?" he asked, enveloping her in his arms as his mouth nibbled its way along her jaw to her ear, his teeth scraping against her lobe, causing a full-body shiver.

"Bed's closer—" She broke off with a startled laugh when he scooped her up and tossed her to the mattress, giving her another thrill as he kneeled at her feet, pausing to take her in, eyes hot, his body revealing exactly how arousing he found her.

Then he slowly climbed up her body, stopping to worship every inch as he went. Breathless, and wanting her own turn, she shoved him off so she could have the top, enjoying wrenching rough groan after groan from him while she repeated the favor, taking her mouth on a tour over his every inch. She'd had no idea how turned on she'd get by taking the wheel. Every pleasured inhale and gasp he made was the most sensual, erotic thing she'd ever felt, and she heard herself laugh in wonder.

"Drunk on the power of driving me out of my mind?"

"*Very* much."

His laugh sounded breathless as it reverberated from his chest and into hers. He had a hand buried in her hair, and just when she could feel him start to lose control, he rolled, tucking her beneath him once more, pushing the weight of his body into hers. "My turn again," he murmured against her skin, working his way down her body.

And, oh, that mouth. Those hands. Slow and methodic. Hitting every part of her, making her squirm and pant and beg as he continued his lazy exploration. And when he finally took mercy on her and shoved her off the edge into release, she lost all sense of time and place. When she managed to open her eyes, she found him watching her, pleasure mixed with something else. *Need*, she thought, and kissed him again, wrapping her arms and legs around him, wanting him buried deep—

"Lex." He lifted his head, his forearms braced on either side of her face, his fingers back in her hair, gentling his grip. "I don't have anything with me . . ."

A condom, he meant, shocked she'd not thought of it first. "I'm . . . It's been a while," she admitted. "I'm clear, and on the pill."

He nodded, running the tip of his nose along her jaw. "Same." He let out a low laugh against her skin. "With the exception of being on the pill, that is." He met her gaze. "You still want this?"

She fisted her hands in his silky hair. "Yes. Now."

"Your wish is my command," he said politely, and then proceeded to take her apart and put her back together again—*not* politely—and she loved every second of it.

THE NEXT MORNING, Heath studied Lexi over breakfast in the hotel café. She hadn't said much since they'd stirred before dawn and devoured each other, again—unless he counted the sweet, sexy, breathless "oh please . . ." and "don't stop . . ." She'd had definite ideas about where she'd wanted his mouth, so he'd let her lead him to all her favorite places. Worked out well, since they were all his favorite places too.

After the guided tour, she'd pouted. "We're up too early."

"I'd feel more guilty about that if you hadn't enjoyed yourself." He paused. Grinned. "Twice."

"Counting is considered rude." She paused. "And it was thrice." He laughed. "*Thrice*."

Now she stole the blueberry muffin from his plate, had a taste, then offered it back to him. Instead of taking it, he leaned forward and took a bite, nipping one of her fingers in the process.

Her stomach did flips, which he knew because she pressed a hand to it and squirmed a little.

But then she went back to being quiet. Too quiet, and he set down his fork. "What's wrong?"

She shrugged, but the look in her eyes belied the casual body language.

"Lex, talk to me."

"There's nothing to talk about. We . . . did some biology together." She paused. "And it was nice. So thank you. For the use of your penis. It was very . . . helpful."

He choked on a bite of his omelet. "*Helpful*," he repeated slowly.

"Yes. Yesterday was a rough day. Stressful. And it got to me. So again, thank you."

"Okay, no." He shook his head. "I call bullshit. It was more than a stress reliever. It was . . ." Soul shatteringly amazing. He shook his head. "Biology?"

"Well, technically . . ." She pushed her scrambled eggs around her plate. "Biology, with a splash of chemistry."

"Flag on the play. I need to take you back upstairs for a replay."

She shook her head. "That would be a bigger mistake."

He set down his fork. "What's really going on here? Because less than a half hour ago, I had my mouth on your—"

"I remember!" She let out a breath. "And fine, it was so much better than nice. Okay? Is that what you needed to hear? That it was the best sex I've ever had? Because it was, Heath. But what happened last night was a one-off. It was . . . Vegas. As in what happens in Vegas stays in Vegas."

He was the best she'd ever had? He almost grinned at the ego boost, but the look on her face, the one that said she was on the verge of tears, is what sent him reeling. He wouldn't push her. Not here. Not anywhere. He'd told her the choice was hers, always, and he'd meant it. It wasn't his place to decide what came next between them. "Okay."

She nodded, not meeting his gaze. "Okay."

They finished their breakfast in silence. Before getting on the freeway, he filled them up with gas and slid behind the wheel.

Lexi had headphones on and didn't so much as glance his way.

Back to the starting gate, then. Good to know where they stood.

AN HOUR INTO the drive, Ashley called Heath. He answered on Bluetooth.

"Hey!" she said, all bubbly happy. "How did it go?"

"We dropped off the check."

She sighed. "Put me on speaker, please. My sister doesn't usually use all that many more words than you, but I am eternally optimistic, so . . ."

He stabbed the speaker button.

Lexi gave him a curious look.

"It's Ash."

"Hey!" her sister said enthusiastically. "How are you doing? Are you having fun? What's going on?"

Lexi repeated his words. "We dropped off the check."

Heath couldn't help but smile, and it was possible, maybe, that she *almost* smiled back.

"Well, duh," Ashley said, sounding annoyed now. "Suzie called me, she was so thrilled to see you. So . . . what have you two been doing since then?"

Well, certainly not each other . . .

Except, oh right, they *had* done each other, spectacularly, and last night would live in his mind rent free as one of the best nights of his entire life too. And also morning, up until break-fast, anyway.

CHAPTER 20

Lexi walked into Daisy's house, mentally exhausted. Physically exhausted too, but that was what happened when one turned into a sex fiend, apparently.

Except . . . Here was the thing about sex. She liked it. A lot. But Heath . . . when he'd touched her, the pleasure had transcended the physical. It hadn't been just her body involved. It had also been her heart. Her mind.

She hadn't known that could even happen.

Worse, she could feel a reluctant smile trying to break free. Last night—and this morning—played on repeat in her head, especially the naughty bits, every last dirty one. There'd been something about the way Heath had looked at her, the way her heart reacted to him, to seeing what he kept buried beneath all his smirk and smolder and easy wit.

And she'd ruined it. Just like she always did when something felt too right, too good—she self-sabotaged. It was in her Eeyore genetic makeup.

In the foyer, she kicked off her shoes, tossed her purse to the bench, then turned to the living room, jumping a little at the sight of Ashley standing there, arms crossed, face dialed to un-happy.

Lexi's heart stuttered. "What? What's wrong?"

"Maybe you should tell me."

Lexi hesitated, trying to read the room. She failed. "Look, my sister-speak is a bit rusty, you're going to have to spell it out for me. Do you . . . want me to leave? Have I outstayed my welcome?"

"Oh, you mean because you never so much as unpacked your duffel bag, instead choosing to just live out of it like you're only going to be here another minute, tops?"

Her head hurt too much for this. Or maybe it was her heart. "Ash, I'm staying in a room the size of a postage stamp with every square inch filled with stuff. Where would you have me unpack?"

"You could've cleaned out the dresser if you'd wanted, but you didn't bother. If it's that hard to be here, maybe you should just go back to that big, fancy life of yours."

Lexi's chest went tight. "So you *do* want me to leave." She shouldn't have been surprised. No one ever wanted to keep her, even now. "We still have three envelopes to go. I promised to stay until we saw this through."

"But you don't want to be here. So much so that you lied to me."

Lexi blinked. "What? When?"

Ashley tossed up her hands. "You can give up the act. I had a little chat with Grandpa Gus. Even though you let me believe you're working remotely, you're not. You took a break from the job. You didn't have to do that, put your life on hold for me."

Lexi shook her head, even as her heart pounded in her ears. "I did not tell Gus any of that."

"No, you told Heath."

Her stomach hit her toes at the implied betrayal, something she'd had way too much of. "And Heath told Gus?"

"No." Ashley's expression softened slightly. "Gus overheard Heath on the phone talking to an old friend. A friend who he thought, along with her siblings, might have need of your services."

A very bad feeling rumbled through her. "Is Heath's friend named Cassidy?"

"Yes."

Lexi sat on the foyer bench. Sat calmly too, even when she felt like screaming. "Heath called friends to ask them to hire me? He got me a pity job?"

Ashley opened her mouth, then shut it with a grimace. "Well, I don't think it was pity—"

Lexi stood again. She couldn't do this. She needed a nap. Food. Booze. And not necessarily in that order. She went to brush past Ashley, but her sister grabbed her arm.

"Wait," Ashley said. "I'm not done being upset with you."

"You're going to have to get in line."

"Why didn't you tell me you'd taken a leave, that you weren't working?"

Lexi lifted her chin. "I have been working." Just, apparently, for friends of a friend. Friends of a friend with benefits . . . And as amazing as those benefits had been, she was embarrassed and angry at what he'd done without telling her. She hadn't asked for help, which meant it had indeed been pity motivating him, and she couldn't hate that more. "I don't see how me working or not working affects you at all."

"Lexi, you lied. You *kept* lying. Does that remind you of anyone in our family?"

Lexi gaped at her. She'd never heard her sister say one negative thing about Daisy, not ever. "Are you saying I'm just like her?"

"No." Ashley softened. "I'm sorry, that was . . . not okay of me. I'm just . . . I'm sorry. But, Lex, if your job's on hold for whatever reason, then you don't have to leave once we're finished with the envelopes, right?"

Lexi must have grimaced, because Ashley drew in a sharp breath. "Except you do have to leave, because you don't want to be here."

Great. They were going to do this now, when she'd gotten maybe an hour of sleep last night for all the right reasons, had picked a fight with Heath for all the wrong reasons, and then been forced to make that long-ass drive home in near silence. Letting out a breath, she met her sister's gaze. "It's because I'm embarrassed, okay?"

"Embarrassed?" Ashley frowned. "About what?"

"There's a lot you don't know."

"So fill me in." Ashley paused, weighed whatever she saw in Lexi's eyes, which was likely far too much. "We're sisters, Lex. We share our burdens."

She'd never been good at that. In fact, she'd never really even tried. *Now or never* . . . Nerves jangled in her stomach and her voice. "There was a guy. A guy I thought maybe might be the One someday. We worked together for several years, he as my direct supervisor." She paused, because she knew how stupid she'd been. "We sort of secretly dated for close to six months before I was accused of stealing from a client. There's an ongoing investigation, but I didn't do it, so they won't find any evidence." She hesitated again. "I'm pretty sure he did it. Dean stole from a client and blamed me, and because I'm so . . ." She gestured to herself. "You know, cold and closed off and all that, they took his side. I'm not on a leave or break. They fired me."

"Oh, Lexi . . ." Ashley looked horrified, and Lexi braced herself to be asked if it was true. Braced herself for it, so much so that when her sister opened her mouth, Lexi started toward the hall to pack.

"I'm so sorry," Ash said as Lexi started walking away. "But they must not have known you at all."

Lexi froze, her back still to her sister.

"You'd never steal, not from anyone," her sister said emphatically.

She hadn't realized how much she needed those words, but she shook her head. "That's not even the worst part." She turned to face Ash again. "After it happened, I realized that I didn't have a single person in my life who knew me enough to stand by me or vouch for me."

Ashley looked stunned for a beat, and then moved closer. "*I* would've stood by you, you amazing, wonderful, beautiful idiot. You don't have to go through things like this alone!"

"Alone is the only way I know."

"Why didn't you hire a lawyer and sue the pants off them?"

"I just wanted it to go away." Lexi scrubbed a hand over her face, feeling stupid, hating to admit this stuff to herself, much less anyone else. "And I know I'm difficult, I do, but I don't know how to change it, or me. I don't know how to open up like you do so effortlessly. And speaking of that, I need you to promise me something."

"Of course. Anything."

Just those few words had a lump growing in Lexi's throat. "You can't tell Heath about any of it."

"Why?" Ashley asked softly. "He'd be furious for you."

She wasn't actually sure that was true right now. "I don't want him to know how stupid I was." And here was when her mouth disconnected from her brain. "Especially after last night."

"What happened last night?" Ashley gasped. "Oh, wait! Oh my God! I saw it but then I got distracted. You have a glow! Like, an all-over glow! An all-over I've-been-screwed-against-a-wall glow!"

"Well, this is embarrassing." Lexi covered her face with her hands. "The glow is accidental!"

Ashley laughed so hard she had to bend over and brace herself on her knees.

"I first noticed it when I was brushing my teeth this morning," Lexi grumbled. "And I can't get rid of it! Same with the stupid smile." She felt it spread across her face even as she said it, and clapped a hand over her mouth. "Seriously, what *is* that?"

Ashley was laughing so hard now that she was no longer making any noise.

"And it wasn't against a wall." She paused. "Well, maybe once . . ."

"Oh—excuse me," a male voice said from the still-open front door.

"Cole," Ashley said, wiping away tears of mirth.

Of course it would be Heath's brother, whose eyebrows had risen so high, they'd vanished beneath his hair. Lexi groaned and covered her face again.

Cole winced. "Sorry. I'll . . . come back later." And he bolted.

"Well," Ashley said. "You got your wish. I won't be telling Heath. Cole will."

"Oh my God. Maybe he won't—"

"If you're harboring some hope that Cole can actually keep a secret, let me assure you that you're wrong."

Lexi rolled her eyes so hard they almost fell out of her head. That was when she caught sight of the opposite wall, which had been empty the last time she'd looked. Someone had hung a framed drawing.

The one she'd done of Heath. "What? Why?"

"Just accept it," Ashley said. "It lives there now. Oh, I'm going to need you to sign it."

"It's practically a stick figure. You can't even tell it's Heath."

"Of course you can. You drew little lines for his disgustingly perfect abs, even over his T-shirt."

Lexi groaned. "We are *not* keeping that."

Ashley beamed. "*We!* You said *we!* And *we* most certainly are keeping it." She tilted her head. "You know, that glow is a really good look for you."

Lexi pushed past her sister and slumped on the couch.

Ashley sat at her side, but turned to face her. "Look, clearly you're . . . besotted, so—"

Lexi choked on a laugh. "Are you thirteen, or ninety-three?"

Ashley just stuck her nose in the air and continued. "So I was thinking . . . Maybe you take this time to stop and smell the roses. You know, with Heath. Take a chance on him, on you both, and let it happen."

"This time? 'This time' implies that I've somehow held back in my life. Which I haven't. Allow me to submit my ex as exhibit one."

Ashley nodded. "Sustained. But what I meant was that maybe this might be different. And even if it's not, who better to practice opening your heart again with than a guy like Heath? He'd never hurt you."

Still stinging from finding out he'd gotten her a job behind her back, she shook her head. "Maybe you should take your own advice." She made a show of looking around. "Because I don't see any girlfriends hanging around."

"Hey, I'm only twenty-three. I'm still sowing my wild oats, figuring out what I might want in a partner someday, so that when I get as old as you and come across a great person like Heath, I'm not too stupid to blow it. Also, I'm not just talking about love, I'm talking about life in general. There are always choices. The trick is figuring out which choices feel genuine and right."

"When you *get to my age*?" Lexi repeated with a disbelieving laugh.

"Is that all you heard?"

Lexi sighed. Ashley was right. There were always choices. She hadn't made the best of them either. One of her biggest regrets was cutting her mom out of her life.

"I think you know I'm right. But . . . and just hear me out . . . what if you and Heath are the real deal?"

"Ash, it was just one night."

"It is if that's what you choose it to be. But you're in the driver's seat." Her phone dinged an incoming text, and she pulled it from her pocket. "It's Heath. He's coming over."

Lexi jumped off the couch. "What? Why?"

Ashley arched a brow, like, *Really? You can't figure it out?*

Cole had most definitely tattled. Dammit. She strode for the kitchen, talking over her shoulder. "Tell him I'm not home. Tell him I can't talk. Tell him—*Oof.*" She'd plowed into a brick wall.

A brick wall named Heath. "Or you could tell me yourself," he said, slipping his phone back into his pocket.

She took a step back and put a hand to her chest. "You scared me."

"Trying to avoid me?"

"Duh!" She threw up her hands. "Take a hint!"

He rolled his eyes. She was wearing off on him.

Ashley eyed the time. "Would you look at that? I've gotta go. I've just remembered I've got something very important to do."

Lexi crossed her arms. "Aerial aerobics?"

Her sister bit her lower lip. "Not today. This is something . . . different."

"Uh-huh."

Ignoring Lexi's sarcasm, Ashley moved to the front door, where she grabbed her purse and keys, and then quietly shut the door behind her.

It immediately opened again. "I put vodka in the freezer. Oh, and our 'Netflix and chill' password is UseACondomKids, no spaces."

At whatever look Lexi gave her, she grimaced and vanished.

Lexi sighed and turned to face Heath.

He cocked his head and studied her, a small smile curving his mouth. "You told her about the wall?"

She felt the heat of embarrassment on her face. "This is all your fault. I'm mad at you."

"Do tell."

"You got me a pity job!"

"No." He gave a single shake of his head, eyes serious. "Nothing about that was pity."

She crossed her arms. "Feels like pity."

"I should have told you. I meant to tell you. I was wrong not to, but I was worried you'd refuse the job—which is legit, by the way. Cassidy was already looking for an appraiser, and not having any luck finding someone reputable."

"Which you now know I'm not."

"Lex." He met her gaze, his own serious, earnest. "I don't

even need to hear the story from your own lips to know I'd bet on you any day of the week."

At that, her spine relaxed. Damn. Her emotions were giving her whiplash. "But?" she asked. "Because I most definitely hear a 'but' coming."

"Look, I trust you. I just wish it was reciprocated, that you knew that you can tell me anything and I won't judge you."

Where to even begin? So many half-truths she'd told, so many things she should have said and hadn't because she'd been terrified of the ramifications, the worst of which would be driving the people she cared about away from her. "Trust isn't my strong suit."

"I get you feeling that way when you first got here. You certainly didn't owe me a thing. Still don't. But it's been nearly a month of us spending a lot of time together. I thought we'd gotten pretty close."

"We did. We have." She had to look away from the hurt in his gaze. "But we both said this wasn't going anywhere."

"I said that because I was scared." He paused. "Scared of getting hurt. You're not the only one with trust issues." His voice, low and sincere, cut right through her. She was scared too. And she wasn't nearly as brave as he was. But she had no idea how to say any of it, how to admit out loud that a part of her didn't feel worthy of his feelings, his trust—or *anyone's*—and maybe never would.

"For the record," he said, slowly moving closer to her, as if afraid to spook her. "I *hate* what happened to you." He slid his hands into his pockets, as if he didn't quite trust them not to reach for her. "Hate that you didn't feel you could tell me. I thought . . ." He shook his head. "Well, it doesn't matter what I thought."

At the pain and regret in his eyes, she had to turn away. Hugging herself, she closed her eyes. "You've met me. Which means you can't really be all that surprised." Her chest felt like it was caving in from the effort of keeping her shit together, trying not to fall apart in front of him. She was shaking with the impending meltdown, one she needed to be alone for.

"I'm here for you," he said, right behind her, so close she could feel the heat from his body. "And I'm not the only one. You don't have to go through the rough stuff on your own."

Didn't she though? Because eventually everyone walked away. The only difference was that this time she was doing the walking first. With that in mind, she forced herself to face him. "But I'm so good at it."

Disappointment flickered in his eyes, but he said nothing. And neither did she as she headed out of the room.

"Lexi."

She stopped, but didn't look back.

"If you ever want to talk, you know where to find me."

CHAPTER 21

Lexi stood on the sidewalk staring at the door to a seedy pool hall in the middle of nowhere, Nevada. Ashley stood at her right, Heath at her left.

It'd been a week since she'd let down the only two people who cared about her. A week of both of them steering clear, obviously trying to give her space and time—which she hadn't used all that wisely. Mostly, she'd twisted in the wind like a tumbleweed, landing wherever the breeze took her.

She'd spent the first day drowning in uncertainty, wanting to talk to her sister, to Heath, badly wanting that, but also knowing she had to get her head screwed on straight first. So she'd worked instead, finishing up both the Sunrise Cove and South Shore jobs, while also clearing out Daisy's garage.

She'd even been hired by a third client in Homewood, only a twenty-minute drive away, all while quietly realizing that this, running her own business, being her own boss, just might be the first thing she could really succeed at.

Wherever she landed.

After this.

But first, she needed to find . . . She pulled out the envelope and stared at the name.

Vinny Ricci Sr., owner of said seedy pool hall.

Heath was studying the building, and just looking at him reminded her what they'd been together, for that one amazing night.

And the next morning . . .

She heard the revving thumping of Harleys before she saw them. A minute later, three massive guys in biker vests and jeans pulled up, parked, and took a moment to give Lexi and Ashley a slow once-over—completely ignoring Heath—before entering the pool hall.

Intensity rolled off Heath in waves. "Lexi, the envelope? I'm doing this one. Alone."

"No one goes alone," she said.

"So *now* you listen to me?" Heath asked.

"I always listen. I don't always agree. Let's just get this over with."

Heath shook his head. "Please, let me do this."

Lexi appreciated the wording. Though there hadn't been a question mark at the end of the sentence, it was clear he was trying to give them a choice. So she was shocked when Ashley shook her head. "We'll be okay." She looked at Lexi. "Right?"

After the week they'd had, Lexi found herself surprised by her sister's almost smile. Had she been forgiven, then? Or, more likely, Ashley had no idea how to hold a grudge. "Have you by any chance learned any self-defense maneuvers in your aerial aerobics adventures?" she asked Ash.

"Me? No. But remember when you took karate? You texted me that pic of you in the getup."

"I won a month's worth of classes, and took them. Ten years ago," she added.

Ashley lifted a shoulder. "Better than nothing."

Lexi had to laugh. "You're right, it's better than nothing." Plus, she wanted, needed, to get this over with. They all did. They'd given this thing a real try, all of them. That it hadn't worked out wasn't anyone's fault.

Well, okay, it was someone's fault—hers.

But not theirs. "We've got this," she said.

Drawing a deep breath, Heath tried appealing to her sister. "Ash—"

"My mom loved this Vinny dude," Ashley said. "She'd never have sent us here if it was too dangerous."

My mom . . . Lexi closed her eyes. It'd taken her over a month, but the pronoun "my" in front of "mom" coming from Ashley's mouth no longer felt strange or wrong. It felt . . . right. What Daisy and Ashley had had together for a whole bunch of years had been . . . well, beautiful.

Lexi didn't begrudge them that. She'd come to understand and accept it over the past week, the past week when both Heath and Ashley had made themselves scarce.

Because she was an idiot.

An idiot who pushed people away.

"I promised your mom that I'd look after you," Heath said to Ashley. "And this is me looking out for you. Come on, we're out of here."

"No," Lexi said.

The both of them turned to look at her. "We're here." She gave them a small smile. "We're doing this."

Ashley studied her for a beat, then nodded. "Yeah, we are."

And Lexi nearly burst into tears. Such easy forgiveness.

Heath didn't object, didn't look mad or annoyed or hateful either. He never had, she realized. Not even when they'd been kids. But he did look unhappy. "Do you have any idea what the logo on the back of those guys' motorcycle vests means?" he asked in a low voice.

"That they love their mama?"

He took a deep breath, but before he could speak, Lexi did. "We'll be quick. We'll be smart. Besides, as Ashley pointed out, Daisy was friends with this guy."

Heath, a muscle bunching in his jaw, took in the building, the entrance, the parking lot. "Fine. But I'm coming with."

"If you insist," Lexi said, ignoring the little quiver of relief. "Let's just get this over with." She wanted to sound confident. Like a girl boss. But her stomach chose that moment to rumble louder than the motorcycles had coming down the street.

"You're hangry, right?" Ashley pawed through her bag and came up with a granola bar. "I knew this would happen. Here."

Lexi eyed the thing in a plastic baggie. Homemade, then. "Tell me those are chocolate chips and that you used a *lot* of sugar."

"They're raisins, and no sugar. Eat it, or I'll shove it down your throat."

Heath's mouth curved in his first smile of the day. "The puppy grew claws."

Ashley growled at him. Lexi bit back a rough laugh, broke the granola bar in half, and handed a piece to her sister. "Hangry must run in the family."

Ashley snatched it and stuffed it into her mouth all in one piece. "If either of you ever refers to me as a puppy again," she said around that full bite, "I'm going to lock you in a closet. Together. And throw away the key."

That wiped the smile off both of their faces as they looked at each other. Heath seemed annoyed. Lexi wouldn't say the same. She just hoped he couldn't see the way her pulse leapt at the idea of being locked together in a closet.

Lexi and Ashley turned to the door, but Heath pulled them back, meeting their gaze, his own serious. Intense. "We stay together. But if we're separated and you get into trouble," he said, "scream. Loudly. I'll find you."

Lexi walked in first, Ashley right on her heels, with Heath at their backs, all of them momentarily blinded by the dark room. It was lit only by tiny lamps over the pool tables and the flickering neon sign that read FUCK YOU.

Okay, then.

Two security guards immediately approached without a word, blocking them from moving farther into the room.

"Hello, gentlemen," Ashley said with a sweet smile. "We're looking for Vinny."

The oversize goons closed ranks, beefy arms folded over even beefier chests, just staring at them.

Ashley had to tip her head way back to see up into their faces, that smile still on her face. "Daisy Fontaine sent us. We're her daughters."

"I don't know who the fuck Daisy is," one of them finally said. "But unless you have an appointment, you're not getting in to see Vinny."

"Then we have an appointment," Lexi said, and lifted the envelope that said quite clearly: Vinny Ricci Sr.

One of the guys shook his head. Quite the feat, as he didn't seem to have a neck. "Vinny Sr. retired to a beach in the Keys eight months ago. Vinny Jr. is in charge now."

"Then we'll see Vinny Jr.," Heath said.

The guys sized him up. "You packing?"

Were they in a bad gangster/mob movie?

"Of course we're not armed," Ashley said.

"We don't take anyone's word for it," No Neck said, then stepped forward with the clear intention of searching them. And, joy, Lexi was the closest.

"No," Heath said, his voice steely authority. "You don't touch either of them."

"To see Vinny Jr., you get searched."

Heath stepped in front of Lexi and lifted his arms, giving them access. No Neck searched him. Roughly.

Lexi sucked in a breath to say something, but Heath shook his head at her to not interfere, his eyes warning that if they wanted to do this, she needed to stay calm.

Not her strong suit.

When No Neck was done searching Heath, he shoulder checked him hard. Heath, his gaze still locked on Lexi, didn't react.

Goon Two turned to Ashley, and Lexi's heart leapt into her throat, but she managed to give a sarcastic snort. "The puppy? You're going to search the cute, little, harmless puppy? She's barely five feet tall and maybe ninety pounds soaking wet. She's wearing leggings and a tank top. Where do you think she's packing a gun?"

The guy didn't crack a smile.

"Okay, first of all, I'm five foot *two*," Ashley said, eyes narrowed at Lexi as she lifted her arms the way Heath had. "And I'll have you know, I'm a hundred and *ten* pounds. Well, maybe a hundred and eleven, thanks to that pizza you ordered last night."

"You ate my leftovers?" Lexi asked, an eagle eye on the guy searching Ash.

"Every last bite."

The guy finished with Ashley and turned to Lexi, a gleam in his eyes. She forced herself to look bored. "When we're done here, I would like to talk to your HR department to lodge a complaint."

No Neck almost smiled, she could tell. She very purposely didn't look at Heath as the guy ran his hands over her. She'd been very secretly dreaming of having hands on her, but the guard's big sweaty meat-cleaver hands were the wrong ones.

Then those hands went to her backside, where she had envelope number four stuffed in the back pocket of her jeans.

"Hey," Heath said, voice cold and commanding. "Easy."

The guard grinned at him, but took his hands off Lexi. "You're all clean."

"Duh," Ashley said.

Lexi was done with this. "Vinny Jr. Now."

No Neck disappeared inside the back office. Just as Lexi was sure they were about to be kicked out on their asses, he reappeared. "He'll see you."

Lexi stepped forward, her hand in Ashley's, Heath at her other side.

The guard put a hand on Heath's chest. "Just the chicks."

"Not happening," Heath said, face blank, expression hard. "Come on, ladies, we're out."

Lexi turned to him and spoke softly. "We're already here."

He opened his mouth, but she knew what he would say, so she gently set a finger on his lips and kept her face even for anyone watching, her voice nothing more than a whisper for him alone. "We'll be quick."

He didn't move a muscle, his gaze still locked on the security guards, who—judging by the tic in his jaw and the hair standing at the back of her neck—were staring at her ass. "We'll be okay, we just need to get it done."

His eyes slid to hers at that. "Right. So you can leave."

"Here?" she asked in disbelief. "You want to do this here?"

"You're not going to back down." He made a sound that was the embodiment of male frustration. "Of course you're not. You've never backed down, not one day in your life."

Very true, so she had no idea why she let that sting. But here was the thing. This wasn't about him, or them, or even her. It was about Daisy. Through these letters and the strangers Lexi had met delivering them, she'd learned so much more about her mom than she'd ever known or thought possible. She'd learned about herself too. She wanted to see this through, but her reasons had changed. She no longer cared about whether there would be money left over for her. Whether she admitted it out loud or not, this trip to Sunrise Cove had changed her life. For the better. "In and out, fast," she promised. "Just stay here, right outside the door."

"A lot can happen behind a damn door, Lexi."

"We'll be fine. I promise you."

Resigned, Heath looked into her eyes and nodded. "I know you will."

Something warm in her chest turned over. Always believing in her, a shockingly powerful feeling. So she took Ashley by the hand and together they walked into the office.

The door immediately shut at their backs. And at her side, Ashley sucked in a breath. Lexi didn't look at her but instead at the man who sat behind his desk looking like a gym rat who ate steroids for breakfast, lunch, and dinner.

And Lexi began to doubt.

But not Ashley. Nope, her tiny little badass sister walked right up to the desk and held out her hand. "Hi, Vinny. I'm Daisy Fontaine's daughter, Ashley. This is my sister, Lexi. It's really nice to meet you. Your dad and our mom were great friends."

Vinny studied her a long moment, then Lexi, face cold as ice. "My dad doesn't have friends."

Still smiling sweetly, Ashley leaned against his desk. "You clearly didn't know my mom. She could befriend a . . ." She seemed to struggle for the right word and glanced at Lexi for help.

"A mob boss in pinstripes?" she offered.

Ashley bit her lower lip, trying to hide her smile.

Vinny didn't look amused, but he took the envelope Lexi pulled from her back pocket. Pulling out the letter, he read it silently, but Lexi, who'd spent a whole bunch of years spying treasures in plain sight, had long ago learned to read upside down.

Dear Vinny,

I once promised you that I was a woman of my word. I know it took me longer than expected to pay you back, but the money's here in full. Thank you for being such a class act and not breaking my kneecaps.

Daisy

Vinny set the letter aside and looked at the check dispassionately. "This isn't enough."

Lexi tilted her head. "So you *do* remember her."

Vinny met her gaze, his still cold. "My dad charged twenty percent interest. I charge thirty. And for every second you stand here, it goes up."

"You do realize we didn't have to deliver this money to begin with," Lexi said, subtly scanning the room for options to escape in a hurry that didn't involve screaming for Heath, who she knew would burn this place down to the ground to get them out safely if he had to.

"And yet," Vinny said, "here you two are, delivered like a Christmas present. And to think, I haven't believed in Santa since I was five years old."

"The debt isn't even owed by us, it was between Daisy and Vinny Sr.," Ashley said.

Lexi whipped her head to her sister, who'd said *Daisy*, not Mom. "Ash—"

"*Not now*," her sister snapped.

Vinny looked amused. And something else, something much darker, that had Lexi's heart kicking into a higher gear—which was saying something, since it'd been close to stroke level since they walked into this office. She quickly grabbed her sister's hand. "We're going now."

Vinny stood up. "You aren't going anywhere until that interest is paid."

"Bummer, because I just remembered I left my oven on." Ashley flashed a smile short of her usual wattage. "I don't like wasting energy."

"You think this is funny?" Vinny's eyes were hard as he came around the desk. "I'll show you both funny—"

"Stop," Lexi said, backing up and yanking Ashley along with her. "Take another step, and we'll start screaming."

"You think one single person out there's going to give a shit? Scream away. Even if someone's dumb enough to barge in here, they'd have to get through Brett and Bones first."

"No problem," Ashley said. "My sister here has a black belt ten times over."

Vinny's mouth quirked. "Brett and Bones are black belts a trillion times over."

Fine, so he had a sense of humor after all, but Lexi didn't, not when he reached for Ashley and shoved her up against the desk.

Lexi moved without a plan, grabbing an industrial-size staple gun off the top of the filing cabinet at her right, as well as a hefty glass baseball paperweight. To get Vinny to turn away from her sister, she said, "Hey, what am I, chopped liver?"

In the movies, they always slo-mo'd these scenes, but in real life, it happened in a blink. Vinny grabbed her wrist, twisting it to try and get her to drop the staple gun. So she chucked the glass baseball.

At his head.

Unfortunately, he ducked, and as it smashed into the wall behind him, he straightened and smiled at her. "You're going to be fun."

Worried someone was about to come running to investigate the noise of the glass breaking, she reacted without thinking, reaching out and . . . stapling his nuts. Actually, she wasn't positive if she'd caught the frank or the beans. Mostly because she might've closed her eyes and hoped for the best.

With a squeak, Vinny keeled over, hitting the floor hard.

Ashley pushed up from the desk, eyes wide, pupils blown with shock. "Oh my God, is he dead?"

The groan that escaped him told her no. It also told her they had only seconds before he called out for help, which would cause No Neck and Goon Two, aka Brett and Bones, to go after first Heath and then them.

"What do we do?" Ashley panic-whispered.

Lexi's thoughts raced as fast as her heart. "We're going to walk right out of here like nothing happened."

They slipped out the door, quickly shutting it behind them. Brett and Bones stood five feet in front of the door, their backs to the office. Lexi tugged Ashley past them, giving a little wave and an everything's-perfectly-okay-and-your-asshole-boss-certainly-didn't-just-have-his-nuts-stapled smile.

Heath straightened from where he'd been leaning against an unused pool table just beyond the guards, facing them. Though everything about his relaxed, calm body suggested someone at ease, there was a tightness in his face, a coiled-up energy that gave away his worry. At the sight of them, he relaxed only marginally as he seemed to linger on Lexi's face, taking her pulse without having to touch her. At whatever he saw, he didn't say a word, just hustled them across the room toward the exit, opening the front door for them.

She couldn't help but let out a breathless laugh. "We're running from bad guys, and you're taking time to open the door for us?"

"Chivalry isn't dead," he said in a calm voice that somehow soothed her nerves.

She still had a grip on Ashley when they cleared the building. "You okay?"

"Yes." Ashley beamed at her. "You were *amazing* back there."

Heath was scanning their surroundings as they moved quickly but casually to the parking lot. "What happened?"

"You should've seen it," Ashley said. "Lexi stapled Vinny's nuts."

Heath's head swiveled to Lexi.

"I told you I could handle myself."

There was a small smile about his mouth as they got to his car. "Get in, badass. I don't want to have to tangle with the B team. I don't have a stapler on me."

"She had a big, heavy glass baseball too. Shattered it against a wall. It was awesome."

Heath smiled, looking impressed. As they tore out of the lot, Ashley poked her head over the center console from the back. "How's your wrist?" she asked Lexi.

Heath frowned. "What's wrong with your wrist?"

"Vinny twisted it to get her to let go of the glass paperweight," Ashley said. "But don't worry. She didn't let go. She threw it at his head. Too bad he ducked."

Heath didn't say anything, but Lexi was pretty sure he was almost smiling. At the first pharmacy they passed, he stopped. He vanished inside and came back out with a bag of supplies. He opened Lexi's door and pulled her from the vehicle. Gently pushing her sweater up her arm, he examined her arm, probing a little. When she grimaced, a twinge of ire hit his eyes as he dug into the bag. He wrapped her wrist, then pulled her into him, pressing his cheek to the top of her head. Just holding on to her. Like she meant something.

"I'm fine," she said, but she held on too. He cared about her, like, truly cared. She'd almost missed it, since his whole vibe was so chill. Even taking care of everyone in his orbit, and some who weren't, he liked to live his life as stress-free as possible. He could do that because he knew what it was like to be over-worked, overwhelmed, and anxious all the time. These days, he made a point of trying to enjoy every moment.

Lexi wanted to learn to do the same.

"You need to rest the wrist," he said.

Ashley leaned out the back passenger window. "You know she's too stubborn to rest, right?"

Lexi huffed against Heath's sternum. "I'm not stubborn."

Heath gave her an amused look. "Only you would be stubborn about being stubborn."

Ashley rolled up her window, giving them the illusion of privacy. Heath said something about being serious that she shouldn't use her wrist. Lexi nodded. He said something about taking care of herself. She nodded. He said something about staring at his ass. She nodded— Oh, damn.

With a laugh, he nudged her back into the car, getting them onto the highway and pointed toward home.

Home . . .

When they'd merged with traffic, Heath slid his gaze to her. "Remind me to never tangle with you."

A pang reverberated in her chest, but she gave a small smile. "Too late for that."

CHAPTER 22

The following night after dinner, Heath stood in his grand-pa's backyard. He'd been restoring an old sideboard for Misty, which had been passed down to her from her grand-mother. The brass accents had tarnished, and were made worse by Cole's fumbling attempts at cleaning before he'd given up and dumped the sideboard on Heath.

He'd carefully mixed up a homemade remedy and applied it to the brass. Since the paste needed to stay on for at least half an hour, he'd stepped outside. Tipping his head back, he stared up at the stars. He'd been to a lot of different places in his various travels, first for work, then later, when he actually had two pen-nies to rub together, for pleasure. But nothing and no place ever compared to Sunrise Cove.

Tahoe at night had to be experienced to be believed.

Especially here, with no city or streetlights, where the sliver of a moon and countless stars scattered across the sky cast the land around him in an illuminating blue glow. A glow that somehow healed something deep inside him he hadn't even re-alized needed healing.

There was something else healing him as well. Someone else. Lexi.

He'd attempted to prevent himself falling for her. He'd failed. And now, every time he closed his eyes, all he could see were the sisters escaping Vinny's office, and his heart stopped all over again. All he'd wanted to do was yank Lexi in close and hold on tight.

And that had been before she'd turned to Ashley with such worry and lingering terror in her eyes, her voice shaking as she demanded to know if she was okay.

The way Ashley had smiled at the question told him that they'd bonded at last.

Not that he could tear his gaze off Lexi, his entire being focused on the beautiful worried heart in front of him, beating and pushing and . . . *trying*.

"He's not listening to us," Grandpa said from his perch on a lounger, his personal favorite stargazing perch.

"Not even a little bit," Cole said from another lounger.

Heath rolled his eyes and reached for the Oreo milkshake Cole had brought as a bribe.

"What I said was . . ." His grandpa raised his voice as if Heath was deaf instead of purposefully ignoring him. "That you only drink your calories when you're moping."

Matty, who'd been snoozing in his dad's lap, lifted his head and zeroed in on what his uncle held. With a gasp, he sat up and gave Heath the gimme hands. "Unkie Heef! Me me me!"

"Wha . . ." Heath hugged the last little bit of the milkshake to his chest. "It's spicy, you won't like it."

Matty catapulted himself off the lounge, straight at Heath, who leapt forward to catch him.

"Pweeze!"

Holding the kid in his arms, Heath looked to his brother. "Your Mini-Me is harassing me."

"Hey," Misty said, waddling out of the house, holding her own Oreo milkshake. "The uncle's supposed to be the good guy and share."

Mentally kissing the last of his milkshake goodbye, Heath pressed his forehead to Matty's and smiled at him. "What's the secret password?"

The kid grinned. "I wuv you."

Heath handed the cup over, then ruffled the kid's hair. "Love you too, little man."

Matty sucked down the drink with loud gulps without breathing, then dramatically stopped to gasp for air before racing off to run in circles.

Sugar overload . . . check.

Mayhem woke up and joined the kid in racing around. Then suddenly he stopped and hunched to poop.

Matty stopped short as well and . . . started stripping.

"Not in the yard!" Misty shouted as Matty crouched low to join in the pooping activities. "Cole!"

Cole was laughing too hard to get up.

"Seriously?" Misty asked him. "We've discussed this a million times." She looked imploringly at Heath. "No one ever told me that when you get a husband, the ears are sold separately."

Heath snorted, but headed for the kid. When Grandpa made to get up too, reaching to unbutton *his* pants, Heath pointed at him. "Don't even think about it."

"Fun-sucker."

Five minutes later, after failing to stop Poop-Gate, Heath held a very pleased-with-himself Matty while simultaneously hosing down the patio. He eyed the wilting strawberry plants he had hanging from the covered patio beams. "Why are you dying?" he asked them.

"Ashley's strawberries are blooming," Cole said. "She claims it's Lexi's doing. I guess she caught her talking to all of their plants, and now they're thriving. You should ask her."

"He can't ask her for help," Grandpa said. "One, because he never asks for help. And two, he likes her. He's especially not going to ask for help from someone he's trying to get lucky with."

Heath rubbed the spot between his eyes where a headache was forming.

Cole, the ass, cackled.

Misty looked intrigued. "How do you know he likes her?"

"He doesn't know shit," Heath said.

"Language!" Misty's head whipped to Matty.

"He doesn't know *shit*," Matty repeated, getting the inflection perfect. "He doesn't know *shit*. Shit, shit, shit."

Misty glared at Heath.

Grimacing, he looked his nephew in the eye. "I'm getting a time-out for using that word, so if you don't want to do the same, don't say it again."

"He doesn't know shit!" Matty yelled cheerfully.

Heath face-palmed.

"Did you know Heath kissed Lexi?" Grandpa asked.

Everyone's head swiveled to Grandpa.

"Yep," the old man said. "Right here in this yard."

Heath's headache arrived in full force. "Your intel is faulty."

"If that's true," Misty said, "why are you blushing?"

"I don't blush." At least, he hoped not.

"You totally are."

"Stop, or I'll teach Matty some more bad words."

Misty jabbed a finger at him. "When you have kids, I'm buying them a drum set." She looked at Grandpa. "How sure are you about him and Lexi?"

"I might be hard of hearing, but I've got the eyes of a cat. I know what I saw. And he most definitely kissed Lexi."

"Actually, technically, Lexi kissed Heath," Cole said.

Heath turned his head to look at him, brows up.

His brother shrugged. "I was checking out the saved footage from the backyard cam, looking to see if I'd left my wallet on the picnic table."

"Violation of privacy much?" Grandpa asked.

Heath threw his hand out, palm up, in Grandpa's direction. "What he said."

Cole rolled his eyes as he looked at his wife. "You're right, babe, he's definitely caught the virus."

"What virus?" Heath wanted to know.

"The L-word virus. *L-o-v-e*." His brother leaned back, hands resting behind his head, cocky as hell. Heath half expected him to kiss his own biceps. He was considering swiping that look off his brother's face with his fist when he heard footsteps. He didn't have to turn and look, he could tell by the way his stupid heart picked up the pace who it was. Surprise hit first, quickly followed by a whole bunch of other emotions that tangled all together.

Lexi appeared, her expression saying she wasn't sure of her welcome. So he straightened and gave her a small but welcoming smile, while flipping his family off behind his back. All while hoping she hadn't heard any of their idiotic conversation.

Lexi smiled at everyone and gave a little wave. "Sorry if I'm interrupting."

"Is this one of them booty calls?" Grandpa asked. "Because if so, we can skedaddle."

Cole shoved his own milkshake at the old man. "Drink. It's a better use of your mouth."

"What, an old man can't say booty call?"

"Please ignore him," Heath said to Lexi.

Lexi smiled at his grandpa. "You enjoying your evening?"

"Better now that you're here. This gang, they're boring. Maybe you can liven things up. How did you meet the big guy here? He's so closemouthed. I heard something about school, but I was working around the clock back then."

"They were in second grade," Cole said helpfully. "He used to come home talking about some girl he could never beat at anything."

"Oh, he beat me at plenty," Lexi said on a laugh. "Actually, I think he beat me at most everything."

Heath shook his head. "Not true. You beat me in the three-legged race in second grade, winning the Lego train set I would have traded Cole for."

Cole rolled his eyes. Heath ignored him. "And then in third grade, you won the cursive writing contest and got to skip that week's test. In fourth grade, you beat me at the jumping jacks competition, and for the next month everyone made fun of me getting beaten by a tiny little slip of a girl who looked like a light wind could knock her over."

Lexi laughed, and there was something in her expression, affection and a warmth that in turn warmed him from the inside out.

"I know you threw that one, by the way," she said. "You let me win."

He shook his head. "You won fair and square. And I didn't even care because it was the first time I ever saw you smile at me for real."

She bit her lower lip, staring at him. "It's funny how, in the moment, you think everything's bad. But then later, looking back, you realize some of what you experienced not only molded you, but made you look at the world differently. Better."

"Agreed. Looking back, I counted on you to push me, to make me try harder, to make me laugh, to give me . . . I don't know, some badly needed comfort in the normal, I guess. And it was . . . everything."

Grandpa had stopped smiling, looking grim at the reminder of what Heath and Cole had been through during those years, but also clearly touched by Heath's words. By realizing how much Lexi meant to him back then—and now. But Heath had given their audience enough, and he slid Cole a look.

Always a quick study, his brother jumped up. "Right," he said. He scooped up Matty and helped Misty out of her chair, before giving a chin jerk to Grandpa. "We're heading out, and I'm taking you with me."

"Aw, but it's just getting good."

"We've got chips," Cole said in a singsong bribing voice, the same he used on Matty.

"With dip?" Grandpa asked.

"With dip."

Cole leaned into Heath. "Veggie chips and hummus, he'll never even realize. And you owe me a babysitting evening the next time I need a date to kiss up to my beautiful wife."

"Friday night," Misty said without missing a beat. "The *whole* night."

Matty, covered in the last of Heath's milkshake, grinned and drooled at the same time.

And then they were all gone.

Heath turned to Lexi. "Sorry about the circus."

"They're not. They're . . . lovely." She shook her head. "Don't be sorry for having a family that loves you enough to give you plenty of shit." At his grimace, she gave him a small smile. "I love how close you all are." She walked over to the sideboard he'd been working on. "Gorgeous." She ran her finger over the inlaid wood that now gleamed under his care. "A vintage 1950s inlaid mahogany and brass sideboard and bar cart. Worth between three and four grand."

"Really?"

"Leaving the brass with the original patina can keep the value high, but you're cleaning it. So now it depends on if you can get that brass to come back to life without damage."

"It belonged to Misty's grandma. Misty doesn't want to sell it, she wants to use it in their home, and she wants the brass untarnished. Cole had a go at it before I could stop him, so now we've got no choice."

She nodded, crouching low to study it more carefully, eyes sharp, mouth soft. She loved this stuff, he realized. Really loved it. "What are you using?"

"Lemon juice and baking soda."

She nodded her approval. Then she reached into the bucket of warm water, pulled out the cloth he had in it, and wrung it out. She looked at him in silent query.

"Have at it," he said.

So she did.

He joined her, and they worked in silence for a while, a surprisingly comfortable one. Or maybe not so surprisingly, since working together on a common goal, be it delivering envelopes or taking each other to bed, had never been their problem.

Their problem was conquering their individual fears.

"That was a nice story you told your family about when we were kids. About me making you laugh, making you . . . feel some comfort." She laughed a little, but it sounded forced. She had her head down, concentrating on the task at hand, which she was amazing at. Something stirred within him, a true affection for her that warmed a spot deep in his chest that had been cold for a long time. "You really sold it too."

"Lex, it wasn't just a story. I've meant everything I've ever said to you."

She nodded as if she didn't quite trust her voice. Then, head still down, eyes on the task, she said, "Dean. My last boyfriend's name is Dean. I told you that we worked together. He was actually my boss."

Above her, he quietly set his forehead to the wood and closed his eyes, breathing through the sudden violence in his blood, knowing he was going to hate this story.

"He was in charge of verifying all appraisals and reporting to the clients on the value of their estates. He had me doing most of it, but he took on the really high-dollar stuff. He always said the powers that be insisted on him overseeing estates over a certain threshold." She paused to rinse out the cloth in the water. "But then there were a few of those in a row, and suddenly he had me do them. Said he was training me to be his replacement when he got his promotion. He'd been working toward that for months. Grooming me. Or so I thought."

Yeah. He'd been right. He was going to hate this.

"Then a set of bronze cherub garland planters from the 1800s, a rare pair in mint condition, easily worth fifteen thousand dollars, went missing. And I'd been the last person to have eyes on them. An internal investigation was launched, and in the middle of that, an early nineteenth-century shaker apothecary worth forty K vanished. And again, I'd been the last one to log it. They, um . . ." She looked away. "At first, I was put on leave without pay, but later let go. They claimed it was budget cuts, but it wasn't. Only I hadn't done any of it. I'd never—"

"Lexi." Slowly he stood, not wanting her to stop talking, but needing to make sure she understood something. "I know you wouldn't."

She stared at him, those honey-brown eyes suspiciously bright as she swallowed hard and nodded.

"Tell me this Dean asshole was caught."

An utterly mirthless laugh escaped her. "How do you know it was him?"

"Because of the betrayal and devastation in your eyes."

She didn't say anything for a moment, then shook her head and looked away. "Everyone assumes it was me, even people I worked with for years, because only two people had access. Me and . . . him. The thing is, he's charming and charismatic. He's got a certain way with people. Everyone loves him, trusts him implicitly."

Yeah, he really wanted his hands around the guy's neck.

"I mean, even I didn't believe it was him at first," she said. "I just couldn't fathom that it might be someone I trusted. Someone I . . . cared about. But I've been over all of it a million times in my head. I don't know who else it could have been."

He felt her pain, felt it like a knot deep in his chest. He couldn't imagine the betrayal, made all the worse because she'd never seen it coming.

"The investigation is ongoing." She shrugged. "If they're looking for proof of my guilt, they won't find it. It's simply not there. As far as I know, they haven't found proof of *anyone's* guilt."

"Why wasn't Dean let go as well?"

"He's never even been under suspicion. It's just my gut feeling, there's no proof. Plus, he's the nephew of the CEO. Honestly, I think he did it for the thrill."

"How long ago did all this happen?"

"Six months before I came out here."

"Is that when you stopped seeing each other?"

"Just before that, yes. He said it wasn't working out for him. A week after he said I might be the One."

"I'm so sorry." He let out a breath. "What have you been doing since then?"

"Unfortunately, word travels fast in the field, and no one was willing to hire me." She shrugged. "Just before I came here, I'd gone through the last of my savings and had been taking on small independent jobs to keep myself afloat." She shook her head. "I still can't believe it happened, that I was *that* stupid and trusting, that desperate for affection. I was an easy mark."

"No."

She met his gaze, enough surprise there that he knew he hadn't done a good job of letting her know how amazing he found her. "You're smart, Lexi. So smart and fierce and . . . incredible." He moved to her as she stood. "The world's brighter with you in it."

"I . . ." She swallowed hard and looked away. "Thank you."

He couldn't imagine the depths of hurt and betrayal she'd faced alone. And then she'd come here, where she'd had to face the hurt and betrayal of her past.

But at least this time, she wasn't alone.

She rolled her shoulders like they ached.

"Are you hurting?" he asked.

"Just sore from going through and moving Daisy's stuff."

"We've got a hot tub that's magic on sore muscles. He gestured to the far side of the patio. Moving to it, he raised the lid, and steam rose in tendrils to the night sky. "Do you want to try it?"

"I . . ." She eyed the water with a longing that he wouldn't have minded seeing aimed at him. She looked around as if assessing how out in the open they were. "I don't know."

He turned to the wall of the house and hit a switch. The patio lights went off, plunging them into the dark, with only the stars above giving off an unearthly glow. The night had gone quiet, the only sounds being a gentle breeze ruffling the trees and the bubbling from the jets of the hot tub.

But he knew Lexi wouldn't do something nice for herself unless goaded into it. So . . . he kicked off his shoes, removed his socks.

"What are you—" She broke off when he pulled off his shirt. "Um . . ."

"I ran hard this morning. I'm hurting too."

Her eyes, which had been satisfyingly glued to his bare chest, rose to his face. He'd given her the magic words—*I'm hurting*.

"How bad?" she asked.

"Enough that a soak will work miracles." His hands went to the buttons on his Levi's, and her eyes widened. "What if someone sees?"

He shrugged. "Grandpa's gone for the night. The closest neighbor is Ashley, and she's at her book club tonight. There's no one to see, but even if there was, all the lights are off." He flashed her a challenging grin. "But if you're too chicken—"

That made her eyes flash. "I'm not chicken—" Her eyes locked on to his fingers, currently on the last button of his jeans. "I just . . ."

He shoved his jeans off, and she sucked in a breath. He raised a brow and prodded her. "You just . . . ?"

"Um . . ." She took in his black knit boxers, fitting a little snugger with each second she stared at him. "I don't have a bathing suit."

"Me either." And then he removed the boxers.

She made a low sound of . . . He couldn't be sure, but it sounded a whole bunch like a whimper of desire. To hide his smile, he turned and climbed into the tub.

LEXI KNEW SHE should walk away. That if she did what she wanted—climbing into the hot tub and straddling Heath— she'd lose herself in him. And that would be . . .

What? Would it be that bad to let herself have this? Him? It was hard to think about any possible consequences when she wanted him so badly. And he very clearly wanted her as well, so why not seize the moment?

Heath leaned back, water swirling around his chest, arms spread on the ledge, watching her with dark, playful eyes and that calm patience.

A panther watching its prey.

"What are you thinking?" his deep voice asked, penetrating her thoughts.

What was she doing? Lusting. Drooling . . . which, given that mischievous gleam, he knew. Time to get him back. "I'm thinking that a good . . . *soak* . . . sounds like just what I need," she said casually, and pulled off her shirt.

Slowly.

His gaze never left hers as she took a few steps toward the

tub. "I'm thinking . . ." she continued, losing her shoes and socks, "how much I want to have that soak with *you*."

Now he was drooling. Good. Her jeans went next, leaving her in nothing but pink lace, which, given that he appeared to stop breathing, he liked. A lot. And when she dropped that lace to the floor, he let out a low, very male groan that empowered her to climb into the hot tub and straddle him.

He slid an arm around her, pulling her into him, his free hand, big and warm, cupping her jaw. She pressed her face against his callused palm, her heart thundering in her chest.

He had once thought of her as comfort. No one else ever had, she marveled, but then he swept her hair to the side, exposing her neck so he could gently nibble the sensitive spot where her shoulder and throat met, and her brain stopped working. At the first touch of his hot mouth, she shivered and her skin pebbled in response, and when he touched his tongue to the spot, she moaned.

"Mmmm. Love that sound," he murmured against her neck, his hands cupping her breasts as his talented mouth traced its way to her ear. "Gonna make you do it again. And again."

"Someone's pretty sure of themselves." Her wobbly voice betrayed her need, and he smiled, a wicked, dirty smile, and kissed her hot and deep.

She heard someone moan his name. Her, of course, and he pulled back to look at her, his eyes roaming over her face and body, his expression pure, raw lust, but also a deep, abiding, warm affection, none of which he tried to hide from her.

This Heath, warm and sexy and highly motivated to drive her insane with hunger and need, heated her blood and stole her breath, right along with her sanity. It stripped her bare, both figuratively and literally as his hands danced over her skin, igniting feelings she didn't know she had. This was the unvarnished version of Heath Bowman. No inhibitions, just one hundred percent sexy, intuitive, driven male intent on plowing through all her caution cones with single-minded focus, and . . .

For once, she was going to let him.

CHAPTER 23

Lexi woke up confused and alone, and not in her own bed. She lay on soft sheets. Pillows from heaven.

Naked.

Her clothes, mingled with the clothes Heath had been wearing last night, were scattered on the floor.

She'd fallen asleep in Heath's bed.

And now the sun slanted in the window, highlighting the fact that she wore nothing but some whisker burns. Then the scent hit her.

Bacon.

Coffee.

God, she could love him for that alone, and she jumped out of bed, pulling on her clothes so fast her head spun. Following the scent of food down the hallway, she could see, through the doorway into the kitchen, something else—something even more delicious than bacon.

Heath, his back to her, wearing nothing but soft black sleep pants low-slung on his hips, hair mussed, standing in front of the stove. The kitchen lighting caught on every muscle, the effect devastating on her self-control. So was the knowing smile he flashed her over his shoulder as he flipped a pancake with an easy flick of his wrist.

"I'm starving," she said, entering the kitchen. "I think we burned at least a million calories each last night—"

A delicate snort sounded, and she nearly died on the spot as she pivoted to find Cole, Misty, and Grandpa Gus sitting at the table eating. Mayhem lay under the table, head on his paws, clearly waiting for food to fall, but he did lift his head at the sight of her and pant a hello. Also under the table . . . Matty, naked, gumming a banana.

The Bowmans had multiplied.

Lexi really hoped that had happened long after Heath had woken her up somewhere around dawn. With his mouth . . . A sound escaped her, like a squeak of a mouse caught in a trap.

Cole's lips tilted up in unrepentant amusement as he studied her over the lip of his coffee cup.

Misty nudged her husband, muttering something beneath her breath about "don't be an ass." She looked at Lexi. "We brought Grandpa home and forced Heath to make us breakfast because out of all of us, he's the best cook."

Grandpa was wearing a Cheshire cat grin. "I'm going to assume you had a good night . . ."

Dear God. Where was a big fat black hole when one needed it? Just as she started to whirl and walk—run—out, Heath gave her a finger crook. His eyes were soft, his mouth too, as he smiled at her like maybe she'd hung the sun and the moon.

"Aw!" Misty elbowed Cole. "You used to look at me like that."

"Still do, baby."

They kissed sweetly as Lexi moved to Heath's side. He'd reached for a second pan on a different burner, flipping the pancakes bubbling there, mashing his lips together to withhold his amusement.

At her.

She shifted to hide her hand as she pinched his muscular ass. Hard. "You could have warned me," she whispered.

"I was being a gentleman and letting you sleep in."

"You know, because of the million calories you burned off all night," Cole said helpfully from the table.

Lexi groaned and dropped her forehead to Heath's shoulder. With a low laugh, he brushed a kiss to her temple. "Don't worry about him. He's not going to say another thing about it in your presence. Not if he wants to keep breathing."

"You two are no fun at all," Cole said around a bite of bacon, clearly not in the least worried about his future breathing.

A drop of pancake batter hit the floor, and Mayhem scrambled out from beneath the table and came running, his tongue mopping up the spill. Then he sat and looked hopefully up at Heath, his tail thumping to remind Heath what a good, well-behaved boy he was.

Heath snorted and tossed him a strawberry. Then he filled a plate with bacon, eggs, and pancakes, and handed it to Lexi. Then, a warm hand at her back, he gently nudged her to the table, pulling out a chair for her. Soon as she sat, he smiled and leaned down, giving her a sweet, smacking kiss before scooping up Cole's still half-full plate and . . . offering it to Matty under the table.

Matty cackled in glee, tossing Mayhem a bite of bacon. The dog gave a joyous bark of excitement and gobbled it up in the blink of an eye.

"You didn't even taste that," Heath admonished.

"Real mature," Cole grumbled at his brother, and, fork still in hand, turned to his wife, eyeing her food.

Misty hunched over her plate, guarding it with one hand as she shoveled in food with the other. "I love you, Cole, to the moon and back and all," she said around a mouthful, "but touch my plate, and I'll stab you with the knife you were dumb enough to leave within my reach. And then I'll finish eating right over your dead body."

Cole blinked. "Did I tell you how beautiful you look today?"

She snorted. "You can relax. I wouldn't really kill you."

"Well, that's good to know."

"Because if I have to go through labor again, so do you."

"Right."

Misty sent Lexi an apologetic grimace. "Normally, I'm a lot nicer than this. Well, nice with a sprinkle of sorry-I-lost-my-shit. I don't usually threaten people with bodily harm. I'm more the type of woman who helps her husband look for his candy that I already ate."

Cole narrowed his eyes. "I knew it!"

Lexi laughed. "No judgment," she told Misty, and then dug in. Stilled. *Moaned.* "Oh my God, this is amazing."

Heath brought her a mug of coffee, running a hand up and down her spine. "Glad you like."

Misty nudged Cole. "My new favorite fantasy is you serving me like that."

Cole smiled at her with the love and affection that came from a longtime, solid relationship. "You've come up with better fantasies than that."

"You're right. Would you like to hear my latest and wildest fantasy?"

Cole smirked. "Oh yeah."

"Me sleeping through the night and waking up to a clean house, a fit body, no wrinkles, laundry done and put away, a full buffet breakfast with no calories, and a million bucks in my purse."

Cole choked on a sip of his coffee. "I was thinking something easier and far more fun. Like your favorite, the pirate and maiden, where I—"

"*Out*," Heath said.

"But it's just getting good," Misty said.

"Which is why you're leaving."

"Why doesn't Grandpa have to leave?" Cole asked.

"'Cuz I live here." Grandpa leaned in and refilled Lexi's cup, gently clicking his mug to hers with a wink.

Lexi had to laugh. He was incorrigible, and she wondered if Heath would be just like him when he got older. And then she wondered why she wondered, since she didn't believe in happily-ever-afters.

Even if a secret little part of her really wanted to.

Cole delayed their leaving to help Heath with the dishes while Misty tried to gather all their stuff.

"I used to be so low-maintenance. I never even carried a purse," Misty said conversationally, picking up toys and diapers, stuffing them back into her massive diaper bag. "These days I'm more a pack mule."

Lexi laughed. "But you have a lovely family."

"I do. Cole's amazing, and Heath . . ." Her eyes danced. "He's been smiling more lately. Which has something to do with you, I'm betting. I think you've reminded him of things he's forgotten."

Something deep in Lexi's belly quivered. "Like what?"

"That he is of value far beyond what he can do for people. He tends to forget that he's loved." She smiled. "You're good for him."

"Oh. I'm not sure what we're—"

Misty smiled. "I'm not trying to pry. I just wanted you to know how much it means to us to see him happy." She paused. "And that if you want a friend in town who you're not related to or doesn't have testosterone, I'm your girl."

That simple act of Misty reaching out, offering friendship with no strings attached, seemed to brush against all the scars in Lexi's heart.

Then Misty surprised her further by hugging her tight before shouldering her bag, taking Matty by the hand, and heading out.

Maybe . . . just maybe it wasn't a secret *little* part of her that wanted to believe in happily-ever-afters. Maybe it was a secret *big* part of her.

CHAPTER 24

At the end of the week, Lexi woke up to find Ashley sitting cross-legged on the end of her bed. Lexi hadn't gotten much sleep—Heath had left somewhere around dawn, which she only even vaguely remembered—and she'd hoped to hit the snooze button three or four or a hundred times.

She and Heath had spent every night since Hot *Hot* Tub Adventure in one of their beds or the other. It'd been the best week of her life, even if she was so tired she wanted to stay asleep all day . . . "Unless you're hiding breakfast behind you, I'm not ready to wake up."

"It's envelope day."

Damn, she'd nearly forgotten. With a sigh, she sat up. "Have stapler, will travel. Where are we going this time?"

Ashley was already off the bed and heading to the door. "Make it quick."

"But . . . where are we going—"

But nothing, because Ashley was already gone.

Lexi showered, dressed, and walked into the kitchen yawning so wide her jaw cracked. Heath stood leaning against the counter, doctoring up a mug of coffee, looking annoyingly fresh and not even the slightest bit tired. In fact, he looked downright chipper. She might've growled at him if he hadn't smiled that just-for-her smile and then handed over the coffee.

He laughed softly at whatever expression she wore. "Cute."

"Cute?"

"The way you look at me," he said.

She narrowed her eyes. "And how do I look at you?"

"Like I mean something to you."

Well, if that didn't cut right through her exhaustion and melt her damn heart, the one she hadn't thought could even be melted.

Ashley poked her head into the kitchen. "Let's do this!"

Just then Lexi's phone buzzed with an incoming call. She stared at the screen in shock. "It's my old work." She paused. "Why is it my old work?"

Ashley slipped her hand into Lexi's. "We've got you. No matter what."

She realized Heath had moved to her other side, his gaze echoing Ashley's sentiment.

"Answer it," her sister said softly, squeezing her hand.

So she did. "Hello?"

"Lexi, this is Bill Swanson." The head of HR. "Is this a good time?"

"Depends on what you're calling about," she said carefully.

And even though she hadn't been kidding, Bill chuckled. "I wanted to let you know, our internal investigation, along with an extensive external investigation, has concluded. Both our team and the authorities have cleared you fully."

Lexi blinked. "External investigation? Authorities?"

"As you were aware, we had missing valuables. From ten different clients. All totaled up, it came to almost a million dollars. Our insurance company insisted on going through the proper channels."

Lexi sank to a chair and let out a breath as wobbly as her knees. "Okay. And . . . ?"

"And . . . the person responsible has been charged and arrested."

"Who was it?" she asked.

Bill paused. "Dean Maddox."

She'd known, but somehow she was still shocked. Shocked to the core.

"I'm sorry it took so long," Bill said. "Even sorrier still that your life was affected."

Affected. Is that what he called losing her job, her pride, her means of making a living, and all sense of trust?

"We'd like to retro pay you for the past six months, and offer you the job back."

Lexi's heart had stopped when she'd seen the caller ID, then immediately kicked into high gear when Bill had started talking. All she could hear was the thump-thump, thump-thump, thump-thump of her own heartbeat in her ears.

"Lexi? You still there?"

"Yes." She had to shake herself. "I'll get back to you." Then she disconnected, set her phone on the table, and stared at it as a shocked laugh escaped her. "That was . . ."

"We could hear everything," Ashley said, and wrapped her arms around Lexi. "It's about time."

She was still shaking her head in shock when Ashley pulled away and it was Heath in front of her. There seemed to be a war of emotions on his face, but he also pulled her in for a warm hug. "Proud of you, Lex."

"I didn't do anything."

"You carried on. You persevered. You didn't let any of what happened break you."

"That's because she's the strongest person I know." Ashley looked at Lexi and smiled, this time with far less wattage. "You've got a lot to think about."

Did she though? With relief still running through her veins instead of blood, she glanced at Heath.

He merely held out an envelope.

Neither of them seemed inclined to push her for what she would or wouldn't do about her job, or future. She didn't know if that was a good or bad thing, but she couldn't think about it right now. Mindlessly, she took the envelope, and both she and Ashley stared down at Daisy's writing. The address was local, and unlike all the other envelopes, this one didn't have a name on it.

"Let's go," Heath said.

Lexi looked at him. "Where?"

Ashley, who'd been staring at the address, suddenly gasped. "Oh! I know! It's the ice cream shop!"

Lexi blinked. "You mean the ice cream shop where we shared that ice cream sundae the last time we . . ."

Ashley nodded. "One of the last times we were all together. You, me, Mom, and my dad. Right before you moved." Her smile faded, and so did Lexi's as they both swallowed hard.

"That's another one of my favorite memories of Mom," Lexi admitted.

Ashley's mouth trembled. "And it's my favorite memory with *you*."

Lexi hadn't realized until that very moment that sometimes really great things could pierce through her walls every bit as much as bad stuff. "How will we know who to give it to?"

"Call me when you get inside and are seated," Heath said.

Lexi and Ashley turned to him in tandem surprise.

"You're not going?" Lexi asked.

He shook his head. "You two got this."

"You're usually so happy to butt your way into everything," Ashley said.

Heath shrugged, and Lexi was pretty sure she knew why he'd backed off. After overhearing the call from her old work, and the offer of her job back, he didn't want to influence her decision.

But how could her feelings for him, for Ashley, for this place, *not* influence her decision? He gave a small, but very warm smile. If Ashley hadn't been there, she might have walked right into his arms. And maybe pushed him against the counter and had her merry way with him.

Her sister snorted. "You do realize I know the two of you have been sneaking around in each other's business every night, right?"

Lexi grimaced. "No." She paused. "Does it bother you?"

Ashley grinned and flung her arms around Lexi, squeezing tight. "Are you kidding? It's the opposite." She cupped Lexi's face. "You've been smiling and laughing so much that I hardly recognize you. I'm just so, so, *so* happy for you both. I *love* that you love each other."

Lexi blinked. "Whoa. It's not— We don't—"

"Ha! Got you!" Ashley said, and snagged the truck keys from Lexi's hand. "And it's my turn to drive!"

"Well, that was just mean," Lexi grumbled, and ignored Heath's snort. "I'm just gonna . . ." She gestured to the door where her sister had vanished.

He brushed a kiss against her temple, and trying not to melt, she ran out after Ashley. Climbing into the passenger seat of the truck, she glared at her sister. "Didn't know you had it in you to lie like that."

"Oh, I wasn't lying. You love him. You just haven't admitted it to yourself."

Which effectively ended the conversation. They drove toward the lake, and Ashley managed to only hit the sidewalk once when she took a right turn too tight.

"Lexi?"

She forced herself to loosen her grip on the Oh-Shit bar. "Yeah?"

"I want you to know I really, really, really want to talk about your phone call. I want to know what you're thinking, what you're going to do. But I also know that this isn't the time or place for that, so I'm trying to let it go. At least until you're ready to talk about it."

Lexi let out a relieved breath. "Thank you."

Ashley glanced, then returned her attention back to the road. "Damn."

"What?"

"That was reverse psychology. I'm pretty good at it too. I really thought you'd start running your mouth."

"Ash—"

"No, don't say whatever you were going to say. I'm rushing you. I need a speed bump between my brain and my mouth. I'm going to stop talking now."

Lexi slid her a dry look. "Are you?"

Ashley mimed zipping her lips and throwing away the key. Which lasted for all of two minutes. "I just wanted to say—"

"But you threw away the key."

Ashley sighed, and ten minutes later, they seated themselves in a booth in the back of the ice cream parlor on Lake Drive, with a stunning view of the granite-rock and pine-lined mountains surrounding the iconic Lake Tahoe.

Once they each had a big bowl of ice cream in front of them, Ashley called Heath on speaker. "We're here," she said. "We're armed with sugar. Who does this envelope go to?"

"Open it."

"Okay, but—"

But nothing, because Heath had disconnected.

"I keep telling him he needs to work on his phone manners," Ashley said, and pushed the large manila envelope to Lexi. "You do it."

Lexi nodded, but didn't make a move to take the envelope. Something told her she'd need more courage than she currently possessed, so she took a big bite of ice cream first, hoping the sugar would convert to bravery.

"Lexi?"

"Yeah. On it." With a deep breath, she opened the envelope and emptied the contents onto the table.

Two smaller envelopes. One labeled *Ashley*, the other *Lexi*.

"Huh," Ashley whispered, leaning back. "I didn't see that coming."

Lexi took another bite of ice cream, savoring a big chunk of chocolate as she stared at her name.

"It's Mom's writing," Ashley whispered. "Just like the others."

Lexi nodded, still watching her envelope like it might be a locked and loaded rattler.

"Okay, well, here goes nothing," Ashley said, and opened hers. There was a handwritten letter and a check turned face down. Her sister ignored the check and started reading the letter. A few seconds later, her eyes welled up.

"Ash?" Lexi reached across the table, wrapping her fingers around her sister's icy hand. "What is it?"

Ashley sniffed and read out loud:

Darling Ashley,

I'm so sorry, because if you're reading this, then I'm already gone. But Lexi's there with you, which means you're surrounded by love. How do I know? Because I know my Lexi, and she feels love more than anyone I've ever met, even though she can't always express it.

Oh, Ash. I miss you already. Having you in my life has made every single day more joyful. Even my shitty days. And I'm a big enough person to admit, there were far more shitty days than there should've been. I'm sorry about that too. But know that I've always fought to give you the best, and I'll never stop watching over you.

By now, you've delivered the first four envelopes. I know it looks bad how I got all this money, but I knew I was sick. I knew there wouldn't be a good ending. And I needed, more than anything, to make some things right. I needed to know you'd be okay, that you'd have a roof over your head no matter what. So when I beat the odds and actually won, the first thing I did was pay off the house. It's in your name. Sell it if you need, or live in it forever.

One more thing. Don't make the same mistakes I made. Family fights for one another, no matter what. *You know I think of you as my own flesh and blood, that I always fought for you. But I'm gone now, and your family's down to one. You and Lexi against the world. I hope you'll fight for her the way I should have. She deserves that, and whether she knows it or not, she needs you every bit as much as you need her. Please stick together, always and forever, in whatever capacity that turns out to be.*

I love you to the moon and back.

Love,
Mom

Ashley carefully set the letter down next to her ice cream. Tears streamed down her face, and she reached for the napkin dispenser on the table. It was empty.

"I've got it," Lexi said softly, glad for the moment to school her expression after the hit of hearing her mom say she'd fought for Ashley, something she'd never done for Lexi.

When she set down a full napkin dispenser in front of her sister, Ashley both cried and laughed. "Good call. Once you read yours, I'll probably start crying all over again."

Lexi didn't sit. She just shook her head as she shoved her envelope into her back pocket.

"Wait." Ashley blew her nose. "You . . . you're not opening yours?"

She couldn't, not when Ashley's letter had triggered all her deep-seated insecurities, the ones she held close to the vest. She wouldn't blame her mom if her own letter was filled with recriminations. She deserved it. She just couldn't bring herself to share it. "I'm not ready."

Ashley's shoulders fell. "Oh, Lex. I shouldn't have read mine out loud. I'm so sorry."

"Why? Because she fought for you, always?" Lexi could hear the ugly coming out of her mouth and couldn't stop it. "Why would you be sorry? It was her truth. It was her dying truth."

"I think . . ." Ashley swallowed hard. "I think you're missing the whole spirit of her letter. She had clear regrets—"

"She shouldn't." Lexi shook her head, nearly choking on her own vitriol. "I was horrible to her. I pushed her away, and I'll have to live with that for the rest of my life."

Ashley stood up and reached for Lexi's hand. "You were just a kid, not old enough to understand the ramifications. She didn't fight your dad for custody. She . . . she hung you out to dry, Lexi. Whatever's in your letter, I promise you it's going to make you feel better."

"You don't know that."

"I do."

Something in Ashley's gaze—guilt?—made Lexi freeze. "How, Ash? How do you know?"

Her sister bit her bottom lip and looked away.

Lexi's stomach jangled uncomfortably. *"Ash."*

Her sister stuffed a massive bite of ice cream into her mouth and then gestured to it with a sorry-I-have-a-mouthful grimace.

Lexi crossed her arms and waited her out, because in three, two, one—

"Ow!" Ashley howled around the huge bite, clenching her head. "Oh my God."

"Brain freeze?" Lexi asked with false sympathy. "That's what you get. Now, spit it out—"

"That's sacrilege," Ashley mumbled, eyes watering, holding her head onto her shoulders.

"Not the ice cream," Lexi said. "Your secret. Spit out your secret."

Ashley swallowed the ice cream and continued to grimace, holding her head.

"Press your tongue to the roof of your mouth."

Ashley did, then after about ten seconds sighed. "Better," she said softly.

Lexi couldn't say the same. "So you read the letters ahead of time. When? Right after she died? Have you known everything for the entire past year, then?"

Ashley slowly set her forehead onto the table. "And to think, I used to want to be an actress."

A horrible thought sank Lexi's stomach to her toes. "Let me guess. Daisy didn't stipulate that it had to be both of us delivering the envelopes, or that they needed to be spaced out. You did that so I'd come. And then stay." She crossed her arms. "How am I doing?"

Ashley lifted her face. "Please don't use this as an excuse to leave and take your old job back."

Lexi nearly staggered back. "So I'm right, then, about all of it." She couldn't believe her voice sounded so calm, so blasé. "You read all the letters ahead of time. Even mine. You made up the stipulation about me having to deliver them with you, then easily discarded that rule when it suited your purposes."

"You're right, but also wrong." Ashley's eyes swam with tears. "You don't understand—"

"Actually, I understand perfectly. You needed to ensure I'd come, so you lied." She held up her hand when Ashley started to say something. "Don't. Just don't. I need . . ." *To be far, far away from here, somewhere I can think.* "I need to go." She eyed her perfect ice cream. She deserved it, so she snatched it up and headed for the door.

"Lexi, wait," Ashley called. "Please, wait." She ran in front of Lexi, hands out. "Yes, I read the letters. And no, I wasn't supposed to. But I needed to make sure that nothing in them would hurt you before I asked you to come out here and do this with me. But the time frame? That wasn't me. Mom wanted that, I swear. The six weeks thing . . . That was what drove me to read the letters. I couldn't ask you to come here for so long, put your life on hold, face the past you hate, if you were only going to get hurt."

Lexi was a lot of things, but unreasonable wasn't one of them. She heard the words, she understood the sentiment behind them, but the sense of betrayal still buzzed through her. "All you had to do was tell me the truth."

Ashley winced. "I made a mistake. I did. We all make mistakes."

Something Lexi knew all too well.

"Please just don't hold my mistake against Mom. She loved you. She loved you so much, Lex. She'd worked on herself, she'd become a better person."

"You sure about that? Because at the end of the day, she did fall off the wagon. So in some aspects at least, she was exactly the same person she'd always been, breaking promises." Feeling her own eyes burn, she handed the truck keys over to Ashley and walked out, still holding her ice cream.

It was a good five miles back to the house. She stopped once to inhale her ice cream and got a gut ache for the pleasure. The trek took forever, mostly because she was in no hurry to face her sister.

Only when she walked in the front door, it wasn't Ashley waiting on her.

Just Heath.

CHAPTER 25

Taking in the sight of Heath waiting for her, Lexi really wished she hadn't eaten all the ice cream. Alcohol might've been a better choice. Because although Heath had looked at her all week with easy affection and a seductive desire, right now he was giving nothing away.

"Let me guess," she said. "Ashley tattled—"

"Are you all right?"

She blinked. "Um . . ."

He wore a pair of faded jeans that lovingly cupped his body, complete with paint splatters and a rip over one knee that she knew was from actual work and not by design. His long-sleeved T-shirt, also with some paint splatter, was the exact color of his blue gray eyes. Whatever he was working on, it was forest green, at least going off the streak just below his jawline. He was looking at her oddly. Right, because he'd asked her a question.

"I'm fine." *Not even close . . .*

He gave a slight shake of his head, his eyes flashing a quick emotion. Sadness? Regret? "You don't have to do that," he said quietly. "Fake it. Not with me."

"But I'm good at it." She actually tried to say this lightly, hoping he'd take the teasing bait and turn this from serious to froth, but he didn't smile.

"Not with me you're not."

That this was true, that he knew her that well, should have sent her running. But her feet had decided they were blocks of cement. "Ashley sent you."

"She was worried about you."

Someone else who knew her, like, really knew her. After years of building her defenses high, so high even she couldn't see over them, no one had gotten through, not really. Except for two people: her sister and the man standing in front of her. But there were things she needed to know. "Did you read the letters too?" He didn't answer until she lifted her head and met his gaze.

"No," he said with quiet steel.

She studied him for any hint of deceit, but she knew him. He didn't do deceit. Something very slightly loosened in her chest. She was wound so tight, she was trembling, but she couldn't break. Not until she was alone. "Did you know Ashley had?"

"No." His eyes flickered. "Ashley is her own person and does what she wishes, but she's also impulsive and doesn't always think things through. If she'd have come to me about it, I'd have advised against it. Strongly."

Another very slight loosening in her chest. She nodded, then shook her head. "When I first showed up, you said there were six envelopes, and that we wouldn't find out who they were for until it was time to deliver them. But looking back, I realize that you never said whether *you* knew who the six were."

He didn't say anything. He was going to make her ask. Fine. She had no pride left. "How long have you known Ash and I were the two last letters?"

"Daisy told me the day she died."

"And you didn't tell me."

"You didn't ask."

Anger was good, she decided. It might keep her from falling apart. "Back in that tent all those weeks ago, you looked me in the eyes and claimed to be an open book."

"Lex—"

"No. You chose a side." A little niggling in the back of her mind told her to shut up and listen, but she couldn't seem to get out of her own way. Self-destruction was so much easier. "And what I know is that no one has ever chosen *me* over everything else."

"You're sure about that, are you?" His voice was low, so lethally calm that she knew he was anything but. "Then tell me this, Lexi. If we didn't choose you, then what the hell have we been doing this whole time? We love you, all of us."

Her throat burned like fire, her eyes too, but she refused to back down. Couldn't. She didn't know how. All her life, she'd had her back to the wall, claws out. She didn't know anything else. "If you loved me, you wouldn't have let me be blindsided."

He dropped his crossed arms, pain and regret on his face now. "I was bound by my promise to Daisy."

We love you. All of us.

Her heart wanted it to be true. And the one thing she knew for sure about Heath was that he never said anything he didn't mean. But in this case, she also knew there were all kinds of love. Panic crawled up her throat, making it difficult to breathe, because she loved him too. She didn't want to, didn't want to need anyone as much as she needed him. Even if deep down, she'd been harboring a secret hope that maybe what they'd shared could become more than anything she'd ever had with anyone else.

But in the end, she was, as always, on her own. It was okay. She knew how to do alone. But she needed to get out, to go somewhere she could take a deep breath without feeling like she had broken glass in her lungs. "I need to—"

"Go. I know. It's all over your face." He gestured to the door. "After all, that's what your mom did to you, so you're justified in repeating her mistakes, isn't that it? You've decided there's no one here worth fighting for."

"I never intended to stay," she managed past the lump in her throat. That lump might be her heart. "You knew that."

"Distance isn't a deterrent when it comes to keeping people in your life, Lexi." There was something in his eyes now, something quietly intense. "At least not for most people. Not for Ashley. Not for me. But you go ahead and use that phone call offering you your job back as an excuse to go and not look back."

She felt her mouth fall open. He really thought she'd . . . "*You* were the one clear with me from the beginning," she said, not able to keep the anger out of her voice. "There would be nothing long-lasting between us."

"Things change. I thought we both knew that."

She shook her head, so far out of her depth, she couldn't even gather her thoughts. Not easy when he was looking at her with worry, confusion, and not a little frustration. She drew a deep breath as some small understanding came to her. "You thought this would be easier. That I'd be easier."

His eyebrows shot up. "Lex, and I mean this in the very best of ways, you're the least easy person I've ever met."

She rolled her eyes, but her brief flash of good humor couldn't stick. "Why didn't you just tell me about the envelopes? I still would've stayed to deliver them."

"Because you would've stayed because you need the money you hoped she left you."

She sucked in a breath at the bluntness, but there was no reason to hide it. "Yes."

He nodded easily, because he'd always known that. "Lex, there are things you don't understand—"

"It doesn't matter." All that did matter was that he and Ashley, and her mom, had made decisions for her. Not with her. She wasn't sure what that was, but it wasn't love.

His gaze was hooded now. "Okay, then."

Okay, then. Feeling her heart cave in on itself, knowing history was repeating and having no idea how to stop it, she said, "I'm going to leave."

"No, this is your house. Allow me."

And then he was gone.

She tried to draw a deep breath, and couldn't. He'd walked, but this one was all on her.

Someone gave a slow hand clap. Ashley, who'd come in unnoticed from the back. "Nicely done," she said conversationally. "You're really good at that, pushing people away. You know by now that Heath thinks people only want him around because he makes things easier for them. As in he's only valuable when he's helping somehow. He's really good at that, but it's a self-fulfilling prophecy, one that triggers a fear deep inside him that those abilities of his are the only reason people want him around."

Lexi's decimated heart tried to squeeze, but being already cracked in two, it couldn't. "That's ridiculous."

"Insecurities aren't logical, Lexi. You know that."

"I just think at the very least someone should have told me about us being the last two envelopes. In a way, I get why you didn't. She was your mom, and you were protecting her. But Heath could've told me."

For the first time since Lexi had shown up, Ashley's expression had gone blank, giving nothing away. "You weren't here when she was dying and making her decisions, so you don't get to judge."

Not good enough. Not when she felt like the fool who hadn't had all the pieces to the puzzle.

"It's not my story to tell, but Heath made a promise," Ashley said flatly. "And promises are important to him."

Because he'd had so many broken promises growing up, and then in his relationships. Her heart, aching and battered, hit her toes. She'd once promised him to be open-minded about her time here, about the things she didn't know or understand about her mom, her sister, their lives.

And what had she done? The minute things had gotten hard, she'd broken her word.

Which meant the only bad guy here was her.

HEATH FOUND HIMSELF in front of his brother's house. Before he could let himself in, Cole opened the door, took one look at his face, and asked, "What's wrong?"

Pushing past him, Heath went straight to the kitchen, because he smelled cookies. Freshly baked cookies.

Sure enough, Misty was pouring chocolate chips into a big bowl of cookie dough with one hand, the other holding Matty on her hip.

"Unkie Heef!" Matty gave him the gimme hands, the universal toddler language for *up, now!*

He lifted the kid high in the air, eliciting squeals of pure, easy joy. "Oh, to be two again."

Misty looked over her shoulder at him. "Really? You want to be a mean little dictator who yells at adults and poops your pants?"

Well, when she put it that way . . .

"I thought so—" She broke off as she turned to fully face him, her smile fading. "What's wrong?"

Cole came into the kitchen. "That's what I'm wondering too."

Heath went to a drawer and grabbed a wooden spoon, which he dug into the dough bowl for a big hunk, then put the whole thing in his mouth. The sugar hit his bloodstream and immediately dropped his blood pressure.

"Me too, me too!" yelled Matty.

The kid's mama gave him an already baked cookie and kissed him on the nose.

Cole was looking at his brother. "You look like shit."

"Shit!" Matty yelled gleefully.

Cole grimaced. "Sorry, buddy, you have to be old to say that word."

"Shit!"

Cole sighed and handed him another cookie, then pointed at Heath. "Talk. Now."

"You do remember I'm the older brother, right?" Heath asked. "I'm the worrywart, not you."

Cole snorted. "Oh good, you're going to play the martyr card again. Awesome."

"Coming here was a mistake." Heath stepped out the back door.

But of course his idiot brother followed him. "It's about Lexi, right? What did she do?"

"How do you know it wasn't me?"

"Because you love her. You wouldn't have done anything to jeopardize that."

"Don't underestimate me. And you don't know how I feel about her."

Cole snorted. "Of course I do. You look like you've been sucker punched in the feels."

"So then why do I feel like *I* punched *her*? I know damn well that she doesn't believe people can care about her, and what did I do?" He shook his head. "I proved her point by walking away."

Cole looked shocked. "What? Why? You've never walked away from anyone in your life, even when you should."

"I guess I didn't want to wait and let her do the walking."

His brother stared at him for a beat. "Okay, so you made a mistake. You're human. Welcome to the planet. Go apologize, if that's what you want to do. Make it right."

Heath turned away, walking to the far south edge of the property to take in a teeny, tiny sliver of the lake visible far below. Cole, never able to leave anything alone, came up to his side. "You could've just sent the sisters to deliver those envelopes on their own, but you wanted to honor Daisy's wishes and help whenever you could. You wanted to be a part of it. You wanted to help fix the relationships, the one between the sisters, and the one between Lexi and Daisy. You couldn't help yourself. That's who you are, Heath, to the core. You've always owned that, so why second-guess yourself now?"

"Because I meddled." He glanced over at his brother. "Would you have let Misty deliver the envelopes on her own, including that pool hall?"

"Man, we would've mailed the envelopes, Daisy's wishes be damned. That was a crazy dangerous thing she asked of her daughters. So I get why you did what you did. All of it. But also, you're being such a hypocrite right now."

Heath gave him a hard look. "What the hell does that mean?"

"You dragged me kicking and screaming into adulthood—"

"Yes, because you were being stupid. I mean, how hard is it to adult? Pay your bills, don't smoke meth, keep a few close friends, wear deodorant, and always tip your bartender."

Cole dropped his head and gave a reluctant laugh. "Right, but at the time, I wasn't ready for any of it. I was screwing up left and right, and heading for serious trouble—until you stepped in, told me how stupid I was, pointed me in a better direction, and made me fix my life. And I'm forever grateful, but . . . you don't have to fix yours?"

"What the hell's wrong with my life?"

Cole ticked each point off on his fingers. "You let people think the worst of you, you go around solving everyone's problems but your own, you're using Grandpa as a crutch to not live life to its fullest . . . Should I keep going?"

"Pass." Pissed off at the world, Heath strode out, no idea where he was going.

"Walking away again, *twice* in one day," Cole called after him. "Maybe you're getting the hang of being human after all."

CHAPTER 26

During the hardest times in Lexi's life, she'd taken solace from driving. Being on the road, behind the wheel, emptied her mind and cleared her heart. Recharged her soul.

But as she purposely lost herself on some of Tahoe's back country highways, bouncing around on the rutted roads so hard it felt like she might lose a kidney, she couldn't seem to empty her mind, clear her heart, or recharge her soul.

So she kept going.

She drove up to the top of Donner Summit, then took a rarely used road to Eagle Falls, a place she remembered once going on a hike with her entire fifth-grade class. She'd hated it at the time, getting all hot and sweaty and dirty, but she thought maybe as an adult, she could appreciate what ten-year-old Lexi hadn't been able to.

She'd been prepared to have to park and walk in to the falls, but at some point in the years since, a fire road had gone in, allowing her to drive Betty all the way to the small lake at the end, and the heart-stopping view of the falls on the far side of it.

It'd rained a bit the night before, enriching all the vibrancy of the forest, the mountains, the water, all of it so beautiful it was hard to hold on to any negative thoughts. But sitting on the tailgate of the truck, she gave it the good old college try, watching as the sun angled itself toward the tallest peak, casting the hundred-foot waterfall in pinks and reds and oranges, all of it stealing the breath from her lungs.

Or maybe . . . maybe that was panic, because now that she was still, it all caved in on her, what she'd managed to do.

She'd blown up the only two relationships in her life that meant . . . well, everything. It made her feel more than a little sick inside. She honestly had no idea what to do. She could leave. She could go back to her life. She'd hate it, but she could do it, pretend she hadn't been changed by this trip. But at the thought, everything inside her cringed. She knew she'd never be happy there again.

She wasn't sure how long she'd sat there when she realized that the sun had sunk much lower now, nearly ducking behind the mountaintops.

Which meant it was time to go. The wild creatures that lived out here prowled for food at night, and she didn't intend to become dinner. But first, she had something she needed to do. She fumbled with her phone for the flashlight app and hoped the glow wouldn't draw all the bugs to her as she opened the envelope that had been burning a hole in her pocket.

A letter and a check slid out.

A big fat one.

She realized she'd stopped breathing when her body took over and forced her to draw a deep breath. Gently sliding the check back into the envelope, she unfolded the letter.

Dearest Lexi,

There's no good way to dive in, so I'm just going to. I realize I'm probably the last person you want to hear from, but if you're reading this, then you've already delivered all the previous envelopes. Thank you. I'm eternally grateful to you for that.

There's so much I need to say, and I've written this at least twenty times. I'm sweating right now trying to figure out how to reach you, when I know I don't deserve to. First . . . and this is the biggie . . . I'm so, so very proud of you, and the life you carved out for yourself. I never should've let you push me away. You were the child, I was the adult. It was me who should've stood up for you. Instead, I did as I always had, and went the easy route. I don't think you've ever done that, not once. Because as you learned far before I did, the hard way is worth it.

Second, and I don't deserve this, but I hope that you can forgive me for the past, and also forgive me for making it as hard as possible for you to walk away from Ashley. That's why I did what I did, why I asked—no, begged—Heath to only give you one envelope every week. I thought if I forced your hand and made you stay for long enough, you and Ash might forge a real relationship. Please know that I did it out of love, for both of you. You deserved more from me, Lexi. So much more. I'm gone now, but you still have Ashley. Please, if you believe nothing else, believe this—you deserve love, and you are loved. All you have to do is reach out and accept it. It's not too late. It's never too late.

To the moon and back,
Mom

Lexi sat on that tailgate, surrounded by endlessly high peaks and clouds, stunned and eyes burning. The only sound was her heart pounding against her rib cage and a few birds squawking at her.

Her mom had taken responsibility for all of it. If someone had told her a couple hundred words would change everything, she'd have laughed her head off.

But they had. They did.

It's not too late. It's never too late.

Wanting, needing, to believe that, she hopped off the tailgate and climbed into the truck, getting back to Ashley and Heath her only goal. Cranking the truck's engine over, she shoved it into reverse. She got maybe ten feet before she felt a thump thump thump beneath her. "No, no, no, no . . . Are you kidding me?"

Knocking her head into the headrest, she stared out the windshield at the quickly darkening sky. Trust her to get herself into this mess. Sliding out of the truck, she took a peek, and sure enough, her back left tire was flat as a pancake. She pulled out her phone.

No service.

"Of course. Not surprised at all." She swore the air blue, even making up a few new oaths while she was at it, then climbed into the bed of the truck to check on the spare. It looked good. All she needed now was the tool kit, but . . . no tool kit. Like a mature adult, she jumped down and kicked the flat tire, then swore some more as she hopped around on her good foot, holding her now aching toes.

When the pain ebbed, she tipped her head back and stared skyward. "Seriously, Karma?" For the first time in . . . well, forever, she had a nest egg—*thank you, Mom*. She could take a deep breath, only she couldn't because instead of being thrilled and excited, all she felt was dread and sorrow bouncing around in her chest.

And loneliness.

Not the usual and vague general loneliness she'd carried around for too long, but a very specific one. She didn't want to be alone, always watching her own back. She wanted her sister. She wanted Heath.

And also, she wanted a damn pizza.

She climbed inside the warm cab of the truck. "Okay, genius, now what?" Her stomach growled, so she looked around for a food stash, hitting pay dirt inside the glove box.

A single-serving-size bag of one of Ashley's organic, no-salt, no-fat plain chips. There was a sticky note on it that read:

Lexi—*EAT WHEN HANGRY!*

She gave a half laugh, half sob. She would've by far preferred fries, but she'd deal. She patted the dash. "I'm going to have to walk until I can get reception or can find help," she told the truck. "Be good."

She started out, lifting her phone high every few yards, checking for bars. She thought back to the last time she'd seen another vehicle—at least a mile back at the last crossroads.

When she got there, she looked right, then left.

No cars.

And almost no daylight left.

She'd never thought of herself as helpless, and refused to do so now. She'd been wrong to push Ashley and Heath away, and the irony of it didn't escape her. Apparently, she'd learned nothing from doing the same to her mom all those years ago.

Each time she'd done it, it'd been an implosion of everything she kept inside, a manifestation of her deep-rooted fears of being alone.

A self-fulfilling prophecy, as it turned out.

Please, if you believe nothing else, believe this—you deserve love, and you are loved. All you have to do is reach out and accept it. It's not too late. It's never too late.

She really, *really* hoped that was true, and with the sudden clarity only the very emotionally challenged like herself would take so long to get, her epiphany hit her in the face.

It wasn't the check that would guarantee her future.

It was the people she'd let in.

She looked at her phone again. One bar! She started moving faster, and after another hundred yards, she had two bars. Sucking in a breath, she accessed her favorites. There were only two names there. She knew she could call either of them. Even after all she'd said, they'd show up for her in a single heartbeat, no questions asked.

No matter what she'd always thought, she was no island of one. For the first time in her life, she wanted a future that included real connections. People who cared about her. She wanted that with Ashley.

And Heath.

She ached to hear his voice, but . . . sometimes you had to learn to crawl before you could walk. Ashley was definitely the easier of the two to face first. Would Heath show up if she needed him? Absolutely. Would he make her work for it, expecting her to talk things through? Also yes.

Baby steps.

Ashley answered on the first ring with a gasped, "Lexi? Is that you? *Are you okay?*"

She blinked back tears. "Yes. The truck got a flat, and I can't find the tire kit."

"Oh crap. Oh crap, I'm so sorry! The tire kit's on the floor in the garage. I had to buy a new one and forgot to put it in the truck. But I've got roadside assistance, hold on and I'll get you the info—"

"I don't think roadside will come up here. I'm up at Eagle Falls. I got off the Eighty at the Summit, then followed the fire road to the small lake there."

Ashley didn't respond, and Lexi looked at the phone.

The call had been dropped.

Uneasily, she turned in a slow circle. An owl hooted. Wind rustled the pines. Or at least she hoped it was wind. Dusk had vanished in a blink, replaced by a midnight blue sky. Fear skittered down her spine as she quickly accessed her flashlight app. The feeble light bounced in front of her as she started running back to the truck. She'd never enjoyed running so every single part of her body protested, but there was that whole not-wanting-to-be-dinner thing.

A buzz of an insect in her face, trying to get into her mouth or up her nose, had her letting out a girlie scream as she tripped over her own feet and hit dirt hard enough to make her knees and palms ache. She jumped right back up, waving her hands in the air, doing the bug dance. It was the howl of a coyote that made her go absolutely still for a single heartbeat before she took off again, going full tilt out to the truck, scrambling inside, slamming the door, and locking it.

Like coyotes had opposable thumbs.

Panting, she leaned back and closed her eyes. When exactly had the call with Ashley cut out? Had she heard where Lexi was? Not knowing played with her mind, made her heart race. Once again, she hugged the small bag of chips to her chest—

Uh-oh. She suddenly realized the truck was listing to the side more than it had been. A lot more. Had more than one tire gone flat? She peered out the window. She couldn't see from here. She'd just take a super quick peek. Sliding out, she shut the door behind her to keep the bugs out.

Yep. Two flats. And that took talent. She ate another chip and went to get back in the truck.

The door was locked.

So was the passenger side. Which made it official, she was an idiot. Probably a dead idiot, but she'd been at rock bottom before. Her survival instincts were strong, strong enough to have her climbing onto the hood and leaning back against the windshield. Eating the chips that she could admit weren't as bad as she'd thought, she stared up at the sky, which was really showing off tonight. Stars twinkling like diamonds and the glow of a few streaky clouds. She sat there, just her and a check that once upon a time she'd actually believed would change her life.

But she'd never been more wrong. Ashley had changed her life.

Heath had changed her life.

She missed them. She missed Ashley making her weird food. She missed Heath challenging her, making her laugh . . . looking at her like she was worth something.

A wind picked up, rustling and riling up the tall pines. The owl hooted again. Insects trilled. Those streaky clouds crept across the midnight sky on the wind, merging, growing, slowly obscuring the stars and moon, until it felt like the sky was closing in on her. Or maybe that was the rustling in the manzanita bushes off to her right. She whipped her head in that direction, blinking as if that would help her see.

"Hey," she called out. "There's nothing to see here, just keep moving along!"

The whole forest went silent at her voice. She fumbled to turn on her flashlight again and aimed the weak beam at the foliage on her right. She saw nothing but . . . oh crap . . . two red glowing eyes.

No, *four*. Four glowing eyes.

Accompanied by a low growl . . .

CHAPTER 27

I f the first rumbly growl hadn't stopped her heart, the second and third most definitely did. Oh shit. This was it. This was how she went out. Except . . . "No, wait! I made mistakes! It wasn't a good run, I need another chance!"

Heavy breathing emanated from the bushes now, and she shivered. Aliens . . . or coyotes? And did she really want to know? She didn't want to be taken back to the mother ship and probed, but she also didn't want to be torn limb from limb and devoured. Very slowly, she looked down at her precious bag of chips. Four left. Making the sacrifice, she threw one of them into the bush as far as she could.

There was a frenzy of snarls and yips.

With a shudder, she chucked the entire bag as well. And when that still wasn't enough, she yanked off one of her boots and pitched that.

Something yelped, and she gave a small smile of satisfaction. "You think that's rough, my hide is even rougher! Trust me, you don't want a piece of this!"

"Lexi?"

At the sound of Ashley's voice coming from somewhere behind her, she whirled and peered over her shoulder, blinking in the harsh headlights of a car she hadn't heard coming.

"Ash?" she called out, then nearly collapsed with relief at the sight of her sister appearing out of the halo from the headlights. She could admit she'd hoped against hope Heath might've come as well, but when she burned bridges, she *burned bridges*.

That Ashley had come in spite of that, when she had absolutely zero obligation to Lexi in any way, shape, or form, just about did her in. "Wait! Stop! Get back in the car, there're coyotes— Well, they could be aliens, I haven't actually seen their faces—"

Instead of running back, Ashley jumped up onto the hood with Lexi.

Lexi gaped at her. "Are you nuts? You could have been eaten!"

"By the coyotes? Nah. They don't bother people much."

"And if it's aliens?"

Ashley looked around them uneasily. "I couldn't leave you out here."

"I'd have followed you!"

"I wasn't taking any chances." Ashley looked around. "Why aren't you in the truck?"

"Oh, because it's a lovely night, not too warm, not too cold, and I wanted to enjoy it."

Ashley gave her a get-real look.

"Fine." Lexi grimaced, then admitted, "I managed to lock myself out." She drew a deep breath. Here went everything. "First, thank you for having chips. Those were invaluable, even if they didn't have enough salt. Second, thank you for coming for me. You didn't have to do that, but you did. Because you care about me. I know that, and now . . . now I need you to know that you're the sister of my heart." She put a hand to her own chest, right over the ache. "I should never have let you doubt that. I'm sorry. I'm so sorry for all the things I said to you when I was hungry—"

Ashley let out a soggy laugh and swiped at her face. "You're an idiot."

"Wait. Why are you crying?"

"Because *you're* crying! It's contagious!"

"I'm not crying." Lexi put a hand to her face. "Ohmigod. What's happening? My face is wet, my eyes won't stop streaming . . . Who's cutting onions all the way out here?"

Ashley sniffled. "You're doing it again, being funny and sarcastic in order to avoid an emotional confrontation."

Lexi wiped her face on her sleeve. "It's an illness."

"No, it's perfect." Ashley threw her arms around her and hugged her tight. "Because now I know it's real. Thank you for that."

"You might wanna hold off on the thanking me due to the impending and aforementioned getting eaten or probed. Also . . ." Lexi hesitated. "There's something else."

The smile dropped off Ashley's face. "There is," her sister agreed. "And it's that I owe you an apology too. I never should have said those things to you at the ice cream parlor. I—"

"Of course you should have said them. Because you meant them."

Ashley reached for Lexi's hand. "Okay, I did. But I didn't have to throw them at you like that. I didn't have to make you feel like you were alone. I should have said it all calmly in a conversation from the very beginning. That way we could've been working on our relationship the whole time. Instead, I held it all in until it burst out of me."

Lexi gave a rough laugh. "It's like we're blood after all."

Ashley squeezed her hand. "Sometimes being blood related is overrated. Sometimes being the family you make is where it's at."

"If you keep that up, I'm going to keep crying." Lexi met her sister's gaze. "While I sat here waiting to die—"

"Or get beamed up . . ."

"Yeah, but I think they've moved off now. I don't hear any of the creepy breathing." Lexi felt her smile slip away. "While I was out here, I realized something. I've been in a holding pattern for a very long time, waiting on life to find me. And I think . . . I think maybe you've been doing the same."

"Are you suggesting you aren't the only screwed-up one? That maybe I took that air aerobics class because I was looking for something?"

Lexi grimaced. "Yes?"

Ashley gave a wry smile. "It's true. I love my job, as much as the other things I do, but I'm very aware that something's still . . . missing."

Lexi reached out for her hand. "When I thought tonight might be my very last on earth, it occurred to me that I had nothing to show for it. I was definitely missing something, but I figured out what."

"You did?"

Lexi nodded. "I've been waiting for some sort of fulfillment to find me. I think I need to go after it."

"How?"

"I'm a little murky on that part," she admitted. "But I think for me, it involves a new start. Like running my own business. And . . ."

Ashley didn't appear to be breathing. "And?"

"Annnnd, I was thinking Sunrise Cove might be the place to do it."

"Don't you tease me."

Lexi smiled. "I'm not."

"You mean we can be each other's ride-or-die?"

"I mean, maybe. But I've always had questions about ride-or-dies. Like, where are we riding to? And do we have to die? Can we get food on the way?"

Ashly laughed and threw her arms around Lexi.

"I'm missing the party."

Lexi froze at the calm male voice. Heath, who'd just gotten out of the car. She pulled back to look at him. "You came too."

Heath's gaze ran the length of Lexi, clearly checking her for injuries. The worry in his eyes didn't abate when he didn't find anything bleeding or missing. Except . . . "Where's your boot?"

She gave a rueful smile. "Threw it at whatever was growling at me in the bushes. You came," she breathed again.

"Of course he did," Ashley said. "He was with me when you called. He'd been sitting on our couch staring at our two phones, hoping you'd contact one of us. He suspected it'd be me, because I'd be easier to face. Turned out he was right."

Lexi winced. She knew she needed to try and make things right, even if she failed. But even now, that persistent fear of not being lovable enough to keep reared its ugly head. "I didn't get any calls before I lost reception."

"Because I didn't call," Heath said quietly. "It had to be your decision, Lex. To go. Or . . . stay."

She jerked in shocked surprise, looking first to Ashley, and then to Heath, not making any attempt to hide their devastation. "You . . . you both thought I'd left. For good."

Neither spoke, and her heart cleaved in half. "Some investi-
gators you guys are," she said in what she hoped was a teasing
tone. "I wasn't leaving. I was . . . thinking. I didn't take any of
my stuff. I also drove Mom's truck. I'd never take your only
vehicle, Ash."

Ashley's eyes filled. "Logical. Unfortunately, I don't always
operate in that area." She gripped Lexi's hand. "And you're allowed to . . . think."

"Thank you?"

Ashley smiled, then glanced at Heath. "For what it's worth,
he wanted to come after you the minute you'd left. But he didn't
want to pressure you. I thought he was going to go gray on that
couch, waiting to hear from you."

"Ash," Heath said softly.

"Yeah?"

"Give us a moment?"

"Oh. Sure." With a grin, she hopped off the hood. "Yell for
me if I'm needed." And with that, she ran back to Heath's car.

Heath watched her go, not turning back to Lexi until Ashley
had shut the door.

"You don't trust her to not listen?" Lexi asked, finding a small
amusement, even as her heart pounded in her ears with nerves.

"I don't trust her to not get eaten." His gaze met hers and
held. "Or probed."

She snorted, and something deep inside her warmed. *Please
don't have given up on me . . .* "I can't believe you thought I'd left."

He gave her a look.

"Okay," she admitted. "I guess I can believe it. Does it help
to know that I have zero intention of taking my old job back?"

That won her an almost smile. "I hope you tell them where
to shove it."

"I plan to." She hesitated. "I don't know how to do this," she whispered, gesturing between them.

"I'm no better at it than you." He reached for one of her hands, wrapping his around it and running the pad of a callused thumb over her knuckles. "But I'm willing to throw everything I have at this, at us. There are things I should've told you, about why I'm so bad at sharing myself. About why I did the things I did when it came to Daisy. And you." He paused, and gave a rare tell by shoving his hands through his hair, pushing it back. "My mom died after being struck crossing a street by a fifteen-year-old kid who'd stolen a car. She was gone before she hit the asphalt. My dad had always been a drinker, but suddenly being responsible for two kids, when up until this point he'd pretty much ignored us, it took its toll. Cole was five." He swallowed hard, pausing. "And things . . ."

"Got bad?" she whispered.

He nodded. "By the time a few years had passed, we were all living with Gus and I was sneaking Cole out of his bed and into Daisy's house. She gave him a bedroom and mothered him half to death, but he was safe."

"What about you?" she whispered.

He shook his head. "I had to stay, or he'd have raised hell over Cole being gone. And then . . ." A ghost of a smile crossed his face. "I don't know how Daisy did it, how she always knew, but on the really bad nights, she started showing up. She'd have a casserole and an easy smile, effortlessly convincing my dad to sit and eat and chat. She'd stay until he passed out, belly full, still more than half drunk, but most of the mean gone."

Her chest felt like it'd caved in on itself.

"She saved my brother. She saved me." He let out a long breath. "More times than I could ever count. But by the time

I was a senior in high school, Cole was . . . wild. I was afraid to leave for college, but Daisy promised to take care of him." He shook his head, his voice marveling. "I don't know how she did it, but she kept him on the straight and narrow through some seriously harrowing dumbass antics, when even I couldn't have. For years, for all intents and purposes, she was the only authority figure in our lives who gave a shit, and it was . . . everything." He held her gaze. "She wasn't perfect. She struggled with her addiction. Sometimes I think that's why my dad tolerated her in our lives, because she got it. She got him and his demons. She understood them."

And now Lexi understood something for the first time too. Ashley having a relationship with Daisy wasn't a reflection of her mom's lack of love for Lexi. And by the same token, Heath having a relationship with Daisy wasn't a reflection of her lack of love for Lexi. And Lexi had been selfish to believe it in the first place.

"That very first day, watching you come down the escalator at the airport . . ." He blew out a breath. "It brought back the grief of her loss. I thought maybe we'd have that in common, but you were so angry. Hurting. And I got it. Your feelings were most certainly valid. But I thought, hoped, that being here, delivering the envelopes to people who'd known Daisy, that spending time with Ash . . . maybe it'd bring to life the mom you never got to see. Not because I wanted or needed you to forgive her, but because it might be a bridge to the family you have left."

"For Ashley," she said softly.

"For *both* of you. Life's short, Lex. Too damn short."

She nodded and mentally pulled up her big-girl panties. "Living with Daisy was . . . chaos. My dad wasn't all that different. It was easier to be angry, I think. At him. At her. I didn't know how to forgive."

"You were a kid. She'd flaked on you a whole bunch of times. She'd gambled away your college fund. Your dad took you, then ignored your existence . . ."

"Yes, but then when I wasn't a kid anymore, when I was a legal adult and she'd changed . . . I didn't." She had to look away. "She got clean and tried to come visit me. I told her not to come. I told her I wouldn't see her if she did. She came anyway. She was outside my apartment when I got home from work one day. And . . ." She closed her eyes, hating this memory. "When she saw me, she . . . *beamed*. She was so proud, so happy. She'd gotten her first-year chip, and she wanted me to have it. I could've taken it with grace, and she'd still have left if I wanted her to, but I couldn't even give her that. I just walked away. She . . ." She shook her head. "She tried once a year for the next few years, but if I'm good at one thing, it's holding grudges."

"Lex," he said softly, pained for her.

"I never saw her again. She passed away, and because of my stubborn pride, I didn't get to say goodbye. I missed out on a relationship with her because I always somehow believed there'd be time." She met his gaze. Not easy, not when she'd just laid her guts at his feet. "I'm ashamed of myself, Heath, and I have no one to blame but me."

"Do you think my brother and I are to blame for not wanting to be with our dad?"

"No. Of course not."

He just held her gaze while she blew out a sigh. "Yes, I heard it . . ."

Hands in his pockets, his gaze again swept their surroundings to assess any threats. Apparently deeming them still safe, he stepped closer, until he was a fraction of an inch from the hood, her knees bumping into his abs.

His nearness, after feeling so very alone, did something to her, something she didn't know how to process, so she closed her eyes.

"Lex." His hands came out of his pockets at last, landing on the hood on either side of her hips.

She opened her eyes to look at him.

"Three things," he murmured. "One, I'm sorry, so deeply sorry, that I let you down, that I hurt you when I didn't tell you about the envelopes. That was never my intention, but—"

"It wasn't your story to tell," she said quietly. "I know, I get that now."

He nodded and gently cradled her face in his hands. "Two . . . I love you."

She'd felt it, she'd known it, but hearing it out loud, spoken with such fierce honesty, made her gasp.

"And three . . ." His gaze slid to her mouth, which had fallen open. "I get that you probably don't, or can't, believe me, nor do you have any reason to after your last experience, but it doesn't make it any less true."

Her heart ricocheted off her ribs so hard, she wasn't sure she hadn't made up the words in her head. "You . . . you really love me."

"I do. I couldn't help myself." He rubbed his thumb gently across her lower lip. "When you first got here, you were so—"

"Irritating?" she asked with a self-deprecating eye roll.

"*Alive.*" He smiled at her surprise. "And when I looked at you, I realized I'd fallen into a rut where I was just going through the motions. You made me feel like a better me."

Something warm flared in the depths of her chest, a slumbering ember sparking to life as her heart fell right into his hands. She realized she'd made room for him between her thighs, reaching out to take a fistful of his shirt as if he might vanish. But his eyes, those beautiful eyes, told her he wasn't going anywhere. Still, just in case, she tugged hard, until he got onto the hood with her.

She climbed onto his lap, straddling him, nearly purring when his hands instantly slid to her hips, yanking her flush up against him.

"I've got three things too," she managed to say. "One, I'm also sorry. You were only doing as asked, as you'd promised, and I took my fears of falling out on you. Two, in spite of that, I did fall. For Sunrise Cove. For Ashley. For your family." She held his gaze. "For you. And three," she said quickly when astonishment flashed in his eyes, "I love you, Heath."

His lips quirked. "Even though you didn't want to."

"It did take me a minute."

His eyes were warm as he nudged her a little closer, and she soaked up his strength and heat. "Doesn't mean it's not real and lasting."

She smiled. "No, it doesn't, and it is."

"For me too." He pulled one of her hands to his chest, set it over his heart. Beneath her palm, his heart drummed. Steady. Strong. And she had to ask . . . "Do you honestly believe that the kids we once were can have . . . *this*?"

"I think we can have this *because* of who we were, who we had to be."

The tightness in her chest released and something filled the void. *Hope.* "So . . ." She smiled. "Are we dating now?"

He smiled back. "Does that work for you?"

Choices. It was always about choices with him, and she could've loved him for that alone. "Very much."

He kissed his way up her jaw to that magical spot just beneath her ear, which he nuzzled. "And where will I find you for these dates? A five-hour flight away, or . . . ?"

"I'm moving."

He pulled back just enough to look into her eyes. "Anywhere I know?"

The look in his eyes said he needed her to say it, and then there was just how badly *she* needed to say it as well. "Let's just say that I think you'll like the commute."

His smile was slow and heart-stopping, and he lowered his head—

"Wait!" She pulled back an inch. "There's one more thing."

He merely rubbed his jaw to hers, like a big cat. "Well, don't hold back now."

She cupped his face, wanting him to see how serious she was. "I know how much you care for the people in your life, Heath. I watch you put your heart and soul into every single one of them, putting their needs first, always. And I also know you'll do that for me too, but . . ."

He arched a brow. "But . . . ?"

"I'll allow it on one condition."

His mouth curved. "You'll *allow* it—"

"*Only* if you let me care for you in the same way."

She'd never seen him truly stunned, until now, his eyes wide, the quick intake of breath. "I mean it," she said. "You have to let me do stuff for you too."

A wicked look came into his eyes, and she laughed. "I mean you have to let me love you in all the ways I know you're going to love me. The way you've *already* loved me."

He seemed almost speechless. "No one's ever said such a thing to me before."

And if that didn't bring her tears back, though she smiled through them. "Consider it a care swap."

He laughed softly as she slid her hands into the silky strands of his hair and pressed even closer. The kiss was just heating up deliciously when Ashley honked.

"Now that you've worked things out with your tongues, let's go to the beach!" she yelled out the car window. "We can come back in the morning with the tire changing kit and get the truck."

"It's one in the morning," Lexi yelled back without taking her eyes off Heath's.

"And . . . ?"

Lexi laughed. Ashley was . . . perfectly Ashley. And Heath, smiling at her, was perfectly Heath. And instead of feeling like the odd one out, Lexi felt like she was . . . perfectly herself. "Let's go to the beach."

Heath braved the bushes to retrieve her boot—without getting eaten or probed—and then they walked hand in hand to the car.

By the time they got to the lake, Ashley was fast asleep in the back seat. When they tried to wake her, she muttered and swore at them. So they locked the car to keep her safe and walked to the beach fifty feet away. The night being thankfully warm, they kicked off their shoes and sat with their toes in the water.

Lexi had a hand to her heart. Heath covered it with his. "Okay?"

"More than." And it was true. "I was just trying to figure out what emotion is sitting on my chest."

"What did you come up with?"

"Contentment." She could hear the bafflement in her own voice.

His laugh was low. Soft. Warm. "Same."

They stared at each other for a beat. She drew a breath. "I've never really imagined myself in a moment like this. It feels . . . romantic."

"You sound surprised."

"I am. I definitely didn't see this coming. I figured we'd challenge each other, maybe chase each other around a bit, and then . . ."

"And then?"

"And then . . ." She gave him an apologetic look. "Maybe once the chase was over, you'd move on."

"I do love the chase," he said, voice low and gravelly, eyes locked on hers. He ran his fingers along her jaw, his thumb gently resting at the base of her throat where her pulse currently raced. A smile slowly curved at the corners of his mouth. "And so do you. But I have no intention of moving on from you, Lex. I want this, I want *us*, for the long haul."

"You want to be with me."

"I want to be yours."

The sweetest thing she'd ever heard, but also terrifying. No, wait. That was her default emotion. The truth was, his words had brought her a surge of adrenaline, and . . . more of that happy contentment. "So just how long is the long haul?" She needed him to clarify. "Like . . . the rest of the summer?"

He smiled. "I was thinking like the rest of my life. But sure, we can start with the rest of the summer. Whatever you want."

"Anything?"

He lightly bit her lower lip. "Do you have any idea how much I love you?"

"I think I'm starting to figure it out," she managed, then shook her head. "And right back at you."

"Scared?"

"I should be," she said, and he laughed. She pressed closer to that strong, warm body she craved 24/7 and bit him back, not quite as lightly as he'd done, before meeting his relaxed, patient gaze. "But I'm not. How about you. Are *you* scared?"

He smiled that just-for-her smile. "Not even a little."

ABOUT THE AUTHOR

New York Times bestselling author **JILL SHALVIS** lives in a small town in the Sierras full of quirky characters. Any resemblance to the quirky characters in her books is, um, mostly coincidental. Look for Jill's bestselling, award-winning novels wherever books are sold, and visit her website, jillshalvis.com, for a complete book list and daily blog detailing her city-girl-living-in-the-mountains adventures.

Read More by
JILL SHALVIS

THE SUNRISE COVE SERIES

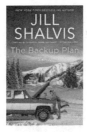   

THE WILDSTONE SERIES

   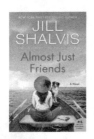

DISCOVER GREAT AUTHORS, EXCLUSIVE OFFERS, AND MORE AT HC.COM.